Winter Concert

OTHER BOOKS BY

Margaret Howe Freydberg

THE BRIDE
THE LOVELY APRIL

WINTER CONCERT

Margaret Howe Freydberg

THE COUNTRYMAN PRESS
WOODSTOCK, VERMONT

SECOND PRINTING

Lyrics from *"Someone to Watch Over Me"* by George and Ira
Gershwin. Copyright © 1926 (Renewed) New World Music CORP.

Excerpt from *The Rainbow* by D. H. Lawrence. Copyright © 1915
by David Herbert Lawrence. Copyright © 1943 by Frieda Lawrence. Reprinted by permission of Viking Penguin, Inc.

Lyrics from *"I Could Have Danced All Night"* and *"on the Street
Where You Live."* Copyright © 1956 by Allan Jay Lerner and
Frederick Loewe. Copyright Renewed Chappell & Co., Inc.

Excerpts from *"Four Quartets, East Coker."* Copyright © 1943
by T. S. Eliot. Copyright © 1971 by Esme Valerie Eliot. Reprinted
by permission of the publisher.

Library of Congress Cataloging in Publication Data

Freydberg, Margaret Howe.
  Winter concert.

  I. Title.
PS3556.R448W5   1985   813'.54   85-10955
ISBN 0-88150-050-X

PRINTED IN THE UNITED STATES OF AMERICA

To Claire Smith
with gratitude

Old men ought to be explorers
Here and there does not matter
We must be still and still moving
Into another intensity
For a further union, a deeper communion
Through the dark cold and the empty desolation,
The wave cry, the wind cry, the vast waters
Of the petrel and the porpoise. In my end is my beginning.

There is only the fight to recover what has been lost
And found and lost again and again; and now, under
    conditions
That seem umpropitious. But perhaps neither gain nor loss.
For us, there is only the trying. The rest is not our business.

From FOUR QUARTETS, EAST COKER,　　　　　　*T.S. Eliot*

Part One

$\backsim\!\!\backsim\!\!\backsim$ I $\backsim\!\!\backsim\!\!\backsim$

A MAN and a woman are about to pass each other in an empty corridor of Boston's Symphony Hall. It is an hour before concert time, and the woman, Celeste Hunter, is arriving for lunch and making her way to the cloakroom, while the man, McCabe Kingsley, having just shed his coat, is heading from there to the bar. It is a Friday afternoon in early January, and outside, in the cold grayness, snow drives softly against the Ionic columns, the terraced steps, the glass doors opening to light.

At that moment, they are the only people in this long wide corridor between the auditorium and the refectory, and as they walk toward each other they are both self-conscious, she as an attractive woman used to being stared at, he as a man staring in spite of himself at an attractive woman. She won't avert her eyes, and so for a moment, as she passes him, she looks this approaching stranger straight in the eye. At the same time, before she looks away, she is aware of his plunging, almost floundering walk, and something else, an instantaneous piercing impression of his being known to her, subtle as vapor and yet protracted and dense as experience. In this second of recognition she has seen a vacancy in his face which is an intense concentration turned inward, so that she thinks, with a feeling of slight relief, that he has not noticed whatever self-exposure may have betrayed her. Perhaps she feels a force in the forward-jutting head, the bemused eyes, later she knows she has. But at the moment she isn't thinking about it. Instead, startled, she is dealing with a little ancient shock which she has no name for and which fascinates her.

He is stunned. As he passes this woman sweeping along, he has a strong penetrating moment in the midst of the grayness of his life, of seeing something wonderful. A large-brimmed hat still glistening with snow sits straight across her brow, and beneath it her hair is shining white from her temples back to a knot. Her eyes are lively, disengaged and kind, her loose coat swings with her stride. It is this that strikes him, that calls his attention to everything else about her, the long swift graceful stride. It strikes him at his center.

He knows she is, if not old, not young. And yet she seems young, young, the zestful stride has all the vigor and fire of youth. And he is stunned. He thinks he has taken something from her which is especially for him. The weight of his age has been lifted, has flown off to lodge somewhere overhead, looking down on him and apart from him. Something in her is now his, a message from her to him, displacing grayness, and lodged in his center like heat.

In the upstairs restaurant, Celeste bought a turkey sandwich wrapped in wax paper, hesitated about buying a drink, which could make her fall asleep during the concert, but then shrugged her shoulders and ordered dry vermouth on ice, which she bore with her sandwich to the broad marble stairs beyond the restaurant where she would sit alone rather than inside at a table of chattering women she did not know. She collapsed onto the stair with a loud relieved sigh and let her shoulder bag slide down her arm to the floor, and then began to unpeel the paper from her sandwich. Two little puddles of melting snow started to gather at the heels of her boots.

A picture of poise. A white-haired woman sitting unconventionally on a low stair with a straight-spined lack of self-consciousness and with an evident confidence that could mistakenly be interpreted as arrogance, biting into her sandwich and sipping her drink with a smiling artless delight in the taste of things.

But inside this elegant woman was a tiredly pumping heart and a train of comfortably inelegant thoughts; she was exhausted after a long meaningless morning which had begun at five o'clock, she had only come to Boston, to the concert, in order to get off the island for a change, "which is reason enough for coming, so don't carp," she murmured. Living alone, she talked to herself. There would be no place to have dinner in Port Stratton at the end of the long bus ride back, and so she would have to sit on a hard bench in the ticket office for an hour and a half waiting for the eight o'clock boat to the island. And the boat trip would be, as it always was at the end of a long day, tiresome and never-ending. Finally home. Maybe some mail in the mailbox? But then the dark house. Empty. Too late for a fire. Too late for a drink. Scrambled eggs. Or a cold chicken leg. And then bed. A flare of incomprehensible but familiar anger shot up in her, tightening her mouth.

"Stop this," she said quite loudly, no longer smiling.

This exhortatory burst of positivism cheered her up, it was a familiar procedure for her, she relied on its taking place, she relied on balance. And feeling gratefully the sharpness of her face softening, she began to ease away from the waste of time that worry was, and stoicly to shift her thoughts to something else.

Finishing the last of her sandwich she rolled the paper into a decisive wad, and wondered where to dispose of it and did not know, and while looking around, came to think intensely for a moment about the mobs of animated women there in the restaurant across the hall. How many of them were here for the love of the music she wondered, and how many of them, like herself in years past, were here because it was what a certain kind of woman habitually did on winter afternoons in large cities?

She thought about the man she had passed in the hall, and now saw that she thought his walk had expressed purpose, perhaps a lonely, desperate, last-minute purpose? As though he were determined to get to some other place? She knew that walk. Where had she known that walk?

She closed her eyes.

Then something happened, briefly, stunningly. This concert hall merged into the concert halls of her past, herself as a part of the stone and plush of them. She was a long, somber-structured, music-pounding flow of opera Saturday afternoons with Mort's Great Aunt Anna, and symphony Friday afternoons with Mort's sister Christina, years and years and years of afternoons, thousands of them. There was no sense of her own self, she was only a thing being helplessly borne along in a flotsam of women and gold-vaulted ceilings and red plush seats and taxis jostling outside in pandemonium downpours. It was a menace of structures, of housings that claimed her and dominated her, but like the other monuments of her past—her grandmother's house,

Mort's family's house—as substantial and as fundamental as the gates of heaven.

She opened her eyes, and sat there on the stair, shaken and awed. "Good *grief*," she muttered. In a minute she tilted the last of her vermouth into her mouth and swallowed it, drew a long breath composed of the waste of the past and the reality of now, and let an amused and resigned sigh steady her.

And then, warmed by her drink, and purposeful in her characteristic way of being able to put aside past pain in favor of present interest, she rose abruptly, brushed crumbs from her dress, hitched her bag up onto her shoulder, and walked briskly, fluidly, elegantly down the marble stairs and along the rose-carpeted hall and into the almost empty auditorium, where she would find her seat and close her eyes and take a little nap before the concert began.

In the downstairs restaurant, Cabe bought a bourbon on ice and a sandwich on a paper plate. Avoiding old Charlie Abbott sitting alone at a table with three empty chairs, and the two Wentworth sisters at a table with an empty place, who were waving and beckoning to "this eligible old widower," nodding courteously to them nevertheless, he went to one of the tall stand-up tables by a window with a view of softly falling snow, looking around for the woman but not seeing her here in this room gradually expanding, growing dense with the crescendo chatter, the ice-clatter, the coffee-pungency, of festive lunching.

It was comforting to him today, in the present disorientation of his life—his recent resignation from the firm, his move from the city, his operation—to be in this familiar room which was more a part of his essential life than any of the Boston rooms he had lived in for the sixty-six years of his existence. It had the familiarity not of thwarting and shadowy complexity, as his mother's Beacon Street house had had, nor of the decorator barrenness of the apartment on Memorial Drive where he and Catsy had lived for all the thirty-six years of their marriage. This room was his room as those rooms had never been, it was the nucleus of himself; it was here that lights were brighter, sounds more heartening, smells more exciting. Prelude to preludes, this room was the moment before the best, it was the promise of the music he would shortly hear.

He had always been able to tolerate all the people he knew lunching here and for whom he would muster grace—his mother's and his mother-in-law's friends, Catsy's friends, his own acquaintances (he had never had close friends), his distant relatives (no close ones were left). He had been able to be gracious without effort to these people because they were, like himself, worshipers of the Boston Symphony Orchestra, either for love of its performances, or for love of the clubbism its performances provided. Though Cabe's passion for music was not confined to the BSO, as "they" called it, nevertheless its divine accomplishment had always given him pride, and given him a base, in this city where other institutions—school, parents, marriage, business—had given him, truly, so little.

He opened his program and read the notes about the man who would play the Mozart piano concerto in today's concert. The young Brazilian, he read enviously, skimming down the page, had begun his career at the age of ten, had subsequently studied with Nadia Boulanger in Paris and had made his debut in 1975 at St. Martin's in the Fields in London under the direction of Sir Neville Marriner.

Nadia Boulanger was a magic name to Cabe. For years

he had convinced himself that Nadia Boulanger could have been his salvation. He believed absolutely that if only he had been able to study piano with her, his embryo talent would have grown, as he was convinced it was capable of, into a great one. When he was very much younger, in his thirties and even forties, still plastic years for him, he had had fantasies about himself as Nadia Boulanger's brilliant student, vivid scenes of himself in her studio, playing for her. In these fantasies, he would be playing for her, for instance, a Schubert Impromptu, feeling it in his heart and mind as well as in his fingers, feeling it, really, in his bloodstream. He would be able, actually, to feel a bond between himself and this great teacher which was like an incandescent cable connecting them, vibrating and crackling with the electricity of interflowing genius. But in spite of the sophistry of these imaginings, their euphoria was true-based in the probity of Cabe's goals. In trance or out of trance, Cabe had never longed to play primarily for praise. And in his Nadia Boulanger fantasy he was playing for her praise only because it would prove to him that the sound duplicated the immensity of what he felt in himself. It had always been his desire, not to win audiences, not to elicit thundering applause, but only to achieve a satisfactory expression of what he knew he was.

All of this came back to Cabe as he stood looking down at the magic name, his full and very sensual lips slightly apart, the glass of bourbon held motionless in one hand. With embarrassment, even with a sort of sad shame, these fantasies came back now to Cabe, along with the various reasons for failure that had always accompanied them—his mother had never encouraged his music, he had been married too young and too impetuously to a girl who had no feeling whatsoever for music, he had had to earn a living at business, he had begun his studies at the conservatory too late.

Nadia Boulanger . . . It seemed imcomprehensible to this aging man who was now disenchanted with binding fantasy, who really despised it, that he could ever have attributed the failure of his life to the absence in it of another person. He now knew that the failure lay, not in what Nadia Boulanger had not done for him, but in what he had not done for himself, in music or in anything else. In the past few months he had come to know this profoundly, but at the same time to sense, on and off, some kind of tenuous encouragement in himself. It was a thing he had to hold on to for dear life, this fragmentary sense of encouragement.

He closed his program and began to think about the woman he had seen in the corridor. And as he stood with the comfort of the buzzing room supporting him again, his furrowed face vacant and loose with thinking about her, imagining that she was in the other restaurant upstairs and wishing he'd gone there, as he stood and wolfed his drink which he didn't taste, and spilled crumbs unknowingly down the front of his old and sagging tweed jacket, feeling the warmth of bourbon expanding in his innards and with the woman's stride inside him like a light getting brighter, suddenly he knew that he knew her.

After the concert, which she hadn't greatly enjoyed because it was all Mozart, Celeste waited twenty minutes in the after concert crush for a subway train that wasn't too packed to board, and arrived at the Greyhound Terminal with only minutes to spare before her four-thirty bus left for Port Stratton. "I'm too old for this," she muttered, striding powerfully and nervously through the crowds in the terminal, and then breaking into a run. But she was optimistic, not too fussed, as she dashed. There was even some fun in the race. And fortunately the bus was still there, its door still open.

Panting painfully, she climbed the steep bus steps and handed in her ticket and started to roam down the aisle looking for an empty seat. But the bus was packed with the quiet staring of the successfully seated. No seats, of course. Yes, a hoarded space next to a window, piled high with the overcoat and the briefcase of the hoarder in the aisle seat. "Is this seat taken?" Celeste asked clearly, pleasantly, imperiously, and while she waited for the man reluctantly to shift his belongings from the seat up to the baggage rack overhead, she looked around her, away, down the aisle.

The man she had passed in the corridor of Symphony Hall was lying back in one of the seats, head lolling toward his shoulder, eyes closed in the peace of sleep. Too big for the space, he lay sideways in it, one long leg thrust out into the aisle, big-booted foot sprawling. There was indeed something familiar about him, clear and yet elusive, as in a dream. And there was a childlike peace in a man's sleeping face that made her feel tender, then sad, then angry at feeling tender and sad, for these were emotions she was uncomfortable with. She tossed her head and unbottoned her coat. "Oh thank you." Her seat was ready.

Through a winsome light descent of snowflakes the bus inched along the choked highway in the late Friday afternoon traffic. Stop. Start. Stop again, this time endlessly, it seemed to Celeste. Trying to relax, she closed her eyes patiently. But in a minute she opened them, and then looked down, pulling off her gloves, and the flesh below her chin became another chin, a soft white velvet cushion. There were fine lines spoking out from the corners of her eyes, and because she was tired there were puffed white crescents beneath them, which still did not conceal their liveliness.

Eyes closed again, she tried to fall asleep, like everyone around her, like the man. There was something familiar about him. He was known to her. But in what way? As a person? No, surely not. Yet he was heavily suggestive of something, perhaps as another body seen in a moment of intense clarity is suggestive of life itself? Was it that? Or was it something else?

Suddenly she was dispirited, and her face gradually fell into an expressionless sobriety, though a certain determination in the jaw never left it, as though the flesh absorbed and reflected emotion, while strength lay in the skull, as though cartilage and bone were interwoven with an obstinate inner strength.

All at once she remembered the torrent of concert halls that had poured through her while she'd been eating her lunch, and now it engulfed her again, but more powerfully and more specifically—a river of stone and plush and gilt and Great Aunt Anna keeping time to *La Bohème* with her cane, the rings on all the fingers of her right hand flashing on its knob, the old red-dyed head bending emotionally from side to side, Christina's imperious blue eyes that controlled, the scent of her Tabac Blond, women, women, furred, chattering, flowing in from martini lunches, flowing out into the lovely early dusk toward the party evenings which would be the same for most of them.

The waste of it gripped Celeste's throat, she felt choked, desolate. Why had she spent one thousand Saturday afternoons with her husband's great aunt in her box at the Metropolitan Opera? Why had she spent one thousand Friday afternoons with her husband's sister at the New York Philharmonic? Oh, that chore of obligatory listening, year after year after year, those places her life had taken her to, Mort's places, which were not of her choosing; that empty pursuit, year after year, of what Mort wanted. . . . It all felt to her like an excretion of things long intolerable, which at last lay here wholly evident, their cumulative decomposition upsetting in a way that actual living of them had not appeared to be.

She remembered that once before in her life, years ago, probably half a lifetime ago, she had had another vivid purgative experience somewhat like this one. She hadn't thought about it in years. She tried to recall it but could only feel a tumbling movement of color, nothing specific. But she did remember that it had immediately changed her life.

She opened her eyes abruptly, terrified at this disorientation which had set her heart to pounding. "Fascinating," she said to herself flippantly, uneasily. "A sort of Johnstown flood," she scoffed. She felt exposed, unsure. Why had that memory assaulted her, stripped her, now, after twenty-four years? That life was gone, replaced by her own. Mort was gone. This was very peculiar nonsense.

She straightened her shoulders and composed her face, and began to dispose of the episode with a typical resourcefulness which could either be her salvation or the means by which she avoided the pitfalls of feeling, or both. She was an indestructibly valiant woman, this was innate. But the tendency for valiance to subordinate insight had always been powerful in her, contradictorily both sustaining and blocking her.

She took a paperback out of her purse, *Minorities: A Sociological Appraisal*, which she had bought this morning in a Boylston Street bookstore. Her work in New York from which she had recently retired had been with philanthropic organizations concerned with the disadvantaged and the persecuted, and she still felt obliged, though with less and less urgency, to read everything written about them she could lay her hands on.

She opened the book and began to read, but with little concentration. After a while she said, "Oh to hell with this," aloud, so that the man next to her stirred from sleep, half-opened his eyes, shut them again. She looked at him. And then, compelled, she turned and glanced back at the man she had seen in Symphony Hall. Sleep made him look helpless, pitiable. She felt something stir in her chest. She looked down the dark aisle of muted people, so many of them gray-haired, aging, like the man, like herself, and all so physically close together though strangers to each other. So helpless, so pitiable. She was overcome with the consuming compassion for the human condition which she carried around in her at all times. And she felt suddenly that this busload of weary people was a declaration of human helplessness she absolutely could not bear.

But no. Just as suddenly she saw this scene as not pitiable at all. She saw it as splendid, heroic. And she saw that this thought seemed to be related to the man. There was something about him, dignity perhaps, or a kind of perseverance in his plunging walk, or something in the sad endurance of his sleeping face, that made Celeste for the moment, not sorry for people, but proud of them.

This was an astonishing new idea for her, and instantly she distrusted it. Yet it compelled her, intrigued her. Was it possible not to despair about the human condition? She had a panic moment of feeling lost without the full bolstering urgency of despairing. She felt a real panic to be questioning compassion at the end of this day of nothing, and with hours of nothing ahead. She felt a passionate nervousness. She raised her chin, set her lips together, took off her large hat and spread it on her knees, over *Minorities: A Sociological Appraisal*, and closed her eyes.

Casting around for something pleasant to distract her, she found her dining room table to think about—rose-colored tulips in the round goldfish bowl in the center of the long table, wonderful the way they stretched out long and slim-stemmed, exuberant and stylish, making the whole room strong with elegance. And this rose-colored splurge in the middle of her table was indivisible from its being the Luhins' birthday present, its beauty spoke of the neighborly attention that took them beyond tulips and made them the center, the heart of the room.

Beyond the tulips was the wall of glass, and beyond that the deck and then the stone dunes and then the sea, sparkling and calm and deep blue. Celeste's face, her shoulders, softened. She loved her new home, she loved where she lived, with the sea sounding so near, all the time that stirring ceaseless sound.

Now she brought Lidi Luhin into the picture. Lidi was coming down the icy driveway, walking with stiff little steps. Lidi walked inquiringly, even when there wasn't ice. She walked slowly and cautiously, as though her feet, and she, were searching. She came up onto the deck and into the living room. Her little pointed face, amazingly unwrinkled for her age, had round pink spots on each cheekbone from the cold. Above the spots, two bead-black eyes were curiously unalive, like stones. Her smiles were always faint. She smiled faintly now.

"Hello, Lidi. Come in. Let's have tea."

Celeste felt warmly now how glad she was to have the Luhins as neighbors. And thinking about them, and about the tulips they had sent her, she had moved into a sunlit place.

Sparse snowflakes fly at the darkening windows, spiral playfully, devilishly in the headlights. Wipers drone in resigned monotony across the windshield, dutiful, perpetual. The bus groans on, the noise of its motors underlying the deep collective silence of its passengers. Dusk. A hush in this close pack of bodies. Few overhead spotlights are on, only a few people are reading or working out of briefcases or murmuring monotonously, only a few alert ones are not being trundled along supine in this day's end washed-out melancholy.

❦❦ II ❦❦

AROUND four o'clock, in the graying afternoon, a few snowflakes were presently over the island. But a lemonish light spot in the sky where the sun was gray-covered, disparaged the sparse flakes, promising that they meant nothing.

Lidi stood at the kitchen window, hugging a scarlet shawl across her chest. I hope it doesn't snow much. I hate snow. Today is Friday. In an hour I will start dinner. Friday. Saturday. Sunday. . . .

The clock ticked at her back. Its slow reliable tock, tock, was alive. Like my heart, it beats like the sureness of my heart.

16

As she stood looking out toward the sea, the pale lemon light dimmed away, and everything now was a flat light solid gray. Why did she keep standing so still by the window, this thin rather shriveled little woman with white hair hanging girlishly to her shoulders?

More flakes were coming, suggesting seriousness. And she stood, held here, as neuter as the gray sky, mesmerized here in a trancelike moment of knowing that whatever it was in her that drove her to action, interest, aliveness, whatever that was, had stopped.

The air was gradually growing solid, like fog. And now there was a driving granular swirling denseness. In minutes, it seemed, the rails of the fence were whitened, the top of the boulder in the field. In no time the wind-tossed ends of the juniper branches beside the gate were like stiff snow-covered fingers, quivering and pointing.

Friday. Saturday. Tomorrow was Saturday, Saturday stretching into long, long Sunday, on which there would be no mail. No mail from Saturday afternoon until Monday afternoon.

Down it came, silent and raging, a texture of crisscrossed, fog-white stitches, muffling the sky, muffling the earth, shrouding the sea. No sound comes through this soft relentless purpose of snow storm so suddenly here, Lidi thought, hugging her scarlet scarf with cold fingers which were chapped and which caught in the loose wool. Except for the ticking clock there was a stillness about this white silent density that seemed to insulate her from life.

Abruptly she turned away from the window.

She went into the living room, where Freddy sat wrapped in a blanket, sneezing. His white hair was on end, this way, that way, like the snow. She smiled her thin smile. "Did you take your temp?"

"A hundred and a half," sepulchrally, triumphantly. He didn't want her to be smiling. He was dramatically not himself, all his sunny vitality hiding off there in the other man, the well man.

"That's lower than yesterday at this time. Mine was like that."

"Well, yours never got to a hundred and two and a half!" His only satisfaction, floating in the misery of flu, was to best her with a higher temperature.

Men are silly when they're sick, Lidi thought. Freddy is very silly when he's sick. Coldly, she felt no sympathy for him. "Would you like me to make you some tea?"

His face eased, pled with her, ashamed of his childishness. Being sick frightened him. "That would be nice."

"And some toast?"

"Please." Then he burst out, "Here I sit, losing *time*. I've lost so much *time*. The Community Services mailing hasn't gone out, I've missed the Planning Board meeting. I couldn't take poor old Mrs. Kline to her Blood Pressure clinic. I'll bet *no* one took her."

Lidi admired Freddy's goodness. He was the only truly charitable person she had ever known. She actually worshiped his charitableness, but with resentment and self-recrimination because she had so little of it herself. She, too, was sorry for poor old Mrs. Kline, but she would never have taken two full hours of her precious day to drive her to a clinic, or to drive her anywhere.

"I *know* no one took her," Freddy howled. "Poor old Mrs. Kline, poor dear old soul." He blew his nose. "Aaaaahhh," a growl of misery. Kleenex was flung into the plastic-lined basket at his feet, his feet set tidily side by side under the mothering blanket.

"Don't be hysterical, Freddy." He mustn't lapse. Freddy

18

mustn't lapse. She desperately wanted him to get well, to be Freddy once more, to be the dependable center of this household. "I'm certain Evangeline took Mrs. Kline to the clinic, she said she would."

"Oh, did someone ask her?"

"Yes. *I* told you *I*'d call her and ask her to. I told you that."

"I don't remember," he said, awed. "Imagine that. I don't remember. That's what a fever can do."

"Well, that could very well be," Lidi said kindly, though she knew it was failing memory not his fever that had done it.

After Lidi had brought Freddy his tea, and smoothed his bed, which she thought he should be in, and laid the fire, she put a match to it, so that suddenly the cheer of an orange snapping blaze flared up, brightening the silence, putting at a distance the downfall of flakes which were larger now, directionless, blown madly sideways and up from the ground, thick big happy flakes crazy in a lighter sky.

Her spirits had risen with this brightening of everything. She went out of the living room, putting a quiet hand for a moment on Freddy's wild white head as she passed behind him. The warmth of his skull, the feeling of helpless stiff unruly hair, stabbed her. But she was so distanced from wanting to allow her hand to feel, or to give, she'd grown so far away from the days when touching was natural and necessary. She was muffled by the snow, by everything. Cocooned. She knew it and pulled her hand away as though she had betrayed herself.

Where else to go but into her little cubicle, her own little room off the bedroom, which was no bigger than a large clothes closet. She lit the lamp by her armchair. And the act of lighting the lamp and sitting down beside the table, began right away to take her into a known, safe place, high and dry. Hungrily, as though it were food, she snatched up a notebook and opened it. She would read, and assess once more, the poem she had sent two months ago to *Viewpoints*. Two months ago. Two months is a long time to wait, when you wake up every morning of it thinking that today will be the day. Maybe tomorrow, she thinks, maybe tomorrow the letter will be there. And if it isn't? . . .

Her heart slips. After Saturday, Sunday. No walking out to the mailbox on Sunday. On Sunday the mailbox is cold, stopped, on vacation. The thought of its cold Sunday emptiness baffled Lidi. How was she to deal with her dependence on it?

She always felt the mailbox by the side of the road to be, as though it were a person, or a governing body, the sovereignty that controlled her life. The mails and the publishers' letters that came through them, ruled and dominated her life. Oh, I hate you and need you, chieftains and messengers, your cruel withholding, your long taunting silences, and then one day, your body blow.

Every day for the past five weeks she had gone to the mailbox at two o'clock in the afternoon. Rain or shine or ice or snowdrift, she had walked out every day at two o'clock to the mailbox, and opened it with her heart knocking, and then had known at a glance that there was no white envelope from *Viewpoints* lying on top of the usual mocking pile of junk mail.

But one day it would be there. It would strike her like an electric shock, that white envelope, lying there, keeping its secret. Oh, that moment before picking it up, when she would be thrilled, galvanized by shock! Her breath, everything, would stand still. And she would stand there, with the envelope in her hand, in that suspended moment before what—joy, despair?—she would stand there and tell herself: Now Lidi, look around you. Concentrate for instance on this milkweed, its bare beauty, the satiny beige silver of the pod. Take one minute to see what's here, to see that the whole world is in a milkweed pod, not a publisher's letter. Take a moment to know what living is, to know where joy is. Know that you live for the sake of this dried flower, that you live for the day, the moment itself. Right here in this moment, she would tell herself, you have the answer to your life. Why must you depend on someone out there to dish out happiness? Stand still here a moment, let everything stand still until you decide that you are not going to let this letter's acceptance or rejection determine your happiness.

But there was never any conviction or any constancy to these dictums. And so it was now. All that was in Lidi now was the emptiness of no mail on Sunday. For a moment she could not find anything in herself to balance the thought of the long stale waiting hours of not going to the mailbox on Sunday.

Except this, the poem in her hands. Yes. Here *she* was, she could go into her self and stay there, shut herself in with her self, and in seconds the mailbox would vanish.

She began to read.

DAWN DEPARTURE
by
Lydia Pratt Luhin

Beyond the dune
the sea is a severe spread of dark gray steel.
Between its strict line of horizon

and the soft dark wall of disappearing night,
a band of pale light widens.

I am transfixed by this spectacle of perfect order,
this deep-colored vast exactness of sea and sky,
straight-lined as though drawn with a ruler.
I am quieted.
I am told to calm down.
I am asked to have no expectation beyond this.
And I am asked why I want to leave,
and where I want to go.

Lidi looked up, and looked out at the dancing snow, but she didn't see it. Her eyes were trying to feel normal, were trying not to blink nervously, evasively, she was trying to put on for herself a nonchalant, an unperturbed face. She bit her lips. Then up through sameness, through an overlay of behavior which seldom let anything unknown to the anesthetizing habit of it be revealed, up through this perpetual blanketing, a small, pale, helpless acknowledgment rose. It doesn't seem as good to me as it did, she said to herself. Her cheeks flamed with shame.

She sat at bay. Where to turn? What to do? This could not be an ending, there were no endings! She tugged at the velvety lobe of an ear, her eyes darting around. She was pursued. But for a moment as her breath came short she really knew that there was no place to run to.

Her heart pounded alarmingly and she got up from the chair with an abrupt movement—to run away. But where? All the rooms were the same. And outside, snow closed the world.

She went into the bedroom and lighted the Limoges lamp on the dressing table and pulled the shades at the three windows hung with ball-fringed muslin—colonial curtains to go with the old maple bed, the early American blanket chest, the polished sloping old floor. She combed her snow-white hair before the mirror, and looked away from her evasive eyes, and wondered whether Freddy would remember her birthday. Her birthday was a week away, and Freddy hadn't said anything about it so far. Would he forget? She looked at this face she thought was fascinating, and saw her mouth tighten and her eyes grow bullet-black.

She *wanted* Freddy to forget her birthday. She pictured the day—at the end of it, he sitting in his chair, she across from him in hers, the fire blazing between them, she lifting her drink to her mouth, he reading the newspaper, everything stone quiet, everything as usual. The telephone rings. She picks it up. "Oh hello! Dearest! Well, thank you. Well, nothing really . . . Well, it's dear of you to call me," and so forth. Hanging up. Returning casually, murderously, to her drink. She raises her eyes to Freddy over the rim of her glass. He puts down the paper. "Who was that?"

"That was Celeste. Wishing me a happy birthday."

She loved this scene. She wanted it to happen. Wonderful, how awful he would feel. Wonderful how it could pad her little failed self with cushions of comforting triumph.

Yet now as she thought of him, his face so aghast, her heart opened and spread.

"I forgot." His face was miserable.

"Well. Yes. You're so wrapped up in your work you forget everything else *but* work. You're so concerned about the poor old Mrs. Klines of this world, you forget about your own wife."

"Oh, *Lidi.*"

She was beginning not to like this at all. She didn't like the looks of her mouth, pulled tight and mean. She got up and flounced away from her mirror. She thought of changing into a long skirt but decided not to bother. Turning away from the closet she then decided immediately that she would bother. A change, any change, even the change of clothes, would be like going forward, not backward, not standing still in this snow-shrouded house.

She trotted into the living room with her little hesitant steps. "Guess what!" she announced to Freddy, who had flung the blanket off his knees and with a crumbled handkerchief was mopping perspiration from the back of his neck, his face. "Oh, your temperature's broken," she cried. "Good."

"Could you get me a clean pair of pajamas? I'm drenched."

She got them. She helped the weakened arms and legs out of the fever-soaked wet pajamas, and into the dry ones. The smell of sickness touched her, and the smell of helplessness. "Anyway," she said, tucking the blanket over his knees again, "guess what? I've decided to have a party for my birthday!"

"I was wondering what you'd like to do. I thought maybe you'd like to go out for dinner somewhere, if I was better by then."

"Out for dinner?" So. Was she sorry, or was she glad he hadn't forgotten? She was both, she saw. But perhaps more glad than sorry. She could have gone either way. If he had forgotten, she could easily have gone down the more exciting, self-righteous, narrow road of being glad he had. But now she could just as easily (and wasn't there some relief in it) go up the widening road of being glad he hadn't forgotten. Yes, there was a faint relief in being denied the closed road, and in being pushed toward the open road. "Out for dinner? Well, Freddo, to tell you the truth, what I've been thinking, I've been thinking I'd like to have a good big smashing party on my birthday. Seventy-two! Boooo! But thanks, dear, just the same."

ᔓᔕ III ᔕᔓ

THE bus labors on, dense with dreams, loud with the surcease from effort. The driver, leaning over his wheel, he and all the forty-seven passengers he is transporting, are deep in the thick silence of no words. Silence, as the bus rumbles on through the fog-thick dancing snow. Deep snow-quiet as the vigilant driver, the sleeping passengers, dream. Soon they will all wake up, and get off the bus, and go home. And begin again.

Cabe had loved the concert. Mozart gave him one kind of musical satisfaction—he listened to Mozart not with his blood but with his brain—and it was always an exciting musical experience to him to be taken into this complexity, this infinity, of erudite elegance. It had been better for him today, he thought, settling into his bus seat, more of a distraction, than Brahms or Beethoven would have been, or Rachmaninoff. Perhaps he could not have easily borne Rachmaninoff today, he told himself. The visit to the doctor, though giving him an entirely clean bill of health, had brought back the depression of the operation in a vivid way that showed him how unreconciled he really was to his new condition.

"Well sir, you're fine. Fine. Good as new."

"It's new all right. It's certainly 'new' to be minus my prostate."

"Don't think of it that way, Cabe."

"You mean what have I got to lose? Well. Nothing now. I've lost it."

"Listen, man. I mean *don't*. Think of it. That way. The surgery as I've explained to you was very minor. You still have years of sexual activity."

Well, it doesn't matter, Cabe said to himself in answer to this, standing across the desk from the doctor. Who cares about sexual activity? And anyway that's not really what I meant. They shook hands across the desk.

But now, in the bus, Cabe told himself that Mozart had rescued him. In prayerful gratitude for genius, he adjusted the bus seat to its ultimate reclining position, fell back on it, and closed his eyes.

He slept all the way to Port Stratton, exhausted by the day, by the effort of this first trip since his operation. At Port Stratton he descended from the bus into softly, steadily falling snow, and went into the Cat Bird Seat and killed time with two small bourbons while waiting for the boat, but it was food he wanted, not liquor. The dark, denlike room shook with noise unbearable to him, the thump and rumble of disco was pervasively under the floor and around the walls and underneath the ceiling, it was in the layers of smoke, it violated his body which was too tired to disregard it. I once liked this kind of thing, too, he thought. But now he felt himself to be entirely distanced from it. Though for a moment, unexpectedly, he did not feel diminished by it. Amazing. He could not feel, as he would have thought he would, that in the youthful roar of this place, and in his own solitary, silent, insulated elderliness, there was a contrast that diminished him. There it was, a robust, young, rowdy vitality, but he felt his own different vitality in no way canceled by it.

This was new. He was greatly interested in this idea of the legitimate, the dignified separation of youth and old age, as he sipped from his stingy little glass of bourbon, trying to make it last. There could be a real satisfaction, he saw, in having a clear-cut, ungrudging acceptance of his own condition, which of course he did not have. He might have slowly accumulated a knowledge of the signs of aging, but not a prevailing awareness of what they meant. He was always wondering what being old ought to feel like, simply because he could not pin down the feeling in himself. He could look in the mirror the first thing in the morning, and see that he was looking at old age. And yet he really had no matching sensation in himself. He suspected that the belief in being old was related to an actual physical feeling of infirmity. After his operation he had told himself that the way he was feeling was the way it felt to be old. His sensations had matched what he saw in the mirror.

But when he had gotten his strength back, he no longer had the feeling of old age. And when he wasn't looking in the mirror, he forgot entirely that he was supposed to be old.

And yet, shouldn't he think of himself as old, he worried, or if not old, then getting there fast?

Most of the time, or really all of the time during these "transitional" days, as he called them, of retirement, of the operation, of the move to the island, he had no clear-cut answers to any of the questions that plagued his days and his nights: Why had he resigned from the firm since he hadn't had to? Why had seeing a man in a subway make him realize, in one moment of vivid clarity, that he did not want to work anymore? What had work meant to him, and what did lack of it mean to him now? What was he to do about himself, a sixty-six year old widower without work and without love, starting life again in a new community? And could he face the uncertain outcome of having music be at last the exclusive occupation of his life? These were the questions that wove in and out of his mind these days, not in Mozartian silver threads, but in Sibelius-like somber rivers.

But for the moment, tired, eased by the bourbon, strengthened and stitched together with lacings of Mozart which still vibrated in him in spite of the bedlam of something else here called music, for the moment he felt in himself and his surroundings something unknown to him before, he felt an equation, a sober and perfectly peaceful recognition of them, out there, those young roisterers, and of him, in here, inside his own skin.

The eight o'clock boat came in and Cabe boarded it gratefully. The snow had become a dense, swirling mist, but after the noxious air of the Cat Bird Seat, he loved it. And fresh salt air was a reprieve. Bed was now only an hour away. He went up to the lunch room and found there the usual Friday evening queue, the usual vibrancy of excitement these off-islanders felt about boarding the boat and crossing to the island—nice-looking people in their weekend jeans and their quilted jackets and their sturdy boots. But even the lively middle-agers were without their early-in-the-morning bounce now. Only the children were wildly unfatigued, swarming and excited, and the older and old, he thought, were just as beat as he was. But he wasn't looking to be comforted, although melancholy lay at the bottom of this observation. He looked with detestation at a white-haired old boy in the queue ahead of him, a back-slapper in immaculate sharp-creased chinos and a parka with fur-lined hood thrown back, exuding a loud grinning cheer. It was false, it was pathetic, it was even brave, Cabe thought, but he hated it. "Old pfouff," he muttered.

He bought a newspaper and a sandwich and a cup of coffee, and turned flounderingly away from the counter, coffee splashing out of his cup, but let it. . . . He saw, then, the woman he had passed in the corridor of Symphony Hall. She was standing silently in the queue, dark blue hat, dark blue coat, very white expressionless fatigued face, too fatigued to care about being expressionless, standing patiently, like all the rest, but what could they do, the line was long.

Cabe stopped. It was as though some mandate from her to him swung out like the mechanical arm at a tollbooth to block his path.

She turned her head and saw him. Her eyes livened from passive exhaustion into a gradual attentiveness. But then the habit, the reflex of lady-like-ness changed them subtly, and they grew civil, pleasant, cool with distance.

Cabe, whose smiles were infrequent and even then faint, smiled, with no intention of doing so and actually with no awareness that he was doing so.

She, then, smiled too, a fresh open smile revealing teeth whiter than her face.

Cabe made a little bow with his head and his shoulders, slopping more coffee uncaringly, but still he stood there beside her. He was too tired to monitor his conduct, and he was unable to move away.

She was arrested by him, his checked cap shading his long gaunt face which sagged, his pale cold eyes, his thrust-out curvaceous lips. For a second she had a sharp full impression of him, sensing that all of the man that lived in that face was heavy with a sagging which was not only physical, but was a brooding a deepening a dropping of his spirit, so that all of him seemed in downward motion. And a quiet about him seemed to point to an intensification of inward focus, as though everything in him was dropping to the bottom and there was amassing and solidifying and clarifying, inspectable; but, somehow he was needful, too. She felt in him a supplicating needfulness that seemed to interfere with all the rest.

She looked at the large weight of demand standing beside her, feeling unequal to it and suddenly quite strongly unwilling to be drawn into even this much conjecture about him. And so she smiled at him pleasantly, impersonally, for a moment, and then let her smile slide over him and away. She turned her head. She suppressed a sigh.

Cabe moved on. He was rebuffed and too tired to care much, and was glad she'd rebuffed him because he was too tired to talk and too tired to even understand why he had had to stop by her. He went down the stairs to the non-smokers' side of the ship, found a row of empty seats, sat down next to the cold dark window and unfolded his newspaper across his knees.

But his exhaustion and the fast-fading support of the bourbon, and the blank black windows, these nullifications were not alleviated by the coffee, or the sandwich, neither of which he paid any attention to. He took the last swift tasteless bite of the sandwich and was crumpling the paper in an apathetic fist, when he saw the woman coming carefully down the aisle, holding a full plastic glass in front of her. He looked away, not to be rebuffed a second time.

"May I sit with you?"

He jumped. Then with an automatic courtesy he half-rose, but wearily, grudgingly.

"Don't get up. Please. Do you mind if I sit here?"

"No of course I don't mind." But he did. Still nursing rebuff, he told himself that this was bold.

She sat down confidently and unselfconsciously and began to unbutton her coat with one hand, keeping the drink unspillably still and high up in front of her in the other hand, which shook ever so slightly, and was white as her face, but blue-veined. Cabe thought of a white kid glove.

He was hard put to it to rally himself, although courtesy demanded that he make an effort. But this was really not at all what he had expected or even wanted when he stopped beside her. What had he wanted? At the moment, alongside the woman herself, he didn't know. He remembered that he had been powerfully attracted to the way she walked, but here in the reality of her presence, this seemed academic. Shrinking into those regions of known and comfortable inadequacy, he wanted to discount the feeling he had had at the concert, and upstairs in the lunchroom. It embarrassed him. It alarmed him that he could have been so moved by a woman's walk, or whatever it was about her that had struck him, and that he himself had been the cause of her coming and sitting down so boldly beside him. And he was wary of her inconsistency—rebuff one moment, friendliness the next. Clearly not a person to be trusted, she sat there in a dark coat that had a warm damp smell, faintly perfumed, oppressive to him, warm and alive and oppressive and too close to him.

But out of the white face, the white parted teeth, words were demanding something of him. A courteous as well as a kindly man, Cabe composed his face and turned to her as best he could, and listened.

"Did you enjoy the concert?" she was asking politely.

"Very much."

"It seems funny for me to come and plunk myself down

like this, but it's because you look so familiar. Is that why you stopped, up in the lunchroom? I'm afraid I was awfully tired and not gracious at all. Have we met somewhere?"

"Possibly," he said, looking at her with the cold detached eyes that were such a contradiction to the flagrancy of his mouth. He was in no mood to go futher with this, in a state of exhausted wariness and feeling absolutely unwilling and unable to deal with the reality of this vigorous, beautiful woman. He took the newspaper off his knees and folded it with a snap and set it emphatically on the seat between them.

Celeste nervously sipped gin from her plastic glass. "Well, don't let me interrupt your reading. I just thought . . ." She took another sip, and then quickly another, embarrassed beyond measure at having given in to some crazy urge to seek this man out in spite of her instincts about him. But now that she was here, she would have to wait a decent few minutes before getting up and leaving. She turned away from him, and sat back in her seat and crossed her legs with a faint silken sound that Cabe took note of. She had stopped talking. Now *he* had rebuffed *her*.

Suddenly he was very sorry. Tired as he was, this wouldn't do. The only thing he could think of to say was, "I like the way you walk." But this wouldn't do either. For a moment he had no idea of what to say to her.

But then, out of and in spite of his reserve, in spite of distaste for her boldness, he said in a sedate impersonal way, censoring whatever interest he might be feeling, "You seem familiar to me, too. When we passed in the hall today, or perhaps soon afterward, I was struck by it. Perhaps that's why I took the liberty of bowing to you up there in the lunch room."

Celeste turned and looked at him. Fine eyes, intent and

innocent, searched his. "Yes. Me too," she said with a rising, eager voice. "I thought that too. I mean when I saw you on the bus."

"McCabe Kingsley's my name."

"My name's . . ." she paused. Then for a second her face was a white mask of astonishment. "Cabe Kingsley! It can't. There aren't. There can't be *two* Cabe Kingsleys! Did you live in Gull Harbor?"

"No. But I visited there one summer."

"Then . . ."

They lay side by side, long-legged and overlapping. And lapping beneath them water softly, scarcely rocked the anchored sailboat. One hour, two hours, three, infinity, the black velvety heat of the night was without beginning and without ending, it was a now composed of timeless absorption, absorption into her of this new substance, introduction into her, through the side of her neck, of a substance that clarified, for the first time, what being eighteen years old was for. Phosphorus in the dark sea of her body. Moonlight made Cabe's face gray. Everything gently, perpetually rocking, cradlelike, in sweetness and blackness and silveriness and sweetness. That new sweetness, new as newborn, sinking into the side of her neck where his mouth moved and kissed and roved, without explicitness, a perpetual tender groping pressure. Stinging her neck and piercing it and pressing down into it and into the canals of her body. Densely sweet. Oh, its sweetness. Hours and hours, only he kissing her, she a river of sweetness being kissed, kissed. Lights from the dock snaking golden in the moving water, continuous as kissing. On the shore, from the roadhouse where Mort and the others were, faint music, continuous as kissing, but another world, Mort's world, lights, loud, real. Here, the first time in her life, eighteen years old, the blistering sweetness that being kissed could be. Never like this with Mort. She was engaged to Mort. And she was lying here illicitly, but beyond thought of illicitness, being infused with this firing, explanatory sweetness.

"Cabe Kingsley!" She looked searchingly at him. Could it be? Yes. It could be. There he was, behind the mask of old age, as though the folds of his face, and the sag of his neck, and the gray hair, were makeup skillfully applied to simulate aging although not skillfully enough to conceal that the man was young. How wonderfully touching and sad. Young Cabe was there. But folds of putty had been piled on and sculptured over his firm young chin and his smooth cheeks, an overlay of it was pressed around the corners of his eyes where fake wrinkles had been grooved; and white powder had been dusted into his hair. She took this all in at a glance before she turned away. But not before she had seen that his mouth was young, young. No makeup on that arresting mouth. It hadn't changed at all. She had forgotten its beauty. Its beauty pained her. And revolted her too. Inappropriate, was it, to the rest of the aging man? A hopeless mouth. Hungry.

She was desperately sorry she had sat down beside him, on some impulse she hadn't wanted to control. She looked down into her glass. She saw a memory of sweetness in it, it was there in the liquid, outside of her not inside of her. Sweetness was a word, the memory of a word. Trying to remember sweetness was like seeing herself in Mort's old cine-kodak movies—jerky motions, giggling young embarrassment—someone she no longer was and had no feeling of ever having been. Sweetness had been a fire she had felt and never forgotten feeling, but now she could only tell herself that this was so, there was no longer even the faintest stirring of it in her sixty-five-year-old body.

She did not want to look at Cabe again. She did not want to tell him her name, which would make everything suddenly physical, intimate, terribly intimate, and what were two aging strangers sitting side by side on a boat, ah yes, side by side on a boat again but what a difference, what were these two people supposed to say to each other when she told him her name? The difficulty, the awkwardness of this was unimaginable, a thing she couldn't handle. She could, of course, treat it lightly. Tell him her name, and laugh lightly, suggesting the evanescence, the callowness, of a few unremarkable kisses in the moonlight. Yes. Shrug it all off, she warned herself. And yet there was a heaviness in her chest, as though her heart were a heavy piece of lead, as though she, he, alone, tired, old, strangers, all sweetness passed, were the faded, dusty terminal of the promise of all sweetness.

"Then we *have* met," he was saying. "What is your name?"

"My name?" In a panicked pause she thought of her middle name. "Brockton," she said. "Celeste Brockton."

"Oh." The heavy head jutting forward, studying her for someone he knew was there, drew back. "Celeste Brockton," he said, perplexed. "Are you from Gull Harbor?"

"Yes."

"That must have been where we met, then."

"Yes."

"It's so long ago." Some memory stirred in him, no color, no shape, only a sense of something, a faint emotion, long gone as this morning's daybreak. "But you *are* familiar."

"I remember *you*, well. But as you say. It was a long time ago." She smiled, her lips curled up, her chin was raised proudly. She was relieved, she thought, that he didn't remember her, correct name or not. Would he have remem-

35

bered Celeste Cunningham? Probably not. Probably he had never even thought twice about that long, long kissing. Life is neuter, she thought with a feeling of great emptiness. One thing does not necessarily beget another. But I am relieved, she told herself. And yet it was inconceivable to her that the long kissing of that night could have failed to have for Cabe the depth and the constancy it had had for her, as inconceivable as the sea without a shore.

However, common sense, her mainstay, now told her placatingly and even comfortingly, that this of course could be so. It had meant nothing to Cabe, and this was life and she was quite used to it, and in a certain way of acceptance, even respected it. And yet . . . A cynical sadness made her look down into her glass again, to the memory of sweetness there in the gin and the melting ice cubes. And she brought the glass up to her mouth, and poured the remains of the memory of sweetness down her throat, saying to herself that this was what she was doing. Her eyes were steady, her hand was unsteady. "Well," she said, and rose briskly. "it's been nice to talk to you."

He rose too. He bowed. "Yes indeed," he said. Suddenly he saw that her spontaneity in sitting down with him was the same thing as her stride, and he held out his hand. Without hesitation she took it. It was cold from her glass. Soft.

She felt large long bones. She smiled genuinely. "Good night."

"Good night."

He watched her stride away. He sat down again and picked up his newspaper. The boat was beginning to roll. Beyond the dark window, through the fog of snow, he could see the white-ridged black troughs of the heaving sea. He did not open his newspaper, but sat uneasily, pouting out his finely formed, lascivious-looking lips, and moving them slightly in response to the confused and directionless thoughts which numbed his tired, his resisting mind. He looked out into the blackness of the sea, snow-veiled, white-streaked. And the boat rolled rhythmically, comfortably, like a fat cradle. A few lights were beginning to sparkle in the far deep snow-glow dark, first the lighthouse, then lights here and there along Outer Neck. Soon, there was the small concentrated glow of Seahaven, an isolated welcoming mass of light in the blackness of island and sea.

Part Two

IT was a coastal storm, and for once the island, not the mainland, got the brunt of it. By midnight—on a rising, melancholy, sometimes shrill wind, which would bluster and then roar off sadly to itself in the woods, or would howl ravenously, or would hammer like a cosmic fist—the snow had become so heavy that the contours of land were blurred, roads had grown indistinct, stone walls were buried beneath drifts blown sloping and smooth.

The storm kept up all night. And then, before dawn, gradually, the flakes grew sparse again, indefinite, as they had been in the beginning, the wind softened, flaring up only intermittently. A few final, meandering flakes persisted, then vanished altogether as the sun, rising from the ocean, streaked the whole eastern sky with persian pink.

$\backsim\!\!\curvearrowright$ I $\backsim\!\!\curvearrowright$

CABE woke up in the bed that still felt strange to him, in the bedroom that he despised because of its "frills and flounces." It was Aunt Tilly's bedroom in her large old house set in a flat meadow with a straight tall line of woods to the south, a beautiful ancient house which she had loved and abandoned with secret sorrow. She had fallen one night at Turck's house and broken her hip, and had stayed there ever since: "The woman who came to dinner" she told everyone a bit defiantly, unable fully to accept what both she and

Turck secretly regarded as unsuitable unconventionality. Together, laughing over their drinks, they called it "living in sin," delighted with the idea. But to the world there was no mention, ever, of any but a caretaker, platonic kind of accommodation between them. Cabe, her long-dead brother's son-in-law, had been the one to urge this arrangement, knowing she should no longer be living alone and subsequently realizing, too, that the fine old house, unoccupied, might be a place for him, for weekends, or even later, for retirement. He rented the house from her for a handsome fee which he told her would keep her in Scotch, and spent a few weekends in it during that spring and early summer. And then, one July morning, he saw a man in a subway. And that afternoon he resigned from the firm.

He had been here in Aunt Tilly's eighteenth-century gray shingle house on Long Creek Road, with its flat fields and its forest boundaries, trying to adjust to living in this strange house and strange bed and strange community, since early in September. And it was now the third of January.

He got out of bed as quickly as the heaviness and the stiffness of his body would permit, crossing to look out of the window and to close it, full of a muted exuberance and expectation because of the deep soft dazzling white world out there, new, full of difference. Across the road Durand's little red house sat deep in snow, its roof blanketed. In the woods a gust of wind roared, tossing the trees and releasing a mist of diamond snow. Cabe felt something fresh, something hopeful, invade him. He felt it, but then immediately disbelieved it. He turned hurriedly away from the pristine snow, from sorcerous hope, toward the safety of known, real, unchanging malcontent, and pulled on his tattered plaid robe with the covert haste of a man who dislikes to expose his body, stepping into his cold slippers and lunging off to the bathroom.

In the mirror he saw the slouched face of Cabe Kingsley, he saw what he considered the reality of an aging man just waked from dreams to an uncertain day, another long day of trying to find in himself and his fingers the music he always believed he could make but was never able to. He stood looking into the mirror, into his strong, unevasive eyes that gave him back no lies. And he sighed heavily because of the truth of Mozart's art, and the truth of his own lack of it.

Music rippled in his head. Music surged into him and away, escaping, leaving him for the moment empty of this reliable need of his life. Then he saw a woman's stride, he saw legs striking forward, scissoring powerfully forward, and he had a peculiar pervasive and profound sense of himself being inert and rigid as wood. *She* was motion going forward. *He* was something stopped. But her radiant walking, for a moment, flickered feebly in him like a little light, so that again he had a sense of taking something from it, of her giving him something he could use. Celeste Brockton . . . He took his toothbrush out of the spattered glass. Celeste. The name tugged faintly, tantalizingly at his memory. But what was the use of trying to remember anything anymore? His memory had become a void, a cloudy obliterating nothing, never an image, a specific in it. Celeste?

He began to brush his teeth doggedly. Every inch of the big man performed this solitary act with a detached but dedicated ferocity. Robotlike he sawed the brush across his open mouth, spat, sawed away again, oblivious to what he was doing, so oblivious that five minutes later he would question having done it, and would have to feel the brush to see if it was wet. The tap dripped, the toilet's flushing died slowly and musically away. There were no other sounds in this large and empty old house. And outside, the quiet was immense, endless.

～～ II ～～

THEY had been lying together spoon fashion in Turck's old four-poster bed, Tilly's back curving along Turck's front, his heavy arm across her waist, their octogenarian faces washed pure and content and slack with sleep. But now Turck stirred, and his stirring communicated itself to Tilly. Softly, pleasantly, then, she was almost all awake. And now they began the ritual of ten years. Tilly gave a short signal, a small movement perhaps, and Turck held open his arms automatically and she rolled stiffly over and into them, gasping a little, settling her head on a certain exact part of his shoulder, a part where her head would be cushioned on yielding flesh, not sharp bone. Thus entwined they both made soft sounds of satisfaction. Their eyes were still closed. Peaceful, they would lie like this and enjoy it for a while.

Time was unimportant. They had all the time in the world, these two old lovers who had never married. There was no hurry about getting up, no hurry about doing anything. Tilly had her garden, she had her clubs, the League of Woman Voters, the Keep Me Informed Club, the Historical Preservation Society, the Friday lunch club. She had her voluminous correspondence with her son and daughter-in-law and six married grandchildren who lived in Australia—every

44

few days she wrote a letter to one of them, or sent a little package, or a funny card, or a pressed flower.

And Turck had his passionately enjoyed activities—hunting and fishing and golf and swimming and his four-mile walk a day; and his hobbies—the collection of old guns and old pipes and ship models in bottles and scrimshaw and arrowheads and antique taxidermed birds that often bore a resemblance to himself.

But in spite of their sidelines, their days were spent for the most part together. When asked by some newcomer who didn't know them, what they did all day, Tilly would say in her explosive, no-nonsense way, "We enjoy." And once Turck had said to Freddy, the only person in the world he would have said so personal a thing to, "You know, Freddy, Tilly and I are inseparable." Daring Freddy to think him sentimental, he had given him a lofty, cold eye whose fierceness only emphasized his sincerity.

After a while Turck and Tilly made long-drawn-out, exhausting love, something they did more frequently than one would expect. Tilly's participation was tepid, almost nonexistent, but it no longer mattered to her that this was so. Her passion was respect for the act, more than anything. To her, the only fragment of illusion in the reality of living was this, this poetic game, this sublime little party. She had never ceased to marvel at "the concept" of it, as though she really believed a deity to have "thought out" this incredible game for the relief of humanity's unremitting misery.

After Turck had come to the long, laborious end of his rapture, and lay stunned beside her, his heart pounding horribly, she said to him, "Did you have a bad dream in the middle of the night, dear? I heard you make a funny strangled sound and you jerked."

"I was trying to run," Turck said promptly.

"Oh, that was it. That jerk was trying to run."

"I could see the boat at the dock. I left the car much too far away from it so that I had to hurry. Walking. Then running. Should I take the street or the beach? I chose the beach. Pleasanter or quicker? The former, I think. Wrong decision. Because I began to see I had only five minutes before the boat left. I began to get worried. But it *was* possible to make the boat, I could see that. I called out to the man taking the tickets to hold the boat."

"Oh, that was calling *out*, that funny sound you made."

"I'm a-Freud it was. Did it keep you awake, Til?"

"No, honey. No. I went right back to sleep again."

Turck closed his eyes. In a minute he was lightly asleep. Faint snores puffed from his parted lips. And with its austere bravado fallen away, his face in stark repose was caved-in, vacant.

This is what he will look like in death, Tilly thinks. She shuts her eyes.

"Well, up I get," Turck said, waking with a start. The room was full of rousing light and chill air. He swung his legs out and sat swaying on the edge of the bed for a moment, then he stabbed up onto his feet and swayed tall there, and then started meekly toward the window. "Blow me down," he said with a sleepy explosion, "must be six, eight inches of the stuff." He stood dazed and remotely excited there by the open window. Snow had drifted in onto the sill, and a light dusting of it lay on the floor beneath his bare feet. Now they felt the icy prick of the snow, and he drew in his breath sharply and took a little clumsy dancing step over to the part of the floor where there was no snow and then he pulled the window down hard. "You should just see this, Til," he muttered in a wondering, respectful voice.

Tilly sat up, slowly. "My," she said. Slowly she came out from under the bedclothes. Slowly, shakily, she walked over to stand beside Turck, "My, it *is* deep. Now you won't go out there and try to shovel, Turck," she announced, "will you?" She put a fussing, trembling, manicured hand, brown-spotted as a bird's egg and beautifully long-fingered, on his arm.

Turck laughed. His laugh was almost soundless, a faint rasping in his chest, accompanied by a shaking of his whole frame, with heaving shoulders thrust up to his flat cold eagle's head. "I could have prophesied that remark," he gasped delightedly.

"And you'll tell me you *are* going out there and shovel, won't you?"

"I will." Happily.

"And *I* could have prophesied *that* remark," she said, turning up her face and giving him a sudden adoring smile that had in it the wisdom of entire knowledge of him. "Now go make the coffee, dear," brusquely, "while I wash."

While Turck made coffee Tilly brushed her teeth and combed her short blue-white permanented hair and put on harsh red lipstick crookedly and then marched back to the bedroom and climbed into bed. Turck brought the coffee on a tray and turned on the television for the *Today Show*, and then he got into bed beside Tilly, and handed her her cup of coffee, and picked up his, and they settled back, shoulder to shoulder.

III

As Lidi pulled up the bedroom shade, the sun struck her full in the face; it blinded her. It was like being struck alive, and from the daze of sleep she exploded into joy. And she heard Freddy moving around in the bathroom with a new step and then heard him come out and head down the hall to his shop. She could tell by his strong step that he was better.

And because the sky was blue and clear, this dazzling white blanket of snow seemed now to her only like a smooth blanket drawn up over sleep, not any longer like a white shroud covering death. Because of the blue sky, because of brightness, not grayness, which was like sound, the loud blue of the sky and the heat of the sun felt to her like sound.

White world, pure world, she said to herself elatedly. And a fresh conviction of unexplored depths in herself came over her, and she was all at once positive that she had it in her to improve "Dawn Departure." She was fired with energy. Freddy was better and heading for his shop, and she would spend the morning writing.

Sun throbbed in the house. She dressed quickly, then hustled through the sun of the rooms, hugged in her scarlet shawl, jubilant in a reliable calm way because of the on-goingness of this house, two people in it planning, working. "Working," she said aloud, and lilted up onto her toes in a sort of skip.

She went into the breakfast room and pushed aside the draperies on their wooden rings, letting in the light. Simultaneously a cardinal in swift flight, mistaking the suddenly cleared glass for space, smacked against it, a sickening alive thug against the glass, then dropped like a stone to the porch floor.

Lidi stood absolutely still.

⌁ IV ⌁

An unusual quiet and a different intensity of light penetrating her eyelids conveyed the fact of deeply fallen snow to Celeste as she came gradually out of sleep, trailing away from the dream and back into herself. Suddenly there was the soft surprise of being awake.

And then, in this first uncomplicated moment of full wakefulness, she was aware, single-mindedly, of a sound— the bedlam of bluejays. For a moment it was as though nothing, not even she herself, existed but this bright outside sound, and she felt how strange it was, and peaceful, to be disembodied, to have there be only two things in the world, this noise of birds, and herself a sounding board in space floating impersonal and flat and feather-light and disengaged from the responsibility of living. Then she began to listen to, and to hear, the sea rattling and sweeping the stones of her beach, she lay listening with the awe and profound satisfaction she always felt, to the pound and rattle and sweep of the surf on her stony winter beach.

She thought of Cabe Kingsley. Then, and now, merged into a floating, absurd, poignant mass of young lips and folds of old skin and the memory of singing blood. It was a disturbing, visceral sensation, akin to the feeling of having eaten something too rich which lies heavily on the stomach. She lay uneasily, wishing these thoughts to be gone, but unable not to go on with them. And then an unbearable and for that reason long-buried feeling of not having been valued at all, of having been discarded as something temporary and not worth keeping, knifed her suddenly, and she felt a surge of hatred for Cabe, because he had begun her life that night, he had shown her, given her a beginning, and then, coldly, carelessly, he had made it end.

She felt a helpless deep sadness as she lay there. And she could tell herself, now, in the first reviving of the memory of Cabe Kingsley she had had in many years, that what she had felt that night was the real thing, and that she had never felt it since, nothing even remotely like it. It had been the awakening of her body in response to the kind of male body hers was meant for.

She sighed, and felt a tired, vague, sour hatred for him.

"I'll call you." He touched her arm, she had never lost the feeling of his sudden grip through the silk of her sleeve. "Tomorrow."

Driving home from the roadhouse, six of them in Mort's open car, she sat wedged between Mort and Cabe in the front seat, Christina and Boy and Girl Birdsell in the back, stone quiet those three, their deliberate, censorious, punishing quiet striking her back like blows. Mort was quiet too, he drove wordlessly and very fast. He was stiff with hurt and incredulity and suspicion—what had those two been doing out there on the boat for hours? He and she were two stiffnesses side by side, but he had nothing to say to her, then or ever. No questions, no rebuke. He wasn't letting her go. Nothing in Mort would concede or permit that she was not his girl, his wife-to-be. The matter would be ignored. Swept under the rug. But the late night was heavy with heat, warm wind tore her long hair back and out straight, the car raced. And exultation lay along one side of her body which was split up the middle—the side sealed against Cabe, rejoicing, conniving, a secret welding, a secret singing of her blood to his, the other side wooden, no life in it, stiff with denial, pressed against Mort.

Split up the middle indeed, she thought now. She moved restlessly under the too-warm electric blanket, and tugged her long white hair angrily from the heat of her neck, flinging it out onto the pillow. Split absolutely up the middle.

She had waked up the next day with only one thought, that the telephone would ring and it would be Cabe. She lay in bed in the room Grandma had just had redecorated for her home-from-boarding school, soon-to-be-married granddaughter, a May-Day-Queen room, overwrought, over-abundantly curtained and quilted and flounced—apple-green glazed chintz bedspread piped in rose, apple-green pleated silk lampshades piped in rose, apple-green carpet, apple-green ruffled organdy tieback curtains, and over them apple-green glazed chintz draperies loud with full-blown roses. Everything brand new except for her old stuffed animals. The room proclaimed to Celeste the position she had come to in this house; this summer-colored newness was the newness of Celeste, was Celeste arrived, given the setting that was now appropriate and her due. She had managed it for Grandma. She had succeeded at boarding school. And then right away, only weeks after graduation, she had succeeded in the promise of matrimony. Mort. She was madly in love with Mort. She thought. When Mort put the square-cut diamond ring on her finger, she had a second of abhorrence, and of terror. But, the ring was an amazing thing. In the prismatic depths of that ring, she saw a world of dazzle. It was the crystal ball of her future with Mort, Celeste at the top of the ladder, Celeste enshrined, Celeste safe. Oh, she was madly in love with Mort. And she believed that this was the intoxicant of the prospect of being Mrs. Morton Hunter. She believed that this new thing, this splurgy excitement, was love. This promise of safety, she believed to be love.

And all the time, this seductive safety had chiefly to do with Mort's position in the world; it was the intoxicant of getting out of her grandmother's aura and into Mort's that gave her this febrile happiness. She had gravitated to Mort because she had been reared to sanctify social prominence, the safe place. She had absorbed her grandmother's obsession with it; it was an absorbed attitude which had grown to be as imperative and as unnoticed as her breathing. She gravitated toward it without even knowing that that was what she was doing. There, one summer night at the Golf Club dance, was Mort, on vacation from law school. There he was, and there it was—Mort and social position. The combination. Fate.

Everyone said that Louise Cunningham had the money and the Hunters the class, and that both sides had gotten what they wanted. Everyone knew this except Celeste. Even Mort, worldly in a way that Celeste would never be, was not unaware of the promise of what *he* believed to be safety, when he fell in love with Louise Cunningham's granddaughter. And he did fall in love with her, deeply. "I'm fortune-ate," he said to himself with happiness and no shame.

"You're the prettiest girl I ever saw. I like the way every-thing in your face curls upward—your mouth, your nose." He had been struck by this the minute he had cut in on her at that Country Club dance. Mort never responded to people or to anything else in terms of metaphors. He would have scorned metaphorical reactions as flowery, female, yet his first reaction to Celeste was not a thought, but a sensation, as though he had walked out of a dark house into the bright sun. Next, more consciously and with utter wonder, he re-alized that her face seemed to offer itself. Unrebuffed was the word for it. It was so enchantingly innocent in its be-stowal. And yet it wasn't weak; in alliance with candor he could see that there was strength and reasonableness there. She chattered on and on, apparently saying whatever came into her head, burstingly joyous and simple. He thought this was a treasure of a girl. He loved her right away.

And Celeste. Her first impression of Mort was that he was exactly like Christina, his eldest sister and Celeste's boarding school roommate and best friend. With Christina, Celeste had found that ultimate ease, an irrepressibly lib-erating and interflowing communion; they talked through the night, they laughed all day. Everything one said the other loved, or agreed with, or giggled at. It was a teeming and high-spirited and stimulating congruence, typically young in its vivacity.

And it was the same with Mort and Celeste. Their per-sonalities kindled each other just as hers and Christina's did, but more so, and more intriguingly so, because he was a man and Christina was not. And he had everything that Christina had, plus that mysterious and coveted organ which

Celeste knew nothing about, and yet in her blood knew everything about. She had felt a kind of delirious safety as she whirled around the dance floor with the panels of her flame-colored chiffon dress floating out, and the same vivid floating sensation in herself. She felt an alliance with his decency, she recognized it and without defining it felt its bond. And, in awe, she listened to his cleverness, which he was making no attempt to conceal. He was not handsome but had a fine-boned, silver-blond quality, a choirboy look, and a beak nose that Grandma called aristocratic, his Yale suavity—those smooth manners—masking a quick and radiant kindness. And his humor!

"He's a riot, Grandma. Honestly, he's more *fun*!"

"Well, sssweetie, that's marr-velous," Grandma said with soft, explosive wonder (though she'd seen no evidence of Mort's humor), raising her eyebrows for the duration of the *r*'s, then letting them drop and giving Celeste a dazzling grin. "And what has Chrissstina got to say about thisss, may I asssk?" A slight lisp made Grandma's *s*'s sibilant, so that this hushed exclamation was a dulcet hissing detonation.

"Oh, she's just *thrilled*!" All through the year of rooming with Christina, Celeste had been told about her huge family and been shown their pictures, but she hadn't met them until this summer when they had spent a month in Gull Harbor. And she had been overwhelmed with the abundance of noisy wonderful family-ness in that household—swarms of girls, all joyous, all arrogant, all immediately fond of Celeste. She had seen them in Boston one day with Mrs. Hunter, before she knew who they were, six little girls in dotted swiss dresses wearing identical cardigans—cherry red so that they would all be visible in crowds, presumably—with black patent leather pumps and short white socks and thin grosgrain hair ribbons hanging to their shoulders over their flat silver-blond hair, six proper little girls strung out in a row, holding hands, two by two, obedient, lordly.

Mort was the only boy. The star, the god of the family. Mrs. Hunter was a tiny, mousy, fussing woman, blurred by childbearing. Mr. Hunter was an elegant, bleakly distinguished man in his early fifties, stony and drained. Living on the vestiges of inherited wealth, he knew himself to be a failure and looked to his son for the luster he had failed to generate.

The family life of the Hunters was a swarming, noisy marvelous wholeness to Celeste. At home, the girls shed their black patent leather pumps and their trancelike manners, and they rioted, the sound of their voices and their laughter rang like a gradation of rippling bells through the rented house on the point. Their feet pounded perpetually up and down the staircases. They chattered, they yelled, they hugged Celeste, their soft alive cheeks brushing hers, their close warm peppermint breath filling her, elating her like wine. They played with her hair, all of them, even the youngest. They undid it and let it fall long and loose and then they pinned it up in awful-looking swoops and buns. And the feather touch of their small fingers sent tickling thrills down Celeste's spine. They adored this pretty friendly girl whose permanence here they sensed immediately. And they all adored Mort, Christina included, for adoration of Mort, the star, the god, was the way it was in this household.

"Oh he's *divine*, Grandma! You should just see how his sisters adore him. *Every*one adores him!"

"Well good," Grandma said in a soft, charged voice. All her utterances were bright and hushed and disciplined, a caricature of lady-likeness. She put her elbow on the marquetry table and leaned the soft white dough of her face into the support of two manicured fingers, yawning, then chewing up and swallowing the yawn, her eyes shrewd. "I hear his father has high hopes for that young man. Well. There's no money in that family anymore. None at all, so I'm told. Well, sssweetie, I'll bet you're having more fun than a barrel of monkeys."

Oh yes, she was having fun, more fun than she'd ever had in her life. Inevitably. She had been a lonely only child or rather grandchild, brought up in a house too big, too quiet, too empty of family, to be happy in. Gabled and turreted and trellised, the large frame house was set back in smooth unused lawns that were always in the process of being mowed and sprinkled. Celeste was not allowed to play on them because they were in the front of the house. Princesses are never seen playing on palace lawns. And she was not allowed to sit on the verandas because they were on the street side, too.

Celeste had loved the house. There wasn't a square foot without interest, without some sort of picture in it. The house was a game. It had a crazy daring, a styleless splash, that spoke of unrestraint, and really of childishness. She was forbidden to touch the china but no one scolded her if she did. "No trespassing, sssweetie," Grandman would say with her sussurant, pressing small voice, and then with a wide disclaiming grin.

She loved the swarm of the house, inside and out it was a tempting, illogical house, frilled, bulging. But it was still only a house, it was not people. And while its excessiveness of architecture and of furnishings had their own clamor, still, there was no sound of people in the house, ever. There was Grandma, of course, but she was always out. There were her stuffed animals, a menagerie loved and hugged to furlessness, particularly a favourite teddy bear named Dearie who talked to her through her own invented gruff bear voice.

There were servants, naturally, but they were somehow noiseless and, except for the cook, a transient bunch. No dogs, no cats allowed.

And so it was inevitable that Celeste should love and crave what she found in the Hunter home. And perhaps it was inevitable, too, that she who had never felt love coming from her grandmother, and had had no experience at all with the sensation of receiving or giving love, should innocently translate the constellation of Mort's attractions, the bounty she found in the Hunter home as well as the bounty she found in Mort, into love for him. Mort was an endearing man. He was a good man. He was radiantly vital. Celeste knew this. She sensed in him what she lived with in herself. Looking at him, talking to him, she felt that she was home in the safest, most basic way. She came to know that he loved fresh air as much as she did, oh more than fresh air, sky, cows in a field, the sea, the world. And so, racing along in the open car with Mort was more exhilarating than just being alone feeling joy, it was she and her husband-to-be feeling joy in the same way and with the same limitless capacity. Their delights, their interests, even their niceties, were attuned. And to her amazement, this sophisticated young man even took to her teddy bear Dearie, entering zestfully and imaginatively into her serious game of make-believe. And he was masterful! She loved that, loved being swept along by Mort's masterfulness, the breezy powerful way he had of showing her, telling her, guiding her, indoctrinating her. "I'm a little lamb who's lost in the wood, I know I could, always be good, to one who'll watch, over me . . ." they would sing together. She loved this shelter of masterfulness. It was a new, undreamt-of experience to have a man in her life, not just Grandma. She loved this spangled shelter. And his mind! She was in awe of his mind.

"You know everything, Mort."

"Well, I know enough to know that we're the best thing that ever happened to each other."

Innocently, she glowed. Since Mort knew everything, he must be right about that. But her innocence, as well as being a vein of gold, was a blind spot, it was purity at the same time that it was ignorance. How could she know this? The nature of innocence lies in not knowing what it is. How could she know that the joy she felt with Mort, the happiness she felt with the Hunter family, the glamor of the Hunter world, was not love? What, after all, did she know about love? Her childlike mind had no way of informing her that sexual attraction is the base of married love, even though after being with Cabe Kingsley her body knew it. Love, to her, was hugging her teddy bear Dearie. She only knew love in the absence of it, as someone knows hunger in the absence of food. She had had no experience of parental love, though in the first four years of her life, before her father died, she had felt something coming from him to her which throughout her life was a tenuous support. And she had had no experience of grandmotherly love. Grandma had no love for Celeste; Celeste was too much like her schoolteacher father, who had been the son of the postmaster. Grandma kept telling Celeste, reproachfully, how much she resembled her father, and how little she looked like her mother, Grandma's only child, dead of flu in her twenties along with the schoolteacher husband. Their elopement had shattered Grandma. She had never been able to be more than civil to the schoolteacher. And after the death of the young couple, Grandma had given her own name, Cunningham, to four-year-old Celeste.

Louise B. Cunningham. A formidable, frivolous woman. And rich. "Dollars keep erupting like Vess-*ssu*vius," she would sibilate, throwing up helpless white hands. Simplistic and rigid, she lived according to a few rules—a woman's day is composed of keeping her house and her own appearance up to the mark; a woman's day is involved with the logical extension of house and clothes, which is society; and her duty, her moral responsibility to her world, lies in giving to those less fortunate than herself. Noblesse—and oh how she wished it were real noblesse—oblige. The Louise B. Cunningham Orphanage for Girls, a monument to the abstract heart of its founder, stood large and cold and institutional on the top of a treeless knoll, gray stone girdled with black iron fire escapes, black driveway winding up to it like a cold deep river.

She had a heart. It was only that she was mystified about how to use it, frightened of using it directly, because of a mild and shallow brain made rigid by rules. Her heart was simply too overlaid with conventional attitudes and social obligations to be given full expression. As much as she had been able to she had cared for her daughter, but the attentions she paid her were insufficient and unstable—she either spoilt her halfheartedly or disciplined her halfheartedly. In the years after her daughter's death she caught herself sometimes with an unexplained haunting sensation of emptiness, like a faint desolation. But a kind of imperviousness, toughness, kept her from letting it amount to anything in terms of undermining the brazen confidence of her nature. She was able to seal it off and forget it for years at a time. She did not seem to be built for a full and uninhibited use of the heart, anyway, even her figure seemed to explain this—it was compact, erect and well-proportioned but with no waistline, she was one straight line down both sides. Her figure was like herself, no swelling hip curving into narrow, poignant waist; no full white breasts belonging to the soft green grass of summer. No curves at all, no subtleties; no poetry; dreamless as cast iron. She came of this cast-iron stock. The women had always endured. Not all of them had rusted. But even the ones who had, had lived it out, somehow.

She had been born and orphaned in this house, married in it, funeraled her husband and her daughter from it. The massive mahogany breakfronts, the fat little tufted velvet chairs framed with carved floral eruptions—this immutability had always been there, she had grown up in the solid dark funerary pomp of this Victorian climate. But she loved to buy, she couldn't stop, and the blond wood of this and that, bulbous caramel-colored chests inlaid with a fluttering of cream-colored birds and garlands, honey-colored game tables with inlaid chess boards, these *she* had added, buying and buying, buying anything, so long as it was antique. "The only thing in this house that's not an antique is the carpet sssweeper," she would say with a whoop of soft laughter. Everywhere there was the padding and the hush of deep-pile dark redness: couches, chairs, portieres, carpeting. And there was an omnipresence of china, in corner cupboards, in glass-fronted cabinets, on mantelpieces, on tabourets, china teapots, china soup tureens, china plates and cups, china figurines. And pictures—the dark paneled, and the damask-papered walls were entirely covered with hand-painted trays, and photographs, and oil paintings of shepherds with flocks of sheep, and stags on craggy mountain tops, and assemblages of grapes and cut-open watermelons on draped tables. There were innumerable steel engravings, too, in lace-like gilt frames, mostly of little girls: little girls embracing kittens, little girls swinging in apple orchards, little girls sitting in a froth of petticoats on grown-up knees. There was one little girl holding herself erect, plump and vacuous as a life-sized doll, head coyly tilted, small fat fingers interlaced confidently on her lap, her dangling ankles correctly crossed. This, Celeste was told, was Grandma when she was six. Little Louise Brockton. And now Louise Brockton Cunningham, grown sixty, held her body in precisely the same way, confident, powerful. Nothing about her had changed at all.

THEY danced, they drove fast in the wind of the open car, they parked on country roads and "petted," their insatiable useless kissing for Celeste only the tender sexless kiss of children. They parked in the dark of night parks and drank sticky liqueurs from Mort's Britannia metal hip flask. They drank a lot, "making whoopee," Mort called it. She, who had never tasted liquor until she met Mort, soon was drinking dry martinis unblinkingly. It was Mort's way. Mort's world. Being drunk was finally fun. They laughed, they chattered nonstop, irrepressibly and freshly fondly delighted with one another. She had never liked anyone better than she liked Mort Hunter. Life lay ahead of her in a trousseau of evening dresses—beaded white chiffon that was one solid glitter, lime green panne velvet lined with gold lamé, tight black velvet with a fountain of black tulle down one side—clothes that Mort had gone with her and Grandma to select, for he took a proprietary as well as a sybaritic interest in what his wife-to-be would wear. Oh, the glamor of having a fiance who liked clinging dresses, who loved plunging necklines, who insisted on lace-trimmed chiffon negligees not warm bathrobes, who gave her a gold anklet to wear under her silk stocking, though Grandma said worriedly, "That's actressssy, Celeste." It was intoxicating to Celeste to be swept out of Grandma's aura and into this one of Mort's, to become so easily, and to Mort's avid-eyed delight, one of those girls she had only seen on the stage, or in the movies, or in *Vogue* magazine. She loved the way she looked in these clothes that Grandma called "fast" and that Mort called "knockout." Life lay ahead of her in all this glamor, in her first fur coat with a little round muff to match, in the bridal parties and the bridesmaids' envy and the bride, the wedding! Life, glittering and bottomless as the diamond, lay ahead of her in the wedding trip to Paris (Grandma's wedding present). Mr. an Mrs. Morton Hunter running up the gangplank in a shower of confetti! Oh, the delirious promise of life as Mrs. Morton Hunter! I love you, she had told Mort, over and over.

But she met Cabe Kingsley. And suddenly there was no bottom, she was adrift and about to drown.

"I don't think I love you, Mort."

They were picnicking beside a little river. Mort sat with his long legs crossed, his blond head flung back, tilting a bottle of white wine sensuously into supporting lips. His Adam's apple, under the white fine skin of his young throat, traveled up and down as he swallowed, his face rapt, dedicated.

She put her paper plate down onto the moss of the river bank, here on this velvet summer noonday, a sky of moving dense green leaves over them, the murmur of the little river. She was very warm, her breasts, the nipples starting up, pricked the silk of her slip. The moss, the river, the leaves, the stirring still heat of the noonday, all had to do with the starting up of her breasts.

"It's awful to say that, Mort."

Stunned, he finished swallowing, slowly, deliberately. In a panic he brought the bottle down and wrapped both trembling hands around its coldness. But then determination shuttered panic instantly, and he turned to her, assuming the face of an astonished, a patient parent. He looked at her with searching blue eyes that had managed to overcome the panic and were now cleverly, even serenely confident. "I. Just. Don't. Believe it." He had a singsong, nasal voice, faintly sardonic, amiable. "Celesty, look, doubts happen to everyone, everyone." He was sure of his worldliness and of her manipulatable innocence, and also, quite rightly, sure of her childlike inability to know her own mind. "Who can love someone every minute of every day, I ask you? That's not the way it is. It's the average that counts, not the minute to minute emotion. I'm willing to bet that tomorrow you'll wonder how you could ever have felt this way. Because honestly, I don't think you really *do* feel this way." And, with a little boy drooping mouth to parody sadness and disappointment, and to shame her out of this, and because, if manliness was not succeeding, little-boyness might, "You promised me. Remember you said, 'Forever and ever, Honor Bright'? Remember our pact? We never say Honor Bright unless we mean it?"

"Yes," faintly, "I remember. Oh, *Mort.*" She looked at him, searching for him. His white shirt was open at the neck. She saw the silver-blond hairs on his chest, and shivered faintly with revulsion. She was lost. She closed her eyes and desperately, adroitly, metamorphosed him into white tie and tails. Then she could respond to him—Mort, sweeping over the dance floor, tails flying out, graceful, like Fred Astaire. The diamond on her finger caught a shaft of sun piercing the shadowing leaves. "I don't know, I don't know."

"You love me." His conviction that this was so was as strong as his fear that it wasn't. "If anyone should know it, the man you're going to marry should. Do you think I don't know how you feel about me? It's written all over you."

"Really?"

"Yes. Really. And listen, Celesty," with his best puckish

look, "I have this great big idea. We're going to have three girls, because girls run in my family and in yours, fortunately for me. They'll be named Celeste the First, Celeste the Second, Celeste the Third, we'll nickname them Prima, Secunda, Tertia. But I won't love them as a father should because none of them will be as nice and as beautiful as you. I'll be a faulty father."

They laughed a lot at this. They lay back and laughed up into the sky of trees. Then Mort stopped laughing and rolled over onto his hip, and put his head over hers and he kissed her. The kiss was wet, tasting of wine and cheese. This transported her to an inside place somewhere, lights, a fire, ice tinkling in glasses. And so the kiss was all right, because it promised all that, and belonged to it. And she was there, not here.

Mort made a soft moaning sound as he kissed her. His thin arched nose dug into hers, his warm winey breath steamed up into her nostrils. "Oh, I love you, Celesty." His voice pled. "Please love me. Please, please love me." An instant's faint connection with a response at her core told Celeste this supplication expressed a rapacious need, and was not something she could rapturously translate into "Mort Hunter adores me."

"Oh, please, please." His lips on hers fluttered with begging.

He was like his spaniel. She loathed that dog, who was always sitting on the floor at her feet, looking up at her with brown liquid asking eyes, putting a paw on her legs as repeatedly as she took it away, begging her to stroke him, to pull his silky long ears, to scratch the back of his neck. Viscerally, violently, she loathed that dog.

She had a moment of loathing this kissing, of fearfully rejecting it as being alien and harmful to her. It was a sense as convinced and as terrifying as sudden disbelief in religion.

She shut it off.

And she was being soaked up by Mort. Helpless. She felt the tonnage of his need lying here beside her, its claim, its omnipotence. Helplessly she told herself that she should be proud to be loved so much by Mort Hunter, and she lay there in acceptance and nullity. She looked up, beyond Mort's head, at the great whispering green cool above them. Her hand lay on the soft moss.

By the time they had packed up the picnic things, gotten into the open car, raced along country roads back to Gull Harbor, and pulled up under Grandma's porte-cochère, she was beginning to leave the witchery of trees and moss, and to return to the sorrowful safety of houses.

In the days that followed, Mort talked to her with the skill of the trial lawyer he was to become, sincerely sure of his love, and determined to be sure of hers. He gave her a book to read called *Love Lies Dreaming*, all about a girl who didn't know she really loved the man until after they were married. He talked to her from the source of everything that she felt was superior, he kept at her with the charm of his smooth assured voice, and with his clever, desperate, winning determination and above all with an iron resolution not to let her go.

Mort had determination (frenetic), and brains, and the obtuse self-assurance of the wellborn. He had done almost everything he had set out to do exceedingly well, and as a result he had an ebullient confidence in himself. But this confidence stopped short in relation to women. There was a dark lack in himself that made him unsure of the manhood he did indeed have and knew he had, and which annulled the display and the proof of it. He had no notion of how to combat this lack, or how to overcome it.

Celeste's lapse of adoration terrified him. But, immediately and bulldozingly, he began to mask his fear of what he did not have, with what he knew he did have, determination and brains and the knowledge of proven capacities. Exerting the masterfulness against which Celeste was powerless, he went about winning her back. Mort's masterfulness was a mixed bag—part an honest self-assurance, part a result of that era in which male domination was taken for granted, part a disguise for his questioned manhood—a mixed bag, but not as far as Celeste was concerned. She saw only an uncomplicated supremacy.

Celeste had a good mind, her marks at school proved that. She also had common sense unusual for a child. Witness the kind of reaction she had as a little girl to an exasperated question of her grandmother's: "Celeste, for mercy's sakes, if you don't keep up your account book, how are you ever going to know how much money you have?" Answer: "But why do I have to keep an account book when all I have to do is look in my pocketbook to see how much I've got." She had a mind which later on was to be respected for its administrative ability. It was a mind intrinsically clear and direct enough to slice through a welter of questions and come out with the logical answer. She was never shrewd, clever, like Mort. His cleverness was manipulative, intricate. But her mind emerged clear, unhindered, decisive, in a way that Mort's would never be.

However, at nineteen, she was too unformed, too dependent, to follow any course but that set out for her by those she was certain were her superiors in every way. A part of this reliance on others was her trust, a quality of sunny, candid positivism which made her see people as they represented themselves to be, to see right before wrong, and to give the benefit of the doubt to almost everyone. "Accentuate the positive, sssweetie," she had learned from Grandma, and this had only reinforced the same tendency in herself.

But since at nineteen she could only use the minds of others, Mort was of course able to persuade her that she loved him. She believed what he told her. Ignoring doubts, she told herself that love lay dreaming and it would come. And in the final suspended moment of accepting this, she felt a rush of elation and relief. Oh, once again the delirious promise of life as Mrs. Morton Hunter!

But that morning in the apple green and rose bedroom, Celeste lay opened, with singing blood and a mind that had forgotten everything but that, and waited for Cabe Kingsley to call.

At ten-thirty he called. "Have lunch with me."

He took her to the Golf Club. Her wedding reception was to be there. He took her into the sunlit dining room where no shadow of the threat of a wedding reception seemed to exist, it was only a big room with tables of people, and by an open window their table, looking out onto jade-green lawns, looking out to the jade-green song of summer.

But it didn't turn out to be what she had expected. It was not darkness and moonlight, it was bright daylight; it was her head, not her body; it was embarrassment and panic and no confidence whatsoever and disappointment, all laced with a growing guilt about Mort, whose sister Isabel sat with a table of shouting little girls at the other end of the dining room. Putting food into her mouth was a self-conscious absurdity, making talk over knives and forks was superficial and not to the point and agonizing. Celeste made bright silly chatter with her heart sinking. Cabe told bragging stories, "I was skulling down the Charles River on the coldest day of the year, and my bare hands froze to the oars."

Oh yeah? Celeste thought now, and over her face, faintly, tenderly, amusement rippled. Last night. Cabe's hand. She felt the placement of her own hand into the momentary keeping of large long bones, the second's pressure of firm strength. Once this was a boy's hand, with male strength yet surely to the touch conveying only the fragile unsureness of the rest of him. But the touch of the grown-up hand was different, no conveying in it now of unsureness, no hint in it any more of the need to spin an improbable tale about male invincibility. "My bare hands froze to the oars." Celeste began to shake with helpless laughter. "Oh," she gasped, "oh. How adorable, how touching. God, what a tall tale." And a warmth, a regard for the man filled her as she thought of his fragile youth, his imagination, and now the strong, sad set of his aging face. Those tall tales were his daytime courtship, she thought. But he was with truth in the dark, not talking with his mouth, just kissing me with it.

After lunch he drove her into Boston to call on his mother. A Beacon Street citadel. Disappointing inside. Stiff, dark, even shabby. Mrs. Kingsley was dour and high-collared as in a daguerreotype, remote in a dark way; like the house, a kind of monument. She guided Celeste's elbow toward a handshake with a dried-up tiny woman in a black taffeta uniform who was lurking in a dark doorway. She was Cabe's old nurse, Miss Stoat, Celeste was told in a tone that warned this arriviste girl, who surely had been raised not to shake hands with servants, to be gracious to this one. Stiff and appraising, though polite, Mrs. Kingsley asked them to stay to tea. But Cabe, having the grace not to prolong the visit, said no.

She never saw him again. She would lie in her room over the porte-cochère, on her apple-green bed, listening for the sound of a motorcycle on the street, Cabe's motorcycle, Cabe driving by—wouldn't he drive past her house just to look at it and imagine her in it? . . . She waited and waited for the telephone to ring again, and for a motorcycle to pound past the house, shaking the porte-cochère, shaking her in the apple-green boughs of her room.

Mrs. Kingsley sent a wedding present (she was an old school friend of Mort's mother), a little portrait on ivory encased in a locketlike brass frame, of a young, epauleted, buff-trousered officer with a crescent of gold curl on a high white forehead. It came in a flat blue velvet box lined with taffeta. After she was married, Celeste hung the little portrait beside her dressing table mirror. And in the blue velvet box, in her dressing table drawer, she kept her earrings.

Impaled along the curved side of a bed in their Paris hotel, Celeste the bride, taken in the middle of the day, after lunch, wine-willing and sadly submissive, her heart empty and rebellious, lay with her legs spread out from her pulled-up skirt, cringing from that bruising persistence that couldn't come to anything more than this because of all the wine of his lunch and because she hated it and he knew she hated it.

A fresh, bitter anger flared up in Celeste. Lying alone in this wasted bed, she felt the sadness, the futility of herself and Mort. Tragedy was the one assimilable word that defined it all. It was like finding an object she'd forgotten about, hidden away in the back of a drawer, and she held it and looked at it as though she had never seen it. It was fully there—tragedy—for her to see. She could see it now, and call it that. Cabe Kingsley had opened the never healed wounds of those twenty wasted, degrading years of her life, and she could be back in them and somehow synthesize them in a way she never had before.

Calling it tragedy had a finality to it that was almost satisfying. To know that it had been this one definite unalterable thing now made Celeste feel, in a calm, yielding way, peaceful. There it was. She had been loveless. And she had been childless as well. She had not been designed to give birth to a beating heart, she had not been designed to bear even one of those girls Mort had wanted—"We'll nickname them Prima, Secunda, Tertia." Being childless had been a deprivation so immeasurable to her that she had buried the reality of it almost at once. But now she had brought it out and looked at it and given it a name. Tragedy. And Mort. Tragedy too, but now that was all only pain worn out. Long ago she had accepted the reality of herself and Mort and the fact that the joining of their lives had been the crime of waste. But for years she had been plagued by the question of who had been more at fault. Was it worse for Mort to love her and to tolerate not being loved back, like his spaniel; and with that bulldozing masterfulness (which she at last, after all these years, saw through), to ignore how she truly felt, to ignore *her*, in effect? Or was it worse for her not to love Mort as a man, and to stay with him just the same, while pretending a physical love that wasn't there and which he knew wasn't there? And why, with so much rapport and so much fondness, had they continued for twenty years to disregard what was best for themselves and for each other?

Finally she understood that their marriage could not be looked at this way. It would be just as meaningless, she saw, to ask herself whether the fault lay with her mother or father, or with Grandma, or with Mr. and Mrs. Hunter, or with Christina, or with Great Aunt Anna, or with wealth, or with the times they lived in, or with society itself. She was no longer concerned with the why of it all. She had gone way beyond the whys, to an acceptance of the inevitable consequences of that marriage. It had taken many years, but gradually she had defined the circumstances of herself, and of Mort, and seen that it couldn't have been otherwise. Even before the divorce, and then very surely after it, she had grown to accept the reality of that insufficient girl and that insufficient boy, and the sad, lacking life they had plunged into.

But how astonishingly long it had taken her to admit this. Twenty years. It had taken her all those precious years of her youth to grow into a gradual admission of the disaster of Mort and herself as husband and wife. She knew from the beginning, of course, that sex was disappointing and sometimes an outrage. But at that time her trusting and stoic mind decided that it was in the nature of things, and she accepted it, made her peace with it and, optimistically, rejoiced in everything else that was so wonderful—her own good health and common sense and great joy in living, her pleasure and joy in the companionship of Mort, in their travels, their innumerable friends, their wealth (Grandma's) which brought them everything they thought their hearts desired. She found that she was pregnant the week Mort was made a junior partner in his Yale roommate's father's illustrious New York law firm. Hurrah, hurrah, what plums from the fruit tree of heaven! "Thisss calls for jeroboams of champagne," Grandma panted, pianissimo, "not magnums, jero*bo*ams!"

Their teddy bear Dearie, now almost as much Mort's as Celeste's, was not enthused. Dearie, it turned out, was jealous. They tried to placate him, but did not succeed.

"He'll come around," Mort said to Celeste, in front of him. Dearie snorted. Enthroned in his armchair in the bedroom, Dearie lived their lives with them. He had his ventriloquial tone of voice, decisive, opinionated. He had his own theme song, "Don't fence me in." He had his gestures, the most characteristic being a paw raised by one of them and held there, then pushed emphatically down along with a disgusted "Humphf!" He traveled to Europe in a suitcase with them, loving France and England but hating—he couldn't "bear" it—Italy because they were dishonest about adding up your check. Feisty, critical, eccentric, harsh about everything to be disliked, adoring them (under his crusty reserve) he was this trapped young couple's extension, he was their discontent made funny, he was their "instead of." His independence, his daring, his openness were instead of their lack of it; even the intimacy he magic-ed between them was instead of a closeness their hearts ached for. And for Celeste, from her childhood on, he had been instead of love. Even with her pregnancy, and the promise of a real child, their Dearie game stayed strong and vital, here to stay.

Celeste enjoyed. She enjoyed, consciously, the fact of breathing. She enjoyed a lilac, the wholeness of a hot poached egg and the plate it was on, cold water from a country pump, bringing sun-dried clothes in from the line, the feeling of velvet. She enjoyed the strong motion of walking forward, the warmth of someone laughing. She was sensuous, sensual, glad. With enormous zest she enjoyed being, she enjoyed what she felt and what she saw. She was wealthy, even her heart was rich, though it was locked away in a vault, inaccessible to her; a treasury of possibilities, locked away. She even enjoyed being in the inner circle, or rather she enjoyed what she took to be its advantages, although, because her natural self-confidence and innate distinction made her feel perfectly at home there and because she didn't feel any different in it than she had out of it, she soon began to wonder why Grandma had put such a premium on it.

Young, beautiful, vigorous, full of the promise of everything that lay ahead, she strode along, chin raised, candid face trusting and mindless, living in the glamor of now and hardly ever wondering where her heart was. Memories of Cabe Kingsley had soon been buried underneath the irresistible glitter of Mort's world. At first, she didn't know she wasn't using her heart. She was too much of a child to know it was unawakened, unused. But soon after she gave premature birth to a stillborn daughter, she began to cry at the movies, in the theater; swollen-eyed and anchorless she would come out from the darkened palace of dreams into the daylight swarm of real life, and she would walk along without any joy at all, disoriented, automatic, dead in the midst of the noisy life of the streets that seemed to have nothing to do with her. At these times the realities of her life, in contrast to the just-glimpsed possibilities of her heart, were coldly, unbearably revealed. What she had to go home to was dead, just as she was. The movie had revealed how much she could not bear what she had to go home to.

Reaching home she would go into the little room she had fixed up as the nursery and which she now used as her own. She would sit down on the bed which was mounded with her old collection of stuffed animals brought here from Grandma's when she was getting the room ready for the baby, and she would pick up Dearie, and press to her emptiness, her forlorn-ness, her disorientedness, this sawdust heart. She would do this while not being able to bear the thought of the evening ahead—Mort coming home, his rousing call from the dark foyer, his ether-sweet gin kiss, and his ritual presentation of the little white waxed paper box with the gardenia in it, "Ohooo, Mort, *dar*ling, thaaaaank you," their customary martinis, one, maybe two, while dressing to go out, Celeste in a mauve taffeta dress with a train that rustled across the floor. None of this could she bear to think about, sitting in the sepulchered nursery, with the late sun stretching down through the apartment window and across the foot of the bed. She would be stopped, made silent, be brought to the threshold which looked out onto darkness.

Yet this was she, and this was Mort, and this was *it*, she and Mort together were *it*. There *it* was. The fact. Reversible? Such a word had nothing to do with Celeste, for it had never occurred either to her or to Mort that the fact of Mr. and Mrs. Morton Hunter was not absolutely and forever unalterable. And so she would sail forth to the party, forgetting. Forgetting would bring her out of it, finally. Along with the martinis. And the faint perfume of the gardenia pinned to the shoulder of her mauve velvet cape. And also her partly unimaginative optimism. Today is bad but tomorrow will be good. There is something wonderful ahead. She was always putting her shoulder to the rock and pushing it back up the mountain.

But she began to have an open, sexual ache, as though she were always hungry, and this ache had nothing to do with Mort. And it went unassuaged. An overpowering, gnawing desire gaped "down there," but there was no one to satisfy it. Except in her imagination. She "fell in love" with movie stars. She had a fantasy affair with Rex Harrison, spun out glamorously in her hung-over mind as she lay for hours in her bed in the mornings. She would develop long, suspenseful stories, lying in her wasted bed, while Mort went off to the law courts, and out in the kitchen the cook stuffed the squabs for tonight's dinner party.

One day, within the space of an hour, all this changed.

"Today is the tenth anniversary of our marriage," Celeste said to herself as she woke up on the morning of that day that both opened and closed her life. She spoke the words aloud, and was surprised to have done this. Why had she done this? She did not want to know the words, hear the words. And yet she had spoken them so that she *would* hear them, and know them.

She let the words stand there, above her, like a black sentence, seeing the words as well as hearing them. Through webs of hangover misery, then, she thought of the words "black sentence." And she let these words sink in, too. In a mind rawly, quiveringly on edge, she let the play on words dance—"sentence," "sentenced," "a black sentence of ten years." She was astonished to be thinking this.

The apartment was quiet. Way off in the kitchen she heard faint sounds of clatter, of running water. The silence pressed, the clock beside her head ticked. She listened to the stalking pressing silence stretching down the long hall. "This is my afternoon to call for Aunt Anna and go to the opera with her." She said this aloud, too. And smiled at the strangeness of what was going on here. Talking to herself. But the sound of her voice was good. She liked this declaring things. "I do not want to go to the opera with Aunt Anna." She spoke clearly.

She lay in a tremulous suspension, faintly sick, hopeless. She knew she did not want to call for Aunt Anna and go to the opera with her and sit in her box with a hangover and watch antic fat bodies posturing as young lovers. The sexual ache, as usual with a hangover, was intense, raging, unassuagable. I would like to be going to a lover this afternoon, she thought, not to the opera with Aunt Anna.

She lay staring up at the ceiling with eyes that felt hard and tight and which ached when she moved them. Nothingness washed over her, vast and empty as space. Obliterated, for a second she had no outline and no substance, she couldn't put her finger on anything that she was. She had spread out into space and had disappeared.

Then she found her mind. Ten years of her life, she thought, all like this. Every morning a hangover, and with every year, less easy to get rid of. And in one month she would be thirty. Thirty years old. Thirty was frightening. "It is my tenth wedding anniversary," she said aloud. "I am going to be thirty and I want a lover and I have the same hangover only worse that I have had every day for ten years."

She lay stiffly, allowing herself to feel desolate. And then a scene drifted into her mind. Behind her tight forehead, developing, emerging out of the aching pressure of her temples, she saw herself in Grandma's orphanage, she was back in the Louise B. Cunningham Orphanage for Girls. She was sitting in the assembly hall, and Grandma was on the platform giving her annual Founder's Day speech.

And now Celeste felt again, as strongly as though it were only yesterday, the sense of barrenness and severity in those rooms, the sense of rules, of pitilessness, of loud shouting that was always being subdued. There was always a sense of subdued riot in those rooms and halls, along with a seething submissiveness. Everything was the color brown, everything was angular, unembellished, unpadded. There was always a smell. How she had detested those orphans, how she had dreaded those Saturdays she was forced to go there with Grandma and "be nice" to those girls who were "less fortunate" than she was. "Just realize they have nothing and you have everything, sssweetie. Try to count your blesssings." And oh, did she! Her home, after that place, had always seemed profligately padded and lush and warm and fragrant, overabundantly everything that the orphanage wasn't.

She lay now in the emptiness of her bone-sore hangover, undergoing a transformation. A crazy brain-soup surged and spattered in her sore head—brown urine-tainted rooms, red velvet rooms and an apple-green one—sense and non-sense ebbed and flowed in her sore head. And then, the whole of her life began to flow through her in colors and textures, the sum of her life flowed through her in velvets and glazed chintzes and satins and tulles and chiffons and taffetas and organdies and damasks, a rainbow of smothering stuffs which felt to her like the very substance of her life, its purpose and its meaning. This was what the essence of her life, and most particularly her married life, had been, this kaleidoscope of stuffs flowing sluggishly, chokingly through her, as though her blood were made of them, as though her heart beat to their thick richly colored flow.

Grandma was on the platform, splendidly all in white: white hair, white teeth, white eyeballs, white diamonds, white cashmere sweater trimmed with ermine and glitter. "You girls are my pride and joy," she was saying with the hushed, intense voice, the penetrating, owlish eyes. "I think of each and every one of you as my daughters." She stopped. Her eyes grew fixed and her broad face smooth as a mask. Tears started to pour down her flat white cheeks.

Celeste's head cleared. The transformation had taken place. These white arms were soft, decadent, her body in its silk nightgown was soft, decadent, this room and the long-ago apple-green room, and the rooms of red plush, all were soft, decadent, padded, obscene, her life was padded and obscene. Angular brown walls and anguish, the clean angularity and anguish of poverty, bone-clean, stark. She felt herself being stripped bare, down to the bone, stripped of padding, of obscene softness.

Suddenly she reared up onto an elbow and reached for the telephone. "Leonora. This is Celeste. I've been thinking about your asking me the other day to be a director of the day nursery. Well, I've changed my mind. If it isn't too late. I've decided I would like to. Good. Yes. Well, not today, today I've got Aunt Anna. But tomorrow. Yes. Fine. See you then."

And so her life changed.

She launched into the minor work of the directorship with all her reservoirs of enthusiasm and zest and practical good sense. Soon the Cloverly Day Nursery took on a new life and eventually the board of directors a new head—Mrs. Morton Hunter. A year later she was asked to join the New York Committee on Minorities and shortly became its executive director. There followed through the years, the New York Friends of Poverty, the Save a Life Fund, the Bowery Project, the International Committee on Hunger, and so forth and so forth. She blossomed like the burst of a roman candle in a night sky. As easily as breathing, she sat in board rooms and found solutions.

Her compassion for the human race had exploded, it knew no bounds. Her tears were now for the victims of floods, of hunger, of racial and political persecution. Pictures of stunned mothers in war-torn villages holding corpses of their dead infants brought on gusts of enraged and desolate weeping. It was unendurable what human beings suffered at the hands of other human beings. Enraging. Her rage fed her compassion and her compassion fed her rage, insatiably.

At first, the rage was abstract in this way, but gradually it began to find closer targets, exploding, to her surprise, in the most unexpected ways. A policeman siren-ing up behind her, making her pull over, sauntering insultingly over to her car and demanding to see her license without even so much as looking at her—this triggered a vitriolic fury she did not know was in her.

Fury born of disillusion began to modify her innocence and became the dark side of it, although she never stopped believing that disillusion could change back to illusion. She didn't call it disillusion. She just knew that something had gone wrong in her which she was sure would end up being all right.

At the same time, using her mind (her heart everyone thought, including herself) for the first time in her life, she began to grow subtly independent, confident, strong in a certain new way that gave her the only surety she had ever had. And yet her breezy imperiousness which had been no more than a spirited expression of confidence, began to grow steely, loud, began to find a source in her which was at home with bossiness. Sometimes she heard the hard sound of her voice, and was troubled. Her mouth, which had known only openness, could tighten now. Once she caught a glimpse of herself in a mirror beyond the head of the person she was talking to, and for a second she didn't know that it was herself. She began more amd more to wear the disguise of flippancy, which seemed to come easily to her.

Work became her focus, even her obsession, along with a growing unwillingness to keep up with the long and late drunken evenings that were the center of their lives. Parties had grown repetitious, their noise no longer drowned everything out. She began to skip the third martini. And then the second. And finally, the first. "Mort, I'm sorry, I can*not* stand the way these are making me feel. I'm tired of drinking. I'm sorry but I'm tired to death of it." Thunderstruck, he looked at her as though she had said, "I'm withdrawing from your life," which is of course what she was saying.

Amazing, how with this rupture, this cessation of the lubrication, as it literally was, of their marriage, their relationship began to reveal its cracks and crevasses, and finally, its putrefaction. Its platonic putrefaction. And the putrefaction was becoming something not to be ignored.

To want Celeste's body and to take it, Mort had always needed the tantalization of something transparent veiling it. Because her persistent aversion to him had only reinforced his uncertainty about his manhood, he had needed more and more to have love-making dressed up. Celeste was absolutely nonseductive. She was all out in the open, unwily, natural, wholesome. She dreamed of making love with some man in a field, naked, under the hot sun. She walked around her bedroom naked. She would have preferred to sleep naked. But Mort had always wanted her in black lace, in bed and after he had had enough to drink, thus circumventing the threat of wholesomeness, the challenge of unadorned woman.

Celeste had at first dressed herself with all this in mind, covering the exquisite decency of her body with those endless transparencies. It had been a wonder to her, at first, that Mort applied himself so intensely to the idea of her looking seductive and that she so easily, so successfully could. But she always felt costumed in the things he wanted her gotten up in, she never felt like herself, and eventually began to realize it, to lose interest in their game, and finally to stop buying that kind of thing. Then Mort sought to provide the allure himself—a black lace nightgown, stiletto gold heels, and even a little satin corset, in style just then, to give a wasplike curve to Celeste's already slim waist. Some high old times were had by him, drunk enough, panting and striving over her lace-shaded body in bed. Afterward, how sad he was. How tired.

He began, guiltily and unhappily, to want someone else. He wanted Leonora Cramm, though he pretended that he didn't. A peach velvet tea gown girdled with sequins, a midnight blue chiffon evening dress open in the front right down to the belt—Christmas presents for Celeste in Bergdorf and Bendel boxes tied with wide satin ribbon—these Mort bought on his annual, seemingly aboveboard shopping tours with Leonora Cramm. Every year Mort had his dual-purpose, long, wine-y lunch with Leonora Cramm after which they went shopping for an aphrodisiac Christmas present for Celeste. The corset was Leonora's idea. Over the oysters Alexandre Dumas and the half-bottle of smoking champagne, Leonora suggested a little corset.

This, the corset, was the final outrage. Suddenly one day Celeste knew it, admitted it as an outrage. And with a breathless, apologetic daring, she picked up the little corset in trembling fingers and turned to Mort, holding it, looking at him, pleading with him. "I can't breathe in it. I can't draw a deep satisfactory breath in it."

Keen blue eyes searched hers. The skin below them was parchment thin and drawn, tinging his kindness and his perpetual weariness with a certain dissoluteness. Deep lines on either side of his thin face seemed to draw the corners of his mouth down. But then the corners lifted. Tolerance, and a kind of condescension softened the lines into a subtly skeptical smile. "Maybe you lace it too tight."

"Well for heaven's sakes if you don't lace it tight, what for heaven's sakes is it for?"

"It's to make you more gorgeous, my love."

"I'm not gorgeous enough without the corset?"

His face tightened, the assured gaiety of his eyes shut off and they were instantly veiled, private. At last he said, "Celesty, you do just what you want." But then he hung his head—the pathetic little boy act—and stuck out his lower lip and whimpered, pretended to whimper, "You're not going to throw it away, are you?"

"It's just that you want me to wear something that makes it hard for me to breathe," she said furiously. "I can't get over that!" But then, seeing his sadness, and shockingly, something that looked insubstantial, she was ashamed. She saw a dryness of skin, a finely lined dryness with the look of nothing firm beneath its surface, as though an impression would remain there if a finger were pressed upon it. There was a tremulous tension about all of him, too, as though his nerves were irreversibly on edge. And he looked as though he were drained of absolutely everything, even drained of red blood, this aging, graying choirboy. She remembered the fresh fine-boned pink and silver of his young blondness, calling to mind white choir robes and piercing pure high voices. And now she saw, for the first time, that Mort had not firmed and grayed into strength, but had somehow muddled into softness. Pity calmed her. For a moment there was nothing omnipotent about Mort at all.

The fast friendship of these two began to grow muted, weary. They were quieter together. Anger exploded too easily in Celeste. Mort hid sadness under suavity. There were fewer parties now, because Celeste too had to get up in the morning and go to work. The little room down the hall in which she lay around all day was seldom used now. Sun slanted across the bed, across the mounds of stuffed animals, the dusty bookcases.

Down that long hall Celeste came one night, home a day earlier than expected from a three-day trip to Washington, down the hall that Mort had traversed every night after work, slapping his newspaper against his leg, bringing the box of gardenias into the bedroom; down this quiet dark hall Celeste came that night, and surprised Mort and Leonora Cramm on the bed, among the stuffed animals.

The divorce was what they both wanted. But it was hard, it was at first unbearably sad.

"Who will take Dearie?" Celeste asked Mort, standing over her open suitcase which lay on the bed in the process of being packed.

"Celeste will," Mort said, in Dearie's gruff bear voice.

Her tears came then in great strangling floods. The armor of the business of living had cracked for a second, letting her see the simple face of her crime. For this second she knew wrong, she felt the hopelessness of having done it, and now of being unable to redress it. Her tears raged on. Years of the evasion of heedlessness, years of sensibilities shut away, all this poured out now.

They held each other until it was over.

He married Leonora Cramm. Celeste, seeing them on occasion, thought they were probably not happy, for Mort looked too old and gray for his age, and Leonora looked too immensely chic, as though this was all she spent her time on. He died early in his fiftieth year, of a heart attack which his life had probably made inevitable. And the finality of death made it easier for Celeste to forget him and to bury guilt and remorse about him and about their life together, in a deep almost inaccessible part of herself.

The process of acquiring autonomy, the ending of her life with Mort and the beginning of her life alone, continued to be somewhat of a stabilizing development for Celeste and to counteract unhappiness. She lived a single, work-busy, people-busy life in New York. She had affairs. Once, she had a brief, dedicated, tense affair with a black man, as a gesture of emancipation from the dependencies of the past and as the most personal way known to woman to live out a belief in equality and fraternity, which did not satisfy the sexual ache, nor any of her unadmitted aches, and which she tended defiantly to flaunt, through sheer bravado and the headiness of independence. After that ended, ashamed of herself, she lay low awhile before having another affair, and then another, with nice men who didn't "excite" her, she told herself flippantly and uneasily. And then, understanding something, she stopped trying for what wasn't coming naturally and began the long yearning wait for what *would* come naturally. Work became time-consuming, it became everything, and it was so successful that a self-esteem based on justifiable pride of accomplishment flourished in her and was a support to her.

She came to know what she didn't want, and was certain she knew what she wanted. Getting used finally to the peace and noncomplication of separateness, she was certain she wanted separateness and not attachment. And in the absence of it (for no real attachment developed, or ever even began), she grew used to the stillness of containment which was now the safe way, the predictable way. So much freer, so much easier—avoidance of that tiring meshing. More flexibility to life without that stone-dead weight of attachment. Free and clear and single, that was the way.

The years passed.

A bluejay came racketing and squawking to the feeder outside the glass wall of the bedroom, landing on it with a force that set it to rocking wildly. Rowdy, Celeste thought, and she began to laugh softly, hysterically beneath her electric blanket which was suddenly too warm. She reached angrily and turned it off.

For a moment she felt suspended, felt nowhere, unable to get out of bed. It was a familiar early-morning feeling now, this sense of nothing happening in her or around her. She was suspended, no motion anywhere. Even the sound of the sea's motion seemed now to come only through muffling layers of unreality, like some remembered long-ago dream.

Cabe Kingsley. Everything seemed all at once absurd and unmanageable and unknowable. She groped for a word, a prop, something that would give her the purpose to get up and get going, something that would mobilize her, reanimate the old familiar generator which had unfailingly gotten her out of bed in the morning and ready for her day, year after rugged year.

Where the hell had her *convictions* gone? Because she knew, had known for some time now, that here in this bare clean little house by the clean sea, and away from the brouhaha of work that had always drowned out what she did not want to feel, those convictions of hers which had been for years the stern prop of her existence, had stopped being urgent, stopped being noisy. They had stopped propelling her, and she needed to be propelled by something. By self-esteem? Yes, she needed most particularly to be propelled by self-esteem. And where the hell was that, she would ask herself? When had it gone? And where was her heart? She simply could not understand the seeming contradiction of a heart that hurt, but yet was hard. Her mind told her that her heart hurt because it was injured, and that it was hard because it had to be. The hurt perplexed her more than the hardness, which seemed reasonable to her under the circumstances.

Is it a condition of aging, she would worry, to have one's heart dry up? And as to that, where had her dedicated compassion for the human race gone to, here by the sea? Because it *had* faded away, no doubt about it. She kept on giving money to the organizations whose solicitations for funds came in the mail, but the writing-out of the checks was automatic and she knew it. She recognized, too, that her rage at what was happening to the disadvantaged of the world, and with those who were making it happen, had shifted over and was now exclusively a rage at those who were making it happen, a blazing, abstract rage. Did all this mean, too, that her heart had dried up?

She had no words to answer these questions. But hazily, uneasily, deep in her gut, she had a sense-knowledge that, long ago, she had contrived to have her survival depend upon the burial of her heart, and that now she was struggling to exhume it.

She gave her electric blanket a mighty kick and then lay there, uncovered, shivering, looking out at the dazzling smooth long ropes of snow on the railing of the deck.

And now, filtering into her came the association of snow

and the removal of it. She would have to shovel! She was all at once energized with the promise of having to go outdoors and shovel a path across the deck and out to her car, she was excited at the prospect of having to cope with this first snowfall on her new land. And she was prepared for it. A new shovel bided in her broom closet, just waiting for this day. She smiled with relief. She loved the thought that a snow shovel could mean so much to her. She, Celeste Hunter, prized a snow shovel, over what? A piece of jewelry, a new dress? Yes. She prized a snow shovel. She prized being alone and free and having the shoveling be up to her. She prized, she thought, looking around this room, the purity and the bone bareness of it, glass-and-wood wall and the red brick of the fireplace rosy warm in this first flood of sun. No trace of apple-green or red plush here, she thought elatedly. She had scuttled every single piece of Grandma's ornate furnishings left in storage for years, and had brought with her from her New York apartment only a few necessary things—chairs, a couch, tables, chests of drawers, a few paintings, some memorabilia. And of course, Dearie. And Dearie's chair.

She looked curiously now at Dearie, sitting in the armchair by the long window. All the years he had been sitting in that chair! It was beginning to look as dilapidated as he was. Both chair and bear had a finished look, and she saw this now acutely, and with tenderness. The sun, here by the sea, had cracked and rent the chair's fabric and faded its rose and beige flower pattern beyond recognition. And Dearie's head was sagging on a neck almost empty of sawdust.

For the first time in the sixty years she had had Dearie, she let herself see that he was transient. For the first time the thought that he needed repair took no hold in her. The words "I must fix his neck" appeared in her mind but went no further, aroused no echo of resolve to fix that neck. Static—herself, and Dearie, she here, he over there. Not connected by resolve. Not connected.

For a second she was suspended again, unconnected to anything, in this new glass-fronted house on the sea which was full of sun on a winter morning. Disconnection felt light, strange, not unpleasant. She heard the sea now, it was loud and real and near, a rousing great hollow sound of waves breaking on the shore.

Part Three

LIKE a rocket, Turck's laugh shot up through the roar of the party. Lidi, in the kitchen rushing hot cheese wafers onto a plate, tense with a listening, preoccupied air, looked at the clock and saw with a little particpating smile of triumph that it was only a quarter to eight and the party already so gratifyingly roaring. In the living room an ebullient Freddy, with his absolute need to have the party resound, was taking very little time to sit and was up and down perpetually, refilling cocktail glasses from a shaker, or pulling highball glasses out of protesting hands to refill them. The tiny living room was dense with people and with smoke and with this gradually rising pleasant bedlam. Tilly and Turck, arriving booted and mittened and cold-cheeked and convivial, had immediately preempted one of the love seats flanking the hearth where the fire snapped and roared in jovial collaboration with the excitement. And now already light-headed, their voices already slurring, Tilly and Turck sat on there, ensconced. They would not be budging from this place, they would remain where they were, nursing the few strong drinks they allowed themselves, Turck claiming the attention of everyone around him with his stories for "not so polite society," Tilly smiling, sipping, nodding her proudly held head.

They stood, packed in groups or wedged tightly together on couches, these happy happy guests, for the most part women. And all of them, the long-skirted women, the ascot-throated men, all these white-haired people loved the febrile exhilaration of being together in this room for this party. Excessively eager, they leaned toward each other, they throbbed toward each other, overdoing their greetings, overdoing their smiles. Overeager, they gaily said what they did not mean and promised feverishly to do what they would never do, sitting hip to hip on the couches, or moving from group to group setting little fires of comradeship.

The room was low-ceilinged and square, a faithful copy of decorator early American—pine, cherry red, pewter, brass, a dark calico wallpaper upon which hung bird and fruit prints in curly maple frames, ruffled muslin at the windows, the fire snapping behind wrought-iron Hessian andirons. It was cozy and very authentic and here was its creator, Lidi, coming with her plate of hot cheese wafers, pushing her way through the sea of people, stopping, waiting, a long full red taffeta skirt flaring out from her little waist. "Oh, Lidi, thank you," a blank look at the plate, an automatic hand picking up a cheese wafer, a vague smile toward her, they were all intent on each other. And here was Freddy, plowing through, cocktail shaker held aloft, wearing for this important occasion his new mail-order English loafers which before putting on he had held beneath his nose letting the smell of new leather steal up his nostrils. "Turck? Come on. Another splash. How about it?"

"I will comply, m'boy."

"Tilly? A cheese wafer? They're nice and hot," Lidi leaning down with her plate. "Is Cabe Kingsley coming, Tilly? He said he would. Do you think he's coming, Tilly?"

"S'far's I know. But he could perfectly well be lost in that piano playing and lose all track of time," tartly. "What a pretty skirt, my dear. Oh, I *shouldn*'t," soft white blue-veined hand with perfect polished fingernails taking a cheese wafer. A smile upward. The sweetest smile in the world, Tilly's was, its sudden radiance lit up the wrinkled face which was serenely inexpressive around dancing black eyes. A blue-white pompadour rose like a wave from her forehead, breaking at either side into sculptured curls which were silver in the firelight.

Lidi drifted elegantly from group to group in a cloud of perfume and a whisper of stiff silk, holding out her plate, smiling her wintry smile, " . . . poetry reading," she was saying to the Durands, "yes, I just heard yesterday. I've been asked to read some of my poems at the Friends of Poetry this month. The twentieth of January. Great excitement. I'm very flattered."

"How marvelous, Lidi."

"Congratulations Lidi."

"I read your seagull poem in the *Gazette*. You certainly conveyed the feeling of the way they soar."

"I read it too. It really grabbed me, as the young say."

Lidi drifted away, holding her plate, listening:

"Make a good selectman. He's young. But solid. I like to see a fellow like that in town government."

"She's having chemotherapy. She's got another month of it."

"Sold for a million five. The lots, I hear, will be ten acres with one subdivision allowed."

"I *lock* my car now. I never used to. Imagine, here on this island."

"All right. But it's not *art*."

"Well, just a teeny, teeny splash. Like a half-inch, Freddy."

"Why don't you go to Johnny's? He's three cents a gallon less."

"Doing pretty well, considering. His whole left side was paralyzed."

"Three times we tried to get off this island in December, and each time the boat didn't come. *Three* times."

"Just so long as that doesn't happen to me on January twentieth," Lidi interrupted, "on my big day," she exulted. "Yes. I've been asked to read some of my poems at the annual meeting of the Friends of Poetry."

"But that's terrific, Lidi."

"Good for you, Lidi."

Her plate was almost empty now, and she threaded her way back toward the kitchen to refill it, but stopped a minute before pushing through the door, just to watch, and to feel the party, away from the center of it. It's literally a howling success, she thought, and then wondered again why Cabe Kingsley hadn't showed up. She wanted him here. For one thing he would have been another man in this overabundance of widows and divorcees, but more than that, he attracted her, something very unusual. She never met men who attracted her, probably because at her age the fires of sex burned low, very low, and also she had had no fundamental need, sexual or otherwise, beyond Freddy, who was her man and who still, in a dim but bedrock way, was as attractive to her as he had been from the beginning.

But, with striking unexpectedness Cabe Kingsley had attracted her. It had been an instantaneous reaction, she had felt her body stir. She had stood looking up at the somber packed presence towering over her, with the loose beautiful mouth and the eyes that told of some compelling worthwhile inner life, and was amazed. Wordless with amazement. Her eyes couldn't leave that mouth and there was astonishingly a permission in her to let this staring go uninhibited. Unabashedly, and really almost with pride, with a recognition of something unknown, unused, unrestrained in herself, she could not and would not take her eyes from his mouth. She had the strange feeling that it was just for her, that it had always been there just for her. Yet it wasn't just his mouth, it was his eyes, it was all of him, it was a total soft thing in him, not a hardness but a softness, which told her of an inner life that was rich and hot. Standing under the precipice of his jutting somber head, she had told herself that here was a man who would listen to her poetry and like it.

But why hadn't he come? . . . Well, never mind, she thought. The party is miraculous. She closed her eyes to get a sharper sense of things, and stood there letting the excitement of voices invade and rejoice her. How wonderful it was to have this happy kind of celebrating thing going on here in her own living room, all these people eager with each other, at ease here in her house, liking to be in her house.

Absorbing the tumult, assessing it, Lidi was exulting not in any single person, or even in persons, but in one overall message emanating from it—the party is a success. Individuality was blurred in this babble and soar of voices sounding at one great voice, all the bodies, sitting or standing in close groups, seemed as one undifferentiated human element, long-skirted, perfumed, permanented, ascot-throated, red-faced, smoking, drinking, eating, shouting, shouting. The party is a success, Lidi gloated. Something, at last, has succeeded for me. But her black eyes were steady, reflecting none of her triumph. The more elated she grew, the stiffer she held her-

95

self, no flicker in her flat face, her flat eyes. And yet she felt she would burst with joy.

But now she began to want to come down out of this. She felt dizzy with it. And a hotness flushed through her, unpleasantly, while two red spots burned and throbbed in her cheeks. And as though toward rescue, she looked at Celeste, who was turned to Evangeline Eliot with a flowing beautiful enthusiasm. And Lidi saw, partly with envy and partly with admiration, how handsome Celeste was with her straight shining white hair and her eager vitality and her fine head held so high and steady on her neck. For a moment Lidi felt translated into something small scale and merely ornamental, she felt herself to be all rustling taffeta and perfume, nothing more.

She sighed. The smoke in this room was awful, and the tables, cluttered with ashtrays, glasses, stray matches, bits of food, had lost all semblance of attractiveness.

Suddenly she was struck with the old age in this room. Everyone was old. Of course. What else? She saw white hair and bald heads and paunches and double chins—oldness, oldness. But in the midst of the weight, in this room, of aging, the inescapable condensed heavy *fact* of it that lodged here like a rock, in the midst of this thing that touched her heart as it frightened her, Lidi said to herself, today is my seventy-second birthday, but I'm not old. I don't look old and I don't feel old. And one is only truly old if one feels old. But at the same time she felt a sort of comfort, a strength in the acceptance of inevitability perhaps, in knowing that she was of these people, that she, whether she looked it or not, was aging too. We're all in the same boat, she thought, and felt a compassion almost tender, looking at these people who were here in her house because it was one of the similar safe enclaves in a tough and brutal young world, people who felt a bond with *her* because *she* was aging. And then she felt a passionate stab of tenderness for Freddy, with his new English loafers and his frenzied hospitality. She yearned toward, she admired, the ease and the outgoingness of this dark-skinned tense man with the wild white hair, who was hers.

But old? No, Freddy wasn't old. She couldn't imagine him ever seeming old. The essence of him was youth, it had been, for all the fifty-two years of their marriage, and she couldn't imagine him ever being without this basis of innocent, volatile confidence. And yet, wasn't his sureness less reassuringly apparent than it used to be? Hadn't a kind of restrained tension crimped those broad sunny areas of his nature, so that his confidence was sometimes shrill, seeming heavily spread on, not natural? Oh, but no, she thought, he is fundamentally the same, he will always be the same. . . .

Freddy is suddenly the boy on the windy top deck of the *Mauretania* playing shuffleboard with a sparkling unassuming energy that brings her to a standstill behind him. She stays to watch him and is transfixed by his snapping, black, incredibly nice eyes, she sees his flat dark hair blowing wildly across his forehead as he lunges with one knee bent, the other leg straight out behind, and with a graceful sureness, smiling, sweeps the puck onto the exact center of the square. She stands and watches him. Does he notice her? Who is he? She wants to know. She will ask someone. She is magnetized by him, by his amiability and his virile artless confidence in winning this game—and he will, he does. He is strong blooded which intuitively she senses; her own dilution is without that strength and purpose, that coalescing generosity. Someone tells her he is on his way to France to compete in the Davis Cup Matches. He will win, she knows.

Looking at him now, she sees that he has hardly changed,

in spite of his tension. Tension in Freddy is not change, she says to herself, it is a superficial mechanism, it is not his center. That absolute fountain of vigorous generosity which is his nature is still pouring out. And in a clear moment of knowing that she could love him and was always failing him, she saw in a way she never had before, that Freddy, with his hands and his mind and most particularly with his heart, was an achiever, that his essence and his motivation was output, that he lived for what he put out and that this was safe and it was sound. While she? Oh, she was almost entirely in the unsound, unsafe way of living for input, for what would come to her from out there. She felt herself to be tethered, and felt that Freddy was roaming free and that this was what their marriage was—she, bound, and he, un-bound, she wanting it all to come from him to her, not the other way around. I fail, she thought miserably. What have I learned in seventy-two years of living?

Tight little woman, tight, tight, tight. Dammed up. Rigid against a world that wasn't giving to her. Tight as a piece of stretched silk, letting nothing out, restrained from letting anything out because the habit of her expectation was that it should all be coming into her from out there.

She would write her poetry, but it had to be received out there. She would give a party, but the only satisfaction she let herself have from it was that they liked her, not the other way around. Any word from out there told Lidi who she was, and that she was okay. With sudden anguish, she would look at Freddy and know that she was stopped, that here was a man she might love whom she didn't know how to love. Stopped, expecting him to determine the spirit of their marriage, expecting that his was the word, not hers.

Yet she never stopped knowing that she didn't have to

be that way. She always carried high up in two hands, in front of her, the cup of herself that could fill and overflow.

The porch chimes rattled. Cold air cut in, then gusted in with the opening of the door. Cabe Kingsley stood in the glare of the porch floodlight, the air around him full of glittering fine particles of blown snow. Clouds of vapor swirled from his mouth. A seaman's dark blue knitted cap was pulled down tight over his skull, his head was thrust forward, and all Lidi could think of, in her astonishment and relief, was that he looked like a turtle. A cold hand grasped hers. "I'm so sorry. I hope I'm not too late." He pulled off his cap. "I do apologize."

"Oh, no, no, I'm *delighted* you came!" Lidi darted around him and closed the door, the wind billowing out her skirt, so that for a moment this great red slashing swirl dominated everything. Behind her, ice rattled in Freddy's glass, which she wished he could put down to receive guests. She was suddenly joyous. Freddy took Cabe's coat, and they each seized an elbow of this special and new guest and swept him between them into the living room.

Celeste and Evangeline Eliot had come to the end of interest in each other, but there they were, side by side on the loveseat, and neither one knew how to get up and leave. But I must, Celeste was thinking, tilting the last of her vermouth into her mouth and looking furtively around as was Evangeline, both of them awkward in the presence of this final silence. I really must, Celeste said to herself now, looking for rescue across to Tilly and Turck, who were both engrossed in the telling of one of Turck's stories, looking calculatingly then around the room, from one dense little group to another. But at that moment Evangeline Eliot rose suddenly, saying, "Well, I'm going to get myself another drink," and departed.

Good for her, Celeste thought, and was about to rise, too, to escape the trap of a loveseat built for two, when behind her she heard Lidi. "I don't think you know Celeste Hunter, though. Celeste," Lidi's hand on her shoulder, "I want you to meet McCabe Kingsley."

Celeste turned, looked up, a sudden little excitement and an instant attentiveness warring against reserves of resentment. But before she could speak, Cabe said promptly and smoothly, "We met on the boat last week," and to Freddy, who had come over with his drink, "Oh thank you, thank you very much." Then, glass in hand, he looked down at Celeste. "Hello," quietly. "May I sit here?" More than anything he just wanted to sit down, but he was struck, too, by the pale shine of her beauty. He did not want to move away from this upward-glowing vitality. Without her hat she was all there to be seen—a shining whiteness of hair, white face—and for a moment he had the same sense of light piercing him that he'd had when he'd first seen her. He found himself thinking that he was glad he'd come—he had had to force himself to—and that the fire was cheerful and that he looked forward to a drink.

"You've met!" Lidi cried. "Really? Well, there you are, that's the way it is on this small island." She came around the loveseat in a clatter of taffeta, and sat down on the firebench next to it. "Freddo," she cried, "fill mine, dear, will you?"

Cabe sank back into the cushions and pouted his mouth into his glass, drinking deeply. The same old tweed jacket fell away from his big shoulders, Celeste noted. She was confused and determined to be cautious, and yet pleased.

And Lidi, tense on the firebench, the fire shimmering on her flat white hair, her scarlet skirt, was jubilant, "Did you know that this man is Tilly's sort-of nephew, Celeste? He lives in Tilly's old house. Do you enjoy it?" she asked Cabe.

"Oh, very much. It's a nice old place. I'm afraid Aunt Tilly doesn't think much of my housekeeping, what she calls my bachelor digs."

"Oh, you're a bachelor!" Celeste exclaimed.

"No." Quietly. "I'm a widower." Cabe said this easily, he had always said this easily, without emotion. But he never ceased to hate the response it evoked in people, especially women, a sudden sympathetic sobering of the face, and then, after a moment's respectful silence, the skillful transition to the here and now of life. He didn't need sympathy. It made him feel like an imposter. When he had to say, "I'm a widower," he would have liked to say it cheerfully. Even perhaps jubilantly. But decency forbade this. He still, after four years, had an accompanying sense of guilty freedom, almost of truancy, when he said, "I'm a widower," as though Catsy's death had let him run away, let him escape. He didn't want to look at Celeste and see this reaction he dreaded and was sure she would have, and so he glanced at Lidi, who of course had it, as he raised his glass to his lips. "Well, well," he said then, before either Lidi or Celeste could speak, "this is very nice. Very nice. Very cheerful. But I think your husband has made me a rather strong drink."

"Freddy's heavy-handed with drinks. He only drinks beer himself so he really doesn't know how to make a drink properly. So. You two met on the boat. Fascinating."

"Well. Actually, we met long before that," Celeste said in a voice which seemed to Cabe insensitively, arrogantly loud. "We met the summer I was eighteen," she said with the same strong breeziness, but now Cabe decided that it wasn't arrogance he was hearing but simply a sort of spirited confidence; there was too much graciousness in her voice for arrogance.

"Yes," Cabe said, shifting around to face Celeste. "Evidently we met. But your memory's better than mine. Mine's a pretty poor thing, anyway."

"That's true of all of us," Celeste said. "My forgetfulness is comic. I keep laughing at it. I don't know what I'd do for amusement without it."

"Oh, mine too," Lidi cried. "Freddy and I almost enjoy ours, it's so absurd. Absurd! We've always got a new story to tell each other, about how we forgot. Listen to this. This is the best one. This is the height. Last summer one day I went over to the beach in the jeep. On the way back, coming into our driveway, I saw the jeep wasn't there but the Chevy was, and I thought, oh, Freddy's gone somewhere in the jeep. Then as I opened that plastic door, I guess because it feels different from the Chevy door, I realized *I* was in the jeep. Don't you think that's really unsurpassed?"

Celeste's laugh pealed out, a natural, easy, rippling sound that pleased Cabe. He smiled, faintly, and nodded his head up and down. "I put my reading glasses in the refrigerator the other day, instead of the butter," he said simply. "I put 'em in the butter compartment and carried the butter dish out to the piano."

Helplessly, Celeste began to shake with whoops of laughter. "Oh look, I'm spilling vermouth all over myself," she gasped, putting her glass down, shaking, erupting with gusts of mirth. "It's the picture," she gasped, "of the butter dish on the piano." She gradually stopped laughing, but with her face still creased with hilarity, excessive perhaps. She stammered, "the thing is, and you just said this, Lidi, it's so entertaining, forgetfulness is. For instance this morning I finished writing a letter. And I addressed the envelope. And then, thinking I'd have to get up and rinse out the taste of licking the stamp, I got up and went into the bathroom. And as I was rinsing out my mouth I realized I hadn't licked the stamp yet. I laughed. It was more fun that way than doing it right."

Now the three of them were quiet for a moment—were they really so amused—the fire roaring softly at Lidi's back, and a people roar packing and shaking the room. They sat, isolated in this violent pulse of sound, their silence acute, odd, noticeable because of it.

"Say, have you heard the one about the absent-minded professor and the farmer's daughter?" cried Turck, who had been listening from across the way. He lit a cigarette and inhaled it deeply and wagged out the match. "Speaking of reading glasses, I caught Til trying to put one set of 'em on right on the top of the other," he shouted, ridiculing as always the other person's memory failure. He never admitted his own.

Explosive laughter again, again excessive, from Celeste, from Lidi; and a chuckle from Tilly. "So I did," she murmured, bringing her lips suddenly away from her teeth in a fresh sweet smile. She had set her empty glass down, and her hands were folded tiredly across her lap. A corsage of three tight yellow rosebuds set in a froth of maidenhair fern and tied with a silver ribbon, rose from one shoulder, and from time to time, as the laughter and stories surged around her, she would lift the shoulder and duck her head to sniff the roses. Even though she knew that yellow roses were awful with the pink and red flowered blouse she wore, she loved them because they were Turck's offering. He always presented her with a corsage on important occasions, ceremoniously, "My love is like a red red rose," he would say without fail, handing her the little white box. "But these aren't red, Til," he had said tonight, "they didn't have red, only yellow," and he had watched her with a fierce, proud, enveloping look as she opened the box, and smiled, and pinned the corsage to her shoulder.

He turned to look down at her now, the old eagle—proud eyes glittering deep-set under bushy white eyebrows, beak nose, white hair growing in a peak on his narrow forehead. Tilly looked up at him and said quietly, not wanting to be overheard, "Should we begin to think about going, dear?"

"Oh, not yet," cried Lidi, who had heard. "Don't go *yet.*" She ducked her head to her glass and sipped, with a sidelong furtive glance at Cabe, who was turned away from her, toward Celeste. She felt a stab of irritation. And immediately, easily, she felt rejection. Something rose up in her that stiffened her shoulders and stiffened her mouth. She saw Freddy making some point importantly, punching a fist up into the air, and she turned away, embarrassed for him, and discontented with everything. "Heavens, I should be doing things about being a hostess," she said in a loud voice, as though to herself, but to be heard, by Cabe, by Celeste, by everyone. Yet she didn't move. "Celeste," she said, leaning out, calling to Celeste across Cabe's back, "how's the concert coming? Have you gotten your musicians yet?"

This came as rescue, for neither Celeste nor Cabe was finding much to say. Celeste's hands were in her lap, gripping her glass, which was empty and which she wished were full. Lifting your glass to your mouth was something to do; sipping, swallowing, could fill silences. She was nervous. There was everything in the world to say to this man, and yet there was nothing to say to him. There was a heaviness in him— she'd sensed it when she met him on the boat—and yet she felt peculiarly drawn to him because of it. It was like a weight, which his cold eyes and accomplished manners would disprove if he were not giving out some subtle signal that failure lay in him like a stone. Still, there was something about him that dignified all this, that made him interesting. She remembered how, last week, the morning after she had met him, she had waked up feeling a stale hatred for him. But she didn't feel it now, and didn't want to. A willing transmutation had been going on in her, and she knew she was letting bygones be bygones. She knew that there was some bond here she didn't want to discard. And so there was nothing in her now that asked for caution, or reticence. Yet this very fact brought self-consciousness, and made small talk impossible. And so Lidi's question was rescue.

"No," she cried quickly to Lidi, "no we haven't found anyone. Have you any ideas, Lidi? The Committee on Hunger," she explained to Cabe, "are trying to raise a thousand dollars for this quarter. There's a bread sale in June. And a walkathon in October. Anyway, I want to organize a benefit concert in March, sometime. I've got the hall, and the piano. Now all I need are the musicians."

"Oh indeed." Cabe was all interest. "What a good idea. You're looking for some local group, I suppose, who'd do it for nothing. What about the Great Pond String Quartet? They're pretty good, I think."

"Well they are. Or so I'm told. I'm not a judge of chamber music. The truth is, I don't much care for chamber music."

"Neither do I. Or only rarely. Only when it's the best. I prefer symphony, or solo."

"Oh I agree. I don't even like opera. I really can't stand opera. I like superb voices all by themselves, not *opera*ting, as Mort used to say. For years I went to the opera every week with Mort's dear old great-aunt. I'm afraid I had no choice. *Every. Saturday. Afternoon.*"

Cabe looked at her curiously. "This was in New York, of course."

"Oh yes. New York."

"I'm confused about your name. Mrs. Luhin introduced you as Hunter." He smiled slightly. "I forget that butter dishes aren't reading glasses, but I don't seem to forget names. Not yet anyway. I thought I remembered your saying your name was Brockton, when we met on the boat."

Celeste looked straight at him. She lifted her chin and flushed. "That's my middle name." Honest, self-possessed eyes stared him down, challenging him to make what he wanted of that. "My name is Hunter. It was Cunningham when I met you, Celeste Cunningham. I married Mort Hunter. Do you remember Mort?"

"Of course I do. Who could forget that stellar fella." Cabe was quiet. He looked away from her, down into his glass. "And of course now I remember *you*, Celeste Cunningham," he said, as though he were speaking to his glass.

There appeared, suddenly, an open space in Cabe's cranium. Like a spot of light. Christina Hunter stood there in that wash of bright light, her white tennis skirt blown sideways by the wind, her blond hair whipping across her face, "Cabe, listen. We were terribly upset by the other night. And Isabel seeing you two having lunch at the club," bringing up the hand that wasn't holding the tennis racquet to lift a strand of hair away from her lips. Fierce blue eyes behind the blowing hair. "Cabe, listen, I feel bound to let the cat out of the bag and tell you Celeste and Mort are engaged. Her grandmother's going to announce it next week. I shouldn't be telling you this, but I'm sure you know why I am. You're surprised? You didn't suspect? That's what I thought."

A sudden slash of taffeta next to Cabe told of Lidi's getting up abruptly from the firebench. He gave this only a fraction of his mind. He looked away from his glass, to Celeste. "I hope Mort's well," he said quietly, ambiguously, directing the intensity of his pale eyes at her.

"Mort's no longer alive," Celeste said loudly, giving as much force to the feeling of rejection—he had remembered her, but obviously with no interest—as to the feeling she would gloss over in speaking about Mort's death. For a second their eyes held together. And in that look, for there was something in his eyes that stirred her, she found a sort of base, something to steady her and to ease her humiliation. "He died twenty years ago," she said, giving him a troubled fullness of gaze in which Cabe saw sorrow without peace, as of something unresolved.

"Celeste luv," Freddy was standing behind the couch, reaching over her shoulder for her glass, "can I fill this for you? Just vermouth, was it?"

"Oh, lovely, yes. Vermouth. On the rocks. Thanks." She turned and gave him her glass. "We were just talking about my concert, Freddy," she said lightly. "We have everything but the musicians. Like that play I saw centuries ago, *It Pays to Advertise*, about two men who dreamed up a clever sales promotion for a special kind of soap, they had its name and wrapper, everything, and orders pouring in, and then one day they waked up to the fact that they didn't have the soap. Anyway, please, everyone, be on the lookout for musicians."

"What about *this* fellow?" Freddy cried, putting his hand on Cabe's shoulder. "This fellow's *good*. I mean good. A super pianist. Tilly told me. I don't know the first thing about music," he said to Cabe, who had turned and was looking up at him with startled, affronted, even frightened eyes, "but Tilly's an authority. Talk him into it, Tilly," Freddy called across to her, for she was leaning toward them, listening.

"You flatter me, Freddy," Cabe said. "But I think this is putting Aunt Tilly on the spot."

Tilly was not one to be told what to do or what to say. "Why, Freddy, I think that's a perfectly wonderful idea. I can't imagine why *I* didn't think of it."

Celeste looked from Tilly to Cabe and then up to Freddy with confusion. Was Tilly really an authority? It seemed so unlikely. She could more easily imagine Tilly liking Strauss waltzes or Sousa marches or "Auld Lang Syne." But she turned quickly to Cabe and said to him with a candid, penetrating look, "That's very interesting." Actually she thought it was. "Let's talk about it."

Cabe settled back in the cushions. He thrust his head forward and put his two hands around his glass and held it loosely in his lap, moving his large lips, pursing them, widening them, pursing them again, his eyes distant, contemplative.

"Oh, Cabe, I wish you would," Lidi cried, too intimately. That omnipresence of fussing taffeta was intrusively there behind him, displeasing him, smothering him.

Ignoring her, Cabe turned to Celeste. "I'd like very much to consider it," he said. "Perhaps you'll tell me more about it, the hall, the piano and so forth. First though, will you come to my house and hear me play? I'd like to think about doing it, but of course you must hear me first."

"Bravo," Freddy said, and carried off Celeste's glass. Tilly smiled and settled back.

"Oh but yes. Of course I'd like to do that. Then we'll both know," Celeste said smoothly. "I'll know with my own ears. And you'll know I know. And then we'll both feel better about it."

"And if you have any reservations you'll say so."

"Yes I will."

Cabe knew she meant this. He had a sudden sense of ease, of a kind of happiness. Celeste Cunningham . . . There was a memory in him of darkness and of kissing. He had kissed this long white neck. The thought had an alarming improbability. Distances, of time, of everything else, made any reality of her and of him ever having been together in darkness and kissing, seem perfectly unbelievable. And yet now, from her to him, from this lovely eager woman with the little pearls in her ears and her tact and her effervescence, there was something he was feeling that was like a transfusion. She was glad, and this made him feel glad. "In that case," he said, "if we both understand that that's the way it will be, do come."

"Fine. Lidi, will you come too?" Celeste thrust a sudden hand up to touch Lidi's arm. "Let's go together," she said kindly, wisely. "May we?" she asked Cabe.

"But of course," he said politely and without enthusiasm.

"Wonderful. When?" Lidi was happy again. For surely, there, in an atmosphere of music, of art, just the three of them immersed in listening to art, it would be appropriate and easy to tell them (tell Cabe) about her poetry, and to be encouraged to read it to them (to Cabe). "I'd love to. I can do it any day next week except Friday. Friday I've my modern poetry course."

And so it was arranged for Wednesday.

The party had reached a concordance of sound, stretched out, sonorous. It was a deeper, mellower, more settled roar, and for a while it had a long loud level musicality that promised to stay that way.

But, gradually, there were fewer people in the room. And the congestion of sound began to be concentrated within smaller groups, isolated little intensities in which individual voices could be heard. There was more space, even a sense of air used up, a sense of a room devoured, with nothing much left in it. And there were more people in the hall, Lidi noticed. With their coats on. Saying loud smiling thank-yous to Freddy. She saw Cabe Kingsley, with his hand on the doorknob, saying his polite goodbyes. Then he was gone. She felt the cold air from the open door on her ankles, here in the living room standing tiredly with Tilly and Turck. The Durands came up to her, "Lidi, you look gorgeous." Evangeline Eliot touched her shoulder from behind, "Lidi! Those cheese things! Dare I ask you for the recipe?" "Lidi," Celeste called, striding with outstretched hands across the room in her very old and motheaten but elegantly swinging fur cape. "My dear. This was a *good* party."

"Oh, dearest Celeste. Well, I loved it myself." And then out it came. "It's the best birthday party I ever had, I think."

"*Birth*day party? Today is your *birth*day? Oh, Lidi. Congratulations!" She leaned to put a white cheek to Lidi's. "Mayn't I tell everyone? Oh please let me."

A little shrug and a little smile from Lidi were really eager permission.

Celeste whirled around with a flare of her cape, soft fur around her face. "It's Lidi's birthday," she called to the people in the hall, in the room, "this is Lidi's birthday party!"

A second's silence and then a torrent of cries and exclamations. Glasses were raised. "To Lidi!" And Freddy, lifting his glass above his head, above the heads of everyone, cried, "To Lidi, who never grows old in spite of her birthdays!"

Lidi's flat cheeks trembled. A wild happiness seized her. She blinked away the sting of tears. "Thank you," she was able to say from a tight throat.

Oh, Freddo, thank you.

The door closed on the last person. And in a sudden flat silence, Freddy began right away to pile glasses clatteringly onto a tray. And Lidi went to the bar table and poured herself another drink and then went over to the firebench and collapsed onto it. "Oh, Freddo, that was such a lovely thing to say. That was a wonderful birthday present. And Celeste, everyone, what heart-warming toasts!" But why to me? . . . She couldn't assimilate it, couldn't believe it, she could not even believe Freddy's toast.

Puzzled, a little drunk, feeling great exhaustion at last, she was held, stilled in this question—why to me?—and she sat on here by the last pale heat of collapsed logs, sipping her drink and saying to herself: "The party was a success, success, success." But these were only words in her head, sounding repetitiously and with no conviction around the startling feeling—why to me?—that had taken entire possession of her. It spoiled the party, spoiled everything. It made her disbelieve the validity of those toasts, totally. And she couldn't even begin to think why.

Part Four

IT seemed to Cabe that everywhere on the island he saw aging. On the town streets, on the beaches, at parties, in shops, driving along the roads. He didn't pay attention to youth at all, only to old age. He selected old age to look at, he concentrated on it, he kept a perpetual sense, or image, of generalized aging within himself without ever letting any perception infiltrate his almost phobic one-dimensional view of it. And because he was on the lookout for it, he saw the signs of aging everywhere, and there were many of them on this island with its large population of retired people.

One day last autumn, rounding a curve on Great Pond Road, he had seen an old roan stallion in a pasture, head bent, alone under a tree. And across the road, in another pasture there was a honey-colored palomino mare, cantering gracefully, youthfully along the split rail fence. He was instantly stunned and moved by this sight, which he saw as a striking example, there just for him, of the pathos of the condition of aging. Another day he saw a young woman on a bicycle, with a child in the basket seat behind her, a dog gamboling alongside. Suddenly adulthood seemed fabricated, arbitrary, ossified even. And old age seemed artificial, made of materials that had lost their pliancy and shine.

And at least once a day, as he drove along in his jeep, he saw in the car ahead of him the backs of two white heads, the white head of the driver, high up, the white head of his wife, lower down—a couple in the lifetime habit, it seemed, of sitting with wordless stoicism side by side, staring stiffly straight ahead, each deep in separate thought. The backs of these white heads exuded, Cabe thought, a giving up, a passivity. He saw this couple as driving patiently along to the library or the fish market or the doctor's office or the bank, numbed by repetition and yet probably expectant over this outing, since it might be the only adventure of the day. Along they went, this white-haired man and his shorter white-haired wife, in their Volkswagen or their Subaru or their Wagoneer, a dog in the back seat as passive and as patient as they, along they all drove, from fish market to library to Blood Pressure Clinic to drugstore to Health Food Store to optometrist. Winter summer spring and fall, up and down these few island roads the white-haired couples drove, day in day out, in autumn the gold leaves of maples sifting down through gold still light, a melancholy thing—the still white heads and the still gold light, and the leaves falling. In spring the white dazzle of beach plum and viburnum blossoms banked the roads, in summer the perfume of wild roses and the brazen orange of tiger lilies, and Cabe wondered whether this bursting profligate beauty might not woo some resiliency into the two white heads. But perhaps not. Perhaps this flagrant declaration of the flowering of life made them all the more aware of their removal from it, told them that they had no relation any more to flowering, even reminded them that they could not remember what flowering had felt like. Perhaps, he thought, they were more content when the autumn leaves were falling, more at peace in the stillness of an ending. And even more content in winter, with the no-color of leafless trees, and the snow, slopes of smooth white cold snow along the roads. Yes, snow was the season of the two white heads, thought Cabe. December song.

He was on the lookout for old flesh, and was not able to see anything about it that dignified it. He would look fleetingly and then away with quick repugnance at his own naked body in the long mirror of Aunt Tilly's bathroom, seeing deterioration while reassuring himself that it was not yet as bad as most. And at the beach, this past summer, his attention had been riveted on aging men—their soft spilling paunches white and liver-spotted, their bright-patterned swimming trunks flaring out so foolishly, so inappropriately from storklike legs stepping cautiously over the stones. He watched them covertly, helplessly, angrily. He watched aging women, stuffed into flowered bathing suits, their dried brown wrinkled skin hanging and swinging from thin arms, thick arms, and he felt a despair. Some were better than others, probably due to exercise, and there was an occasional miracle. But with few exceptions he thought naked old bodies were pitiable, they were nature's bad planning. Here it was, in the flesh, literally in the flesh. And it was worse, in a way, than the two white heads in the car. Here was the nakedness of aging, the whole thing, not just the head. A jacket and a tie and trousers covered up so much, and long skirts. But on the beach! . . . It was almost indecent he thought, to expose disintegration and decay like this. The human body in its final years is an outrage, he thought, a blasphemy.

The fact that Aunt Tilly and Turck were lovers, for he was certain they were, embarrassed Cabe. Once or twice, looking at them together, he had tried to imagine their two old bodies in the act of love, and had veered away from the idea with utter disgust. But at the same time, looking at Aunt Tilly, with her fine head held so proudly and so strongly, he felt a faint undefined reassurance that possibly it wasn't the way he thought it was, that possibly neither one of them was troubled by their bodies, or embarrassed by them. Though the next time he saw Aunt Tilly in a bathing suit he reverted quickly to his usual embarrassment and condemnation. Her upper arms swung like hammocks as she raised them to fit on her bathing cap, her white plump thighs were lumpy. And Turck, all skin and bones in his tall raging emaciated way, was like a predatory ancient bird. It was impossible to imagine these two bodies locked together in union. It enraged Cabe to have to consider it at all.

He was more obsessed with aging flesh than with any other aspect of aging. He knew it, and was astonished by himself, often trying hard to see the whole of these white-haired people, not just their flesh. Look at their eyes, he scolded himself, look at their spirits, look at their minds, their hearts! Sometimes this admonishment worked, and he could be distracted from paunches to personality. At such times he despised his fear of old flesh, and was able to see the weakness in his present state of mind. Then he felt like an absolute simpleton. However, feeling himself to be a simpleton only compounded his confusion, and far from enlightening him, made him feel worse.

He was in a time of crisis. Reason and emotional dignity had deserted him. The newness of everything in his life, all the new situations happening more or less at the same time, or rather within a few years of each other, were too much for him—the newness of nearing seventy, the newness of no job, of no wife, of a strange house, a strange place, of the loss of what he considered his manhood, of the challenge of being left alone at last with his music and had his capacity for it always been only fantasy—all these changes bludgeoned him ceaselessly.

Sometimes he knew that he had never really felt otherwise, and that the way he was feeling now was not basically different from the way he had felt all his life. It was more apparent now, that was all.

He knew with guilt, for instance, that he was glad to be without Catsy, that in the deepest part of himself he had wanted to be without Catsy from the first months of their marriage. Even, from the first days of it—Catsy, the spirited girl who had thrown the turkey pope's nose at him across his mother's Thanksgiving dinner table. He remembered that moment forever, the spot of grease on his necktie and the glow of the silver pheasants in the candlelight and the bitter fragrance of yellow chrysanthemums.

"Catsy's a prom trotter," he had said to the table at large.

"Whatever does that mean, dear," his mother asked smoothly, but looking sharply for a moment at Catsy.

"It means she has a route from Yale to Princeton to Harvard to Cornell to Williams to Amher . . ."

Smack! It him him on the chest, and splashed back down and into his wineglass.

"Hey!" He picked up his napkin and began to dab at his tie, and while he was doing this, he looked across at Catsy with wonder. Who was this girl who dared to do such a thing at his mother's table, at anyone's table but particularly at his mother's? He was stunned. He felt a strange exultation. He would have liked to fish the pope's nose out of his wineglass and throw it back at her.

But he felt a different dare rising up through layers of repression. He felt the omnipotence here at this table being shattered, dispersed. He looked across at Catsy's round face with its halo of brown curls and the faintly protruding candid brown eyes. She smiled, her wide fresh sudden smile.

"Marry me!" He threw this across his mother's table to Catsy, recklessly challenging omnipotence. "I'll only forgive you if you'll marry me," he cried, and the whole world seemed open and possible.

He always remembered the look on Catsy's face—astonishment, fear, a flicker of triumph, before she said in a lilting, mock-little-girl voice, "I'll have to ask my father." And then grinned.

The pope's nose which had sunk to the bottom of the wineglass, the faint sweet bitterness of chrysanthemums, the stunned look on his mother's face, the silence. Marry me . . . Now, forty years later, he knew that what he had meant was: Join me, lift me out of this, give me your daring spirit, make me like you are. Help.

But he had not changed. And he had never been happy. His life with Catsy had been a drab sorrow. From the beginning.

"But I'm writing thank-you notes, Cabe."

"To hell with thank-you notes. Some brides wait months before writing thank-you notes. Maybe a year. Come to bed."

"But it's the middle of the *day*."

"What difference does that make?"

"Well someone might come in. Adelia might come in."

"Adelia's out today. Today's Sunday. Today's Adelia's alternate Sunday off."

He had a hangover, and he wanted feverishly to make love. The ceaseless murmur of traffic on Memorial Drive, beyond their apartment windows, drove into his tremulous body a sound and a sense of monotony that seemed to him the counterpart of this room, this life. His marriage, and his life, were no more than the muted sound of something endlessly passing outside of him. And the room had the same coloration and tone of something not of him but outside of him, all new, and monotone, neuter, sterile as a hotel room—beige slipcovers, beige Chinese rug, beige damask curtains falling in strict columns to the floor, all done by a decorater and paid for by Mrs. Turnbull. Bachrach photograph of bride and groom in a silver monogrammed frame, standing on the mahogany drop-leaf wedding present table. How pretty Catsy looked with the train of her wedding dress arranged across her feet, her low full breasts caught up in the transparency of net and lace, her head turned to him with a spontaneous look of trust and happiness. And how guarded he looked, stiff in his cutaway. Already prepared, was he, for the monogrammed guest towels and the monogrammed blanket covers and the silver cigarette box with little matching monogrammed matchboxes? Portrait of a young man prepared for a monogrammed marriage, was it?

Monogrammed marriage. This was what Cabe secretly labeled it, castigating with this contemptuous slogan not only Catsy but her massive mother. He liked Mrs. Turnbull, but resented, though of course passively, the indefatigability of her overseership, the stiff sterile perfection of what she established and nurtured here—Adelia taught to serve from the left and to use a clean folded napkin while doing so, Adelia taught to remove the service plate along *with* the soup plate with the left hand and simultaneously to put down the warm dinner plate with her right.

Having a daughter married and turned into a housewife was heaven to Mrs. Turnbull and began her life all over again. She was a massively obese woman who spent her life sitting because it was too difficult to move around, and because her life's occupation, anyway, was within the four walls of her home. In a polished house in Brookline, with a mild silent man who was her husband, she seemed even to sit *on* her house, to hatch out the bowls of fresh flowers, the cedar-scented closets, the soup to nuts dinners, with the same brooding, overspreading concentration as a hen hatching out eggs. She lived for spring and fall housecleaning, for the change of winter velvet to summer chintz, and back again. Winter orientals were rolled up in May, and straw rugs put down, a week of labor supervised by Mrs. Turnbull sitting in tentlike folds of silk on a Chippendale sofa. In the autumn, same thing in reverse, oh blessed occupation. Clothes closets had matching quilted garment bags and storage boxes. Linen closets were stacked with monogrammed bath towels and guest towels and sheets and pillowcases that had never been used and never would be.

Thus. The inevitability of matching quilted clothes bags and storage boxes in Cabe's closet in the apartment on Memorial Drive. Chintz curtains substituted for damask in the summer time, and back again. Cabe's new habitat, The connubial bed turned down every night by Adelia after she had served the dinner with the left hand and then the right hand, Catsy's nightgown folded and placed on one side of the bed, Cabe's pajamas on the other. On top of the monogrammed blanket cover.

Even the bed, in this dwelling, was not of Cabe. In any way. In one sense it was not even Catsy's. It was everything she had learned, and everything that in bed she *was* through everything she had learned. It was a should, Catsy's marriage bed. It should, before everything else, look right, it should have a quilted chintz bedspread to match the chintz curtains, it should have a crepe de chine blanket cover in winter and a seersucker one in summer, both with a monogram in the center. It should have the nightclothes laid out upon it. It should then be gotten into, slept in. And of course, love should be made in it, but as little as possible because there was nothing in it for Catsy but endurance and undignified struggle. She could feel nothing. Intercourse was the greatest disappointment of her life. She had burst into tears on her wedding night, that happy bride in the silver monogrammed picture frame. As far as she was concerned, intercourse was all for the male—he, literally and figuratively on top, enjoying, she underneath, passive and patient and scornful. In this bed, Catsy learned submission. She learned to grit her teeth.

But she was wrong about Cabe's enjoyment. His participation in their lovemaking was an insatiable need forever unfulfilled. Her pretty body, her full pearlike heavy soft breasts, aroused him, at first continually. But in the act, she was simply a vessel for his ejaculation. Afterward, emptied, he would lie quiet and ashamed and hopeless before falling asleep.

He respected Catsy. Respect had been the basis of his attraction to her. But after the promise of his deliverance in marrying her had faded, he came to see that their dissimilarities were fatally unfruitful. He could always remember the day he had first understood this. They were driving along the highway to the Cape, Catsy at the wheel of the Packard roadster her father had given her for a birthday present. The roadster was gray. Polished, inside and out. Pearl gray. The chrome trim blazed white in the sun. Catsy's hands on the wheel were smooth and tan and beautifully slender, her fingernails painted a lustrous pink. He began to pay attention to her hands, to everything. After giving thought to the immaculate gray of the car, he gave thought to the immaculate capable beauty of Catsy's hands. Guiding. In control. Then he had a second's knowledge of being removed from those hands, of a positive and necessary separateness from them.

Her foot on the accelerator was long and slender. A very long foot for a girl. Her shoe was white, with black patent leather on toe and heel. Pure white. There would never be a smudge of dirt on the pure white of her shoe which was capably, expertly playing on the accelerator.

"Catsy." He turned to her and had to look slightly up. She was a shade taller than he. She seemed very tall to him at this moment. Too tall.

"Dear?" She threw him a short glance, because she shouldn't take her eyes from the road. In that glance, her brown eyes were instantly, dutifully, but warmly at his disposal. A quick smile raised her cheeks so that her eyes were momentary slits, then the cheeks dropped back down. Smile over. The smile in her eyes was warm, but the smile on her face was automatic. "Yes?"

"Nothing." He felt a faint sickness touch his innards. What am I doing with this tan, lean, grinning girl? There is nothing in that hand, on that polished wheel, that I know. And nothing in those nice brown eyes that knows me.

"I want to stop somewhere and get a plant," Catsy said.

"A plant?"

"Yes. I want a plant for the bedroom. A pink geranium. I think, to match the pink in the chintz. Don't you think that would be yummy?"

Again that visceral uneasiness. "Why must a plant match something?" he asked quietly and ominously. And why for God's sake should she think he would *care* about a plant matching the bedroom chintz? Didn't she know him at all?

Why didn't she know he would despise the idea of buying a plant to match something? It depressed him to see she had no knowledge whatsoever that this was so. And then it depressed him even more to see that this was the way she was and always would be, and he hadn't really known it, or at least hadn't admitted it to himself in his urgency to marry her. Still, there was nothing wrong with a wife telling her husband she wanted to stop and buy a plant to match the bedroom chintz, was there? It was a perfectly harmless insignificant thing to say, wasn't it? Why should he feel that Catsy was the one at fault here, not he?

And then he saw that of course she wasn't any more at fault than he was. And in a moment of fathomless despair he saw that this whole ridiculous plant pother was simply an ultimate definition of Catsy, and of himself, and of the two of them together.

They were on their way to the island to visit Aunt Tilly. It was a clear August morning, the sky was blue and without a cloud. They sped along. "Do you want to change over?" Catsy said, dismissing the subject of the plant.

"Not particularly." He was ashamed of his outburst. "I like doing nothing for a change. Unless of course you're tired of driving."

"Heavens no. You know me. I could drive from here to California nonstop."

And she could, too, Cabe thought, with despair giving way to a grudging admiration. Even if she were exhausted, that incredible energy and duty and just plain guts would get her nonstop to California. She would drive the two hours to Port Stratton, she would mend his socks because that was not Adelia's job, she would cajole him out of a depression with that great grin (not an automatic smile but a genuine open grin). She would arrange a dinner party to include someone her father knew on the board of directors of the BSO, in order to further his "musical career," as she called his playing. He would know that this was inappropriately and uselessly wide of the mark and that it was simplistic of Catsy, and even crass, to have the idea. Yet behind what he thought of as her crassness was a force, a strength which, though misguided, felt like the ground under his feet. And so, squirming, he would consent to having the director of the BSO invited for dinner, both hating himself for agreeing to it, and half-believing that something would come of it. And after dinner, Catsy would make him play. "Play that thing you did so well for Mummy and Daddy the other night, that thing by whosis, oh Lord, you know me, I never remember the names of pieces." Cringing, loathing himself for playing, yet wanting enormously just the same to play, not just for the BSO man, but to play, to play, Cabe would play. And not play well. Naturally. Polite applause. Insincere words of praise from the other guests, talk about his music prolonged by them because it was expected of them. The BSO man would say nice bland things, and leave shortly thereafter. Adelia would come in for the coffee cups, substituting a tray of liqueurs.

End of party. "I thought you played beautifully, dear."

"For Christ's sakes, Catsy, how can you say that? I played abominably. For Christ's sakes."

She came over to him, tying the belt of her long flannel wrapper as she moved, her eyes determined and lively and warm, a growing mischievous grin on her confident mouth. He was sitting dispiritedly on the edge of the bed, the shoe he had just taken off dangling in one hand. She removed the shoe from his hand. "Gimme," she said softly. Then she sat down beside him and put her arm across his shoulders and tilted her head to rest against his, and she gave him a quick hug. "C'm on, boy. None of this. You know you can play. If you think you didn't play well tonight that doesn't mean you think you *can't* play well. You *know* you can play well." She put a warm hand, smelling of perfumed soap, along his cheek. The hand was comforting. Like her words, like the kind warm strength of her face, the hand calmed him. "Listen, boy. Go on out there and play it again. Play it the way you can. I'm going to bed and you're going to play. Hear?"

There was a complacent comfort for Catsy in the durability of her wifeliness. She felt, and in one way she was right, that Cabe was hers. She knew she would always help him and that he would always need to be helped, even though his music declared their hopeless separation. Music was outside of her, it was no part of her, it all sounded the same to her because that's all she heard—sound. And Cabe in his music was something she couldn't reach. She felt helpless, often strangely sad about this. Yet she was unfailingly strong in other ways. Sadness and strength together composed her.

Cabe was the center of her life. She adored him, idolized him. Part of his attraction for her was the grandeur of his somberly private, art-seeking, love-seeking nature, which she worshiped the more doggedly really because it was "light years" (her words) beyond her capacities or her comprehension. His music was the only overt demonstration of this, and so she was pained, for his sake, that she was so insufficient about it, so separate from it. With a touching dogged seriousness she kept on trying for all the thirty-six years of their marriage to share with him this single part of him that was open to being shared. When he played, or at the concerts she dutifully went to with him, she gritted her teeth and tried to listen, to feel something. But she couldn't, she couldn't. She always drifted away from it because all she was hearing was loud sound. Still, she was determined to memorize the names of the pieces Cabe played, and the names of the works she heard at concerts, and the names of the composers. And she would remember them for a while. But soon she would forget them, and Sibelius' Symphony #7, was "that long gloomy thing by Whatshisname, drat, what *was* it? Oh, well, you know *me*."

Yes, Cabe knew her. He was at first touched by these efforts to share his music, but finally galled, even affronted by her obtuse persistence which was accomplishing the reverse of what she was striving for. She actually detracted from his pleasure in concerts, he would have much preferred to go alone; she dozed off, she sorted out the contents of her purse, she made lists on the margins of programs. Once— it was during Ravel's "Bolero"—Cabe couldn't help but see, the program was propped on her purse, the pencil was in her hand. "Cream of mushroom soup," he read, "leg of lamb with mint sauce, roast potatoes, peas, baked Alaska."

Their life went on.

Cabe liked his work, he liked figures, he enjoyed the problem of finance. The job he got after Harvard Business School, in the small brokerage house of Chisholm, Clark and Stone, was an interesting enough, undemanding enough pastime, and well enough paid to keep Catsy in winter and summer blanket covers, also remunerative enough to see him through long-drawn-out, part-time piano study at the Conservatory. He did not complain. He was practical and conscientious about his job, and a series of promotions was inevitable. Eventually the firm would be Chisholm, Clark, Stone and Kingsley.

Catsy kept house, like her mother, obsessively; she played bridge, she played tennis, she sailed, she served on little committees, she made needlepoint pillows and spectacle cases and bedroom slippers and summer bags. She was a solid best friend to a handful of girls she had grown up with, and she had lunch with one or several of them every day of the week.

They lived a conventional young-married life, more affluently than most of their friends, due to the Turnbulls' money. They were a popular couple; between them they knew "everyone," both having been born and raised and for the most part educated in or near Boston. Their dinners, with excellent food served by light-stepping Adelia, were outstanding, especially in the fall when Mr. Turnbull went duck shooting, and were thought to be glamorous by those couples who were still struggling to live well on a young husband's earnings. They danced, they weekended, they drank. They were dutiful about their parents. "What have we got for tonight, Cats?"

"Oh, tonight's Father's birthday, remember? Guess what Mother's giving him? She's giving him a first edition of *Little Dorrit*, it's in little magazines the way it first came out, nineteen of them. Dickens in parts, it's called."

"That's nice I suppose. But what will he do with it?"

"Why it's a part of his collection."

"So it is. Do they come here or do we go there?"

"We go there."

"What are *we* giving him?"

"Oh I got him a camel's hair bathrobe at Brooks Brothers. *Vedy* English lord looking."

"Monogrammed, I suppose."

"Oh yes. In brown, on the pocket."

Catsy was pregnant six months after the wedding, although she never used the word "pregnant," which no one used and which was too physical anyway. Her friends said, "I'm going to have a baby," but Catsy said, "I'm with child" or "I'm enceinte," with a gleam in her eye that made this the fun she wanted it to be, and not pretense. She was so tall, and so wide-boned, that her pregnancy didn't show at all for the first seven months, and then showed for the last two only in a slight rounding of her abdomen, as though she had eaten too large a meal. Mrs. Turnbull bought her expensive flowing dresses, which concealed even that slight manifest of life inside. Catsy told everyone she felt weird about it, "I'm a freak," she said, but actually she was wonderfully relieved not to have that great bump thrusting out. "I'm the exact opposite of the girl who swallowed an olive, and all the boys had to leave town," she said with her comradely grin. She would say this to Cabe's mother without batting an eyelash, with Cabe looking on aghast and dumb with admiration. And Mrs. Kingsley, who had always secretly admired Catsy's spunk, would nevertheless pretend not to know what Catsy was talking about and change the subject smoothly.

A son was born to them. McCabe Turnbull Kingsley. Cabe's mother was outraged at the "Turnbull," this presumptuous linking of a high-up and a middling name. She thought it arriviste; she blamed not Catsy so much as the Turnbulls for taking advantage of the birth of *her* grandson to glorify *their* name. "The family are up in arms," she told everyone. Mr. Turnbull was a distinguished and respected banker, but no matter. The Turnbulls weren't Kingsleys.

"Little Cabe" died at the age of three, a puny pop-eyed baby, unsuckled by his flesh-hating mother, bottle-fed by a baby nurse who at first allowed no one to come, unsanitarily, anywhere near the bassinet without a nose mask. "What's he *for*," Cabe said with laughing exasperation, wanting his child to receive human contact, though he himself had no wish to give it. This was not the era of Spock, it was the heyday of a mechanical man named Watson, and Cabe, in this thirties wasteland of loveless child care, was both behind his time and ahead of it in knowing that the prohibition of touch and kiss was against nature.

The household hardly altered at all, except for the faint sounds, from the nursery, of a baby's wails, and the more frequent presences of Mrs. Turnbull and Mrs. Kingsley. With scorn and yet with a flashing fervor, "He's all Turnbull," Mrs. Kingsley said of this extension of her son, her self. And with equal grandmotherly fanaticism, Mrs. Turnbull provided exquisite monogrammed baby-boy clothes, blue, and saw to it that the nurse wore a uniform and that the carriage, which was the finest money could buy, had a navy blue broadcloth carriage robe with a large gray monogram in its center. Catsy, liking the *idea* of having a baby but uncomfortable with the fleshly reality of it and frightened of the responsibility, held little Cabe tensely in her arms, with a gentle look downward, in the Bachrach photograph of three generations—grandmother, mother and child. She bought a row of glass jars with hand-painted blue bunnies on them, for the shelf above little Cabe's rubber bath table—one for cotton, one for nose swabs, one for talcum, one for baby oil. On the nurse's day off she had to cope, nervously and resentfully, with what was in all of them. She did have a deep feeling for this baby. But his pallor, his incessant crying, terrified her. And as for Cabe, "I'm never allowed to see him," he would say, pseudo-protestingly. He had no feeling at all for the pale child with the Turnbull pop eyes.

Music became the focus, the vital center of Cabe's life. Mrs. Turnbull, to replace his old secondhand Baldwin, gave him a Mason and Hamlin baby grand piano for his thirtieth birthday (the Buddha-like woman adored him, also thought his musicianship appropriate to everything Bostonian).

Abe at thirty-five.

A taciturn young man, going through the motions with less and less to say. Remaining courteous—he was a man trained in courtesy—remaining tiredly charming, but growing remote.

And Cabe at the piano, blazing into life, all his passion pounding behind the blank face and the vacancy of the strange cold light eyes. And yet, his playing could not grow. He was not up to what he felt was in him. Technically, he began to reach perfection. But there was an unrealized quality in his playing. He told himself that if he were all of a piece, he could put himself wholly into music and become the full pianist he knew he could be. But as yet, something was absent which could transform the fire of what he felt into the fire of performance. And so there were no performances for Cabe, except as accompanist.

The years went by. Life never changed, it was always the same, monotonous as the traffic on Memorial Drive. Dinner on Sunday with the Turnbulls, dinner the next Sunday with Cabe's mother, Christmas and Thanksgiving with both families, Cabe's mother looking down her nose at the nouveauness of Mrs. Turnbull's perfection. Summers on the island. An occasional trip to Europe. Commonwealth Avenue, Beacon Street, Newbury Street, Boylston Street, Mass. Avenue, the brokerage firm, the Conservatory, the Boston Symphony, Memorial Drive, Brattle Street.

Even though Cabe was the sternly raised, sternly adored only child of a widowed mother whose powerful parenting dominated him tragically, he had still managed all his life to hold onto the belief that he had a center which was his own. A half-admitted loneliness at school, and again at college, at first worried him, but then strangely he made his peace with it, an innate good sense telling him that he was different and private. And he had the strength to abide with this knowledge. In his junior year at school, he asked to have a single room. The idea of having no roommates felt quiet. And it turned out, almost excitingly, to be the way he needed it to be. The black-slapping "Hi-ya, boy,"and the improbable tales of prowess, gradually died away, and by the time he was midway through Harvard he had found three substitutes for these flamboyancies—a growing absorption with music and a love of literature and mathematics. The passion which had seemed a part of personality, was no longer on display, was internalized, and became the dynamics for musical creativity. He discovered Walt Whitman. Hungrily, in utter rapt astonishment, he read Walt Whitman. "I am not what you supposed, but far different."

He was too attractive to be a loner. How often does attractiveness distract from a man's own sense of privacy because the world makes claims on him and he feels a responsibility to respond? All his life Cabe was claimed, because of his kindness and charm, by both men and women. In his youth, girls were exorbitantly attracted to him, to his loping walk, his seal-like head thrust forward, the sudden charming smile of his sensual lips, the queer light turquoise color of his eyes, his genuine warmth, and his quality of secrecy, of elusiveness. And he was also intensely male. Boys liked him because he had the dashing confidence of being likable and therefore was, and because he was competent at sports. However, he had no close friends. His treatment of everyone was more or less superficial. And he never quite made the top, in anything. He was proficient at the piano but continually lacking in what he wanted to make of it. He was good at mathematics, and literature, and got by in his other courses. But no honors, ever. He failed, just, to make Porcellian, perhaps because of that superficiality which was really a declaration that he did not care very deeply for who he was with, and what he was doing. Even his marriage, in his mother's view, was second-rate.

Second-rate. An accompanist. That's how Cabe ended up, and that's what he knew himself to be. Second-rate, but with the unshakable conviction, even in his sixties, that he was capable of his own kind of first-rateness—a capacity for music for its own sake, music that gave him satisfaction; and a capacity for love. These were convictions that had sustained his pride all his life, even though all the evidence was to the contrary.

The wrong man to be married to Catsy. He was gentle with his decent wife, and remote, considerate, wearily amused. Yet in a certain way, her strong insensate cheerfulness was an antidote to his mute despair. She was a fine, sensible, spirited woman and she carried him along, not toward what he wanted to become, but as the conformist he had to be in order to survive at all in the prosaic and inflexible circumstances that controlled his existence.

Each appreciated and loved the strengths of the other. Cabe's heart was like an aching stone, yet it was unthinkable to him that they separate. Unseat Catsy Kingsley? He couldn't conceive of it. Though after his mother died and with her his fear of what she would think or do or say if he were to tell her he wanted to leave Catsy, and after the Turnbulls, that impregnable fortress around his marriage, died, Cabe let himself dwell on divorce, but only in fantasy. It was simply not something he could do, or had any heart for doing. He had grown fond of that splendid woman, but like a sister. And even though he had endured for thirty-six years the melancholy of being married to a sister, the desperate sadness of going to bed (until he was no longer able to) with a sister, of making love with no passion, only with fondness aided by liquor, he could never seriously entertain the thought of telling Catsy he wanted to leave her. Passivity, affection, misguided loyalty, family, conformity, fear of alternatives, need of Catsy's strength—these were forces too powerful for Cabe to challenge. And Catsy? She adored Cabe, and never so much as dreamed of turning her marriage inside out to inspect what was there.

And so, with the drab surety that it would be frivolous to break up a marriage because it lacked rapport, that it would be a declaration of the ascendancy of carnality over probity to desert Catsy because of the lack of good sex, Cabe, finally unable to feel anything for his sister-wife, even with the aid of alcohol, in his mid-fifties, overnight, it seemed, grew impotent.

Catsy died. And Cabe was free. But it was too late for freedom, he thought. He was too old, too spent, he had played a game for thirty-six years and it had dulled his capacities, or even his desires, for anything real. He felt as neuter as though he had been castrated.

He fired the maid and lived alone among the monograms. He went to work, he practiced, he went through the motions at dinner parties; a single man, he was in much demand. At little concerts he, the accompanist, stood up with the soloist and took self-effacing bows, waiting with decorous humility for him or her to leave the platform first.

Summer vacations on the island with Mr. Turnbull's sister, Aunt Tilly. An occasional trip to Europe. Commonwealth Avenue, Beacon Street, Newbury Street, Boylston Street, Mass. Ave, the brokerage firm, the Conservatory, the Boston Symphony, Memorial Drive, Brattle Street. . . .

Then one day, standing in the subway on his way home from the office, swaying there as the trolley rattled comfortably along, he saw a man. Right away he found himself looking devouringly at the man. The man stood straight, with a strong stillness that seemed to Cabe to create a nimbus around him so that he stood out, in dimension, from the background of other people as markedly as though he had been pushed into the foreground and was lit from behind. He was looking out of the window, but with such a calmness that it seemed to Cabe his eyes, by means of muscles and nerves and tendons, were attached to a solid weight somewhere in his body, keeping them that steady. It was as though he had a powerful, a very powerful automized stabilizer in his center that kept him so immovable and so calm. He was singular in this, apart from other people in this tranquil stability, this sureness. And it seemed to Cabe that everything anyone ought to know, or rather, that the most important thing in the world for him to know, was in this man's eyes.

He could not stop looking at the man. He thirsted for knowledge of him.

As he looked at the man, the thought that he would resign from the firm, entered Cabe's head and went through him like a peaceful purge.

II

On the morning of the day Celeste Hunter and Lidi Luhin were to come to hear him play, Cabe shaved more carefully than usual. And he took a little rusted scissors out of the medicine cabinet and clipped the hairs out of his ears, something he hadn't done in years. Then, as he did every morning before stepping into the shower, he darted a scared, hopeful look at the body in the long mirror on the door. This time he decided, in that one furtive look, to be reassured by what he saw—his flesh was going but it wasn't gone, a paunch was beginning, but it wasn't hopelessly full-fledged and like a bowl of rising white dough, his legs were still muscled, though there were knots and lengths of coiling blue veins in one of them.

Shamefacedly, he distanced himself from the mirror in order to get a different perspective of his body, and now he let himself be even more reassured by what he saw. Squinting his eyes, he blurred the body in the mirror, and thus indistinct, it seemed almost presentable to him. Presentable. . . . He straightened a little. He stepped into the shower and turned on the steaming needles of water. Presentable. . . . Soaping himself in the roar of the water, he acknowledged that word. And the significance of it sent a little shock through his chest.

He began to hum the Brahms Intermezzo he would play this afternoon.

At three o'clock, Cabe sat down in the kitchen to wait. He had given the living room a tidying of sorts, removing last Sunday's New York *Times* from the couch and plumping up the cushions with mighty swats that sent out clouds of dust. He had debated about whether to offer tea and decided positively against it, since it would be a distraction from his music, and make the occasion not serious but social.

The old kitchen was aglow with deepening winter sun. From the plant stand next to his chair, Aunt Tilly's red geranium which he was pledged to water, sent toward his nostrils a faint lively astringency. He took a nail file in a leather sheath from the breast pocket of his wool shirt, and began to file his brittle nails. He noticed that his fingers were shaking and, dismayed, ashamed, he put down the file and sat up straight and tried to force his shoulders to relax. Then he noticed the silence of this sun-still kitchen, it had a pressure, a weight which he thought of as emptiness, and all at once he felt it as a self-imposed solitude he didn't want. A conjunction of aloneness and of anxiety over his recital seized him, and for a moment he was acutely conscious of uneasiness that was a sort of fear. It is so crucial to him to play today, to play well today, to play acceptably. Is this a thing that will never happen? It is too late for it to happen? Is this empty kitchen, and these inexpert hands, the reality of himself, now, in this dwindling part of his life? "But where is what I started for, so long ago?/And why is it yet unfound?"*

Cabe's surroundings were always in the process of absorbing and giving back to him the vibrations of his emotions; he experienced the rooms he walked into as an extension of himself, mirrors of himself. So that now the kitchen, the

*Walt Whitman

geranium, the warming sun and himself he experienced as one thing. Sitting there tensely in his rocking chair he experienced sun and geranium and himself composed of a commingling of the substance of finality and nonfinality—an absolute conviction of being ended along with an equally absolute sureness that he could get beyond being ended. He existed in this inner and outer climate of failure-hope. He and the furniture and the walls and the fields beyond the walls of this house are composed of the absoluteness of being something stalled, ended, and yet, just as absolutely, of being something with infinite promise.

He got up abruptly and went over to the sink and began to wash the breakfast and lunch dishes piled there. As he was hanging the damp and very dirty dish towel on the rack, he heard the squeak of tires on snow, and turned to see Lidi Luhin's car stopping by the front walk, and Lidi opening the door. Just Lidi.

His first instinct was to hide. He would not have Lidi here alone, he would not play for Lidi alone. It was unthinkable. Hide. She would think he had forgotten the appointment. Run for it.

But she was already out of the car and walking slowly across the driveway to the front door. "Damn," he said, explosively. Then setting his face into lines of politeness, he strode to the front hall.

"Hel-*lo*!" Lidi stood stiffly like a little mannequin, wide and short and stiff in a fat quilted brown coat. "Don't be appalled at just me. I've got to go down-island afterward and pick up Freddy, so Celeste's coming in her own car."

"Oh? Really? Fine. Fine. Well. Do come in."

Lidi stamped the snow off her little shiny boots, and stepped in. She pulled a mitten off and gave Cabe a cold dry hand that was all bones.

"Here. Let me help you with your coat."

"Oh mercy, don't bother to hang it up, I'll just dump it on the bench if I may. Oh, I'm *so* looking forward to this."

Stiltedly, they accomplished the disposal of the coat; awkwardly, they advanced together into the living room, neither of them speaking. Then Cabe, at a loss, turned to her. "Would you like a fire?"

"Oh. Why yes. That would be nice."

"It's all laid. Here, I'll just put a match to it."

"What a lovely old room," Lidi cried brightly, falsely, aware of the fine proportions of it, though appalled at its shabbiness and neglect, for to be sure Aunt Tilly's antique-filled house needed an upkeep Cabe didn't give it. Without a daily dusting, without weekly applications of wax polish on the drop-leaf tables and tabourets, without an eye, and a needle and thread, to the fraying ends of the oriental rugs, these gentle old rooms had a look of decline, even of poverty. The noble scale of the rooms, the beauty of the furnishings, even these seeming infallibilities were unable to maintain any dignity in such disregard for them. Sunlight chalkily reflected on the dust-encrusted prisms of a girandole—this was a poor thing, a failure of both sunlight and prism, and more, of intent.

To others, the room spoke of failure, though not to Cabe. To him, the room was perfectly all right, he could see nothing wrong with it. Aunt Tilly had a hard time coming into the house, and didn't if she could help it. But Cabe never noticed the white rings beneath the dust of the mahogany coffee table, or the lusterless china, or the blackened silver, or the unreflective prisms. He tripped on the frayed ends of the oriental in the front hall, and cursed, but only at the perpetual inconvenience of tripping. A meticulous cleaning woman, who had worked for years for Aunt Tilly, had lasted only one day here; her incessant talk and her incessant vacuuming drove Cabe wild. And now a high school girl, who gave everything a careless once-over, came on Thursdays for two hours, Cabe's afternoon for errands and the only time he allowed himself away from the piano. "She gives it just a lick and a promise," Tilly told Turck with a loud, sad sigh.

Lidi could not bear shabbiness, particularly in her own house. It spoke of failure, decline. "Oh look, this is Gaudy *Welsh*" she cried, "my favorite china."

The door knocker sounded. It tapped once, loudly, and then once again, and Cabe, stopped by the fire with the matchbox in his hand, felt a hard loud pounding start up in his chest, as though it was his heart that the knocker had struck. The matchbox still in his hand he turned abruptly, with uncharacteristic incivility, away from Lidi, and then remembered to say, "Oh, excuse me," to her as he strode past her to the front hall. He saw the matchbox shaking in his hand, and flung it onto the hall table. He drew a stabilizing breath and then opened the door.

In the living room with the two women, the fire lighted and beginning to snap encouragingly, Cabe's poise came back to him. He seated them with ceremony, Celeste in a wing chair by the fire, Lidi across from her on the couch. Bowing toward each one with a tarnished silver box, he offered them cigarettes, which they both declined. He asked them if they would like a drink of something, which they both said no to. "Oh not at the moment," Celeste said cheerfully, and Cabe took this to mean that she planned to stay a long time. She wore black slacks, and a black turtleneck sweater upon which a flat silver pendant caught the firelight, a heavy half-moon swinging from a black cord,

Cabe saw. It rested on a promontory that was neither large nor small, he noticed. Standing between the two women's quiet—Celeste's poised, anticipatory, smiling, Lidi's tense and eager—he brought his long hands slowly together with a nervous, washing movement, then, noticing that they were damp, he fished out a handkerchief from his pocket and mopped at them. He wanted to play right away, without the nonsense of preliminaries, yet he was held back by the sense that there should be a little more talk before getting down to the music. His abruptness, he felt, would seem to demonstrate his preference for music over people, and even emphasize his nervousness.

"I'm looking forward to this," Celeste said, smiling widely, wanting to put Cabe at his ease. "This is a treat. A *private* concert. You and I should feel like ladies at court, Lidi. Who could we be? Let's see, Madame de Pompadour. And you're"—pointing to Cabe—"Couperin. What a fun afternoon."

"Isn't it," Lidi said loudly, thinly. She thought Celeste's frivolity insensitive, though she knew that Celeste used flippancy to cover up feelings, her own and other people's. Lidi was tense. She was nervous for Cabe and nervous for herself and what she would say after he had played, it should be right, it should be sensitive and beautifully expressed and she knew it wouldn't be. She was tight with these responsibilities.

"Well," said Cabe. "I'll begin, I think." He bowed very slightly toward them, then turned and went across to the piano beside a window through which late sun poured richly. Outside, the snow was gilded, and long deep blue shadows lay beneath the trees. Beyond the fields was the stretch of the sea which sounded distantly in this silence of waiting. Cabe heard it and thought about it and felt himself backed by it. He pulled out the stool and sat down. He looked up, across the piano to the women over by the fire.

Suddenly he knows that he will play a Chopin waltz instead of the Brahms Intermezzo. He wants to, he must play the Chopin waltz, because he feels that its wistful, purling young lightsomeness is what needs to be sounding here, not the ancient tranquility of the Intermezzo.

"I'll play Chopin's Grand Waltz in B flat minor," he announced. He cleared his throat raucously. He slid his hands, which were still moist, back and forth over the wool of his knees. Then he brought his hands up to the keyboard.

Chopin rippled out.

Celeste settled back and brought the palms of her hands purposefully and soundlessly down onto the arms of the chair, her lips tightening. She was going to be impartial and practical about listening to this recital. She had already decided that if Cabe's playing was impossible, she would say to him that she would have to take it up with her committee, and that he would be hearing from her, then tell him the committee had met and felt they needed an ensemble, not a soloist. Difficult, but necessary. She was prepared to find Cabe Kingsley amateur. But of course she was keeping an open mind. In any event, she was determined to listen critically. She owed the Committee On Hunger a good enough concert to raise the thousand dollars she was aiming for.

But the first notes of Chopin swept away her practicality. She had not reckoned on Chopin. The airy plaintiveness, the lament of Chopin meant only one thing to Celeste—it was Paris and mimosa and spring and unattainable desire, it was she and Mort sitting in a sidewalk café on the rue du Bac. The first awareness in her life of Chopin had been there, sitting and hearing it and having a thorough sense-recognition of an unresolvable something which that haunting music declared, along with an identical unresolvable something which was the condition of her life. *"Tristesse,"* her word for Chopin, and for herself and for Paris, had the sounds and feelings of Chopin and of hopelessness in a way that "sadness" didn't. *"Tristesse"* was palpable, like tears on your cheeks.

She was powerless now to prevent this waltz from coming down to her through the open window above the café on the rue du Bac, she was totally there listening to the sound coming with a halting, tinkling lyricism from a bad piano and an inexperienced player. The thundering traffic of the buses and taxis and cars and motorcycles almost drowned out the sound of the music, and yet a persistent sharp-sweet trickle of it kept floating out over the street. Mimosa wrapped in a paper cone lay on the marble-topped table, and from time to time she would pick it up and sink her nose into the furry yellow fragrance of the little balls on gray-green stems. Mimosa. Mort had bought it for her. In Paris it is mimosa, not gardenias, he gives her. Mort smokes his pipe, his head sunk into it. There are tiny red blood vessels in the corners of his eyes, and the hand that grips the pipe shakes slightly. He is wearing his just-purchased Charvet necktie, maroon with a silver-gray pattern, very elegant, very conservative. She is wearing her just-purchased Alexandrine kid gloves, cream-colored with little pearl buttons at the wrists. They have been "flanné-ing" as they call it, up and down the rue Saint Honoré all morning.

She plunged her head into the mimosa, her head was tight and light with hangover pain. This was salvation. The entirety of the invasion of this fragrance, antidote to what was, intimation of what could be, was salvation. Yet what was there to do but put them back down on the table? She did this, resignedly, and sighed and looked up at the French sky which was lavender-gray and massed with purple clouds. In a minute it would rain.

"*Garçon, encore deux pernods,*" Mort called to the waiter, speaking for her since it is he who makes the decisions about drinks.

One more, two more, whither thou drinkest, there will I drink. . . . She broke off a spray of mimosa and brought it up to her nose. This way she was with Paris and love and everything that was not here at this table between these married people who were raw with hangover. Mimosa could tell her of possibilities, French possibilities, that resolvable thing she saw in couples walking with their arms around each other, the man's head ducked down to the woman's turned up to him adoringly, their hips knocking suggestively together as they strolled and sometimes lurched. Celeste inhaled the mimosa and sipped the pernod which blurred reality. It was *she* looking up so adoringly into that man's face, it was *her* hip rubbing sensually against his. They would go to his apartment. The door would close. He would begin slowly to unbutton her blouse. He would put his head down between her breasts. She would untie his necktie, slowly. Slowly she would unbutton his shirt. They were both now naked. And the seeking hot hard knock of his sex against her opening softness . . .

"*Violà*, Monsieur-Dame." The waiter was putting two soupçoups on top of the two already there. "*Ça fait dix francs, s'il vous plaît.*"

"Drink up, Celesty. We're late."

Cabe's fingers flowed up and up and back and up, his arpeggios rippled with sure dulcet precision, the sustenuto sang with sweet-toned effulgence, hopeless and haunting, from the center of himself. And he was comfortable; elatedly at his ease. Knowing that he was playing surprisingly well and easily, his confidence accumulated, encouraging rarely revealed depths of expressiveness. Transcending inhibition, glimpsing new capacities, exultant, he was letting himself go with a certainty that his fingers were reliably, and with an imagination he couldn't believe, doing what his senses wanted done on this keyboard.

At first Lidi was not listening to the music, but was lost in a churning uncomfortable assault of thoughts—Celeste's black suede espadrilles were new, the coffee table was dusty, the poems were in her bag but when and how was she to show them to Cabe. Did she dare, did she even want to? She knew that Cabe was not interested in her. Acutely, she had sensed his polite reserve with her, and his guarded strong eagerness with Celeste.

She watched Cabe's head, bent low over the keyboard. His large lips were thrust out, and parted. There was a dangerous happy absorption over his face. He had forgotten everything but the music.

But now, suddenly, Lidi saw that this was wonderful. She knew what such absorption felt like, she herself had it when she was in her cubicle writing poetry. She could touch this, be this, she felt a happy bond with it. This is what it's all about, she said to herself. This is it. Easy tears were in her eyes because of the recognition that this was the secret source, his and hers, of the meaning of their lives.

She began to pay attention to the music, and then to hear it. His Chopin sounded expert to her, though she knew she was no critic of music. Yet she could tell when music was poor, mediocre or good. And this was good. She could feel in her bones that it was even very good. Dancing, slowing to tenderness, exploding in sweet bursts, it raised the little hairs on the back of her neck.

She felt moved and excited. Shivering, she saw the man at his piano—he loved it, he loved it, he was playing totally, nothing of himself was being held back.

And then she had a stilling recognition, which took her by surprise. The man's music, she thought, is of himself. She had an entire, gripping sense of what she meant by this. His music was something that he had caused to grow in him and out of him, as though his life had been directed toward the fusion of mind, senses, fingers, arriving finally at the triumphant expression of that pursuit. She saw here the dedicated direction of a life and its accomplishment. For a moment Lidi was immersed in a knowledge of what creativity is, and she said to herself: "He has caused that to grow. He has made that happen." And she felt another, stronger flow of kinship toward him, finding in herself the sense that this is what she, what everyone, had to feel. Everyone, everyone, she thought, has to play Chopin, or look at a rosebush, or a poem, or a child, and say, "I have caused that to grow."

Knowing that she had touched base for a moment with a universal truth, she sat back against the couch pillows, amazed and relieved.

She looked across at Celeste, and was shocked to see a look of intentness that was almost pain darkening and tightening the clear sunny mildness of that face. Celeste's head was bent toward her lap, her lower lip was caught in white teeth and her hands were locked tight together at her knees.

Accelerando. The waltz was ending. Two deep suspended smashing chords. A pause. Then the simple surprising conclusion of seven strong octaves.

For a moment there was silence. Then Lidi, who had worked herself up into a shivering emotion, cried out in a strangled voice, half-theatrically, half-earnestly, "Oh, oh, I can't speak, I . . ."

"I'm going to play one more thing," Cabe cut in. He was looking up at nothing. "Would you mind waiting until that's over to comment. Thank you. I'm going to play Bach's Italian Concerto."

Bach wasn't Celeste's dish, as she would say, but she was glad to be freed from Chopin, and now she did listen carefully and critically. And she thought Cabe's playing was excellent, facile technique, a quite moving expressiveness, capable interpretation, and with that male force which she preferred to the nongutsiness, again her words, of women pianists. It wasn't great, she decided, but it was certainly good. She even found herself really drawn into Bach during the Andante, for Cabe played it, she felt, with an emotional intelligence which interested her. Through layers of resistance, she was almost moved by it. She was relieved that she would be able sincerely to congratulate him, and invite him to perform at her concert.

Lidi was sliding into her quilted coat. The three of them stood in the front hall, Cabe holding Lidi's coat, Celeste reaching for her quilted jacket. "Goodness. Aren't we a bunch of Michelin men," Celeste said airily, with a crisp smile. A blank look from Lidi. "You know, those pneumatic men in the ads for Michelin tires."

All this airiness. Celeste had risen, after the Bach, Lidi had sprung up, too. And Cabe, slowly, had gotten up from the piano stool. Then Lidi, the first to speak, cooled down somewhat by the Bach, had cried, with lamentable inadequacy she had thought, "Oh, I can't even *begin* to tell you what your playing has meant to me. I simply don't have the words." And Celeste, quietly, had said, "Thank you. Really. I liked it. I hope you'll be our soloist." Then facetiously, "You will, won't you?" And Cabe, still deep in his music and barely listening, said only, "Thank you. Thank you both."

"He hasn't answered my question," Celeste cried with imperious-sounding flippancy. "Do we, or do we not have a soloist, Lidi?"

"Well, of course I'm very pleased to be asked," Cabe said detachedly. "Of course I'll play."

"I'm glad the concert's not as early as the twentieth. That's the day I go off-island to my poetry reading," Lidi said with her stone eyes expressively wide, suddenly jubilant over this so-called opportunity to tell Cabe about the reading without seeming to make a point of it. "I've been asked to read a few of my poems at the Friends of Poetry meeting on that day. Very exciting, of course."

"Oh, indeed," Cabe said politely, vaguely.

"Yes. I consider it an honor," Lidi said shortly. Then, "Heavens, I must fly," looking at her watch.

"Me too." Celeste raised her chin. She was now quiet.

And then they were all in the front hall. In a minute both women would be gone, Celeste would be gone. This was not at all what Cabe had imagined of the afternoon. The thrilling satisfaction of his playing—that was not enough. There was something that had not happened here, had not developed. In a minute he would be standing here alone, in a sort of hole, in an empty house that would rebuke him for what had not happened.

"Goodbye. And oh, *some*time, I hope to be able to tell you how I feel about your playing. What I'll do, I'll write you about it. I can never talk. That's why I write. Poetry I mean. Thank you. I *must* dash. Goodbye to both of you."

And Lidi was gone.

The minute the door closed, Cabe turned to Celeste. "Must you go? Won't you stay and have a drink?"

Without preamble Celeste let her jacket drop back onto the chair. "I'd love to."

Cabe was bowled over by this forthright acceptance. "I'm delighted you will. What will you drink?"

"Dry vermouth. Please. If you have it."

"Yes. Here, I'll just go out to the kitchen and get the drinks. Go on in, won't you, and sit down by the fire. I won't be long."

"Can I help?"

"No. Thank you."

"Mayn't I see Tilly's kitchen?"

"You'll wish you hadn't. Or rather, Aunt Tilly'll wish you hadn't. She told me the other day, in her unmistakable way, 'Dear, it's a pigsty.'"

"Then I'll save everybody's sensibilities by not looking at it."

Cabe brought drinks into the living room in both hands, gave Celeste hers, turned on some lamps, and then sat down across the fire from her. "I washed your glass carefully before filling it," he said, smiling a little, "I thought I might have scared you about the sanitary conditions out there."

"Oh that was nice of you," Celeste said softly. She held the glass up. "It sparkles." Then in the next breath, suave, airy, she began talking, talking in a high smooth voice about this and that—how kind it was of Cabe to ask her to stay, how delightful it was to be here, how pleasant fires were in winter, what beautiful old things Tilly had. She rattled on, trying to steel herself to be cautious and reserved while being dismayed at what she had let herself in for against all her resolutions, and at how eagerly she had agreed to stay because she had so much wanted to.

She stopped. A second of quiet had arrived in her, a little space had opened in which she saw, and understood, that the unbelievable had happened—she was with Cabe Kingsley. She was here, in a room, on an island, after endless years, at the age of sixty-five, sitting and talking to Cabe Kingsley. She felt panic, but a kind of elated amusement too.

Then, out of this awesome moment, she said to herself humorously: Well, for goodness' sakes why not? And at the same moment she saw, startlingly, that Cabe was a very attractive man. Even more attractive than he had been as a boy. Because of something inner? Yes. Because of the way he wore the fearful quiet of his composure with such dignity, and really with distinction. Still waters, she thought. How he had changed. All she remembered about that boy was his kissing and his extravagant stories. But there was nothing in him now to remind her of him then. And yet, when he smiled his ghost of a smile, there was the same astonishing charm in the ingenuousness of that sensual, sculptured mouth, even though beneath his firm chin, the skin of this throat ran down loose and cleft like two mountain ranges with a valley in between. She looked at the long deep folds in his cheeks, and, yes, she remembered now that those cheeks, young, had been lean and sucked-in looking, a part of the charisma of his smile, which then had been rash and brilliant. But they were still, those crevassed cheeks, a part of his charm.

She was tempted to feel pity for aging flesh until she recognized that there was no need to at all. This man's aging flesh had not really defeated the display of his charm. Flesh has nothing to do with it, she thought. It's only what animates the flesh that matters. And anyway, his charm, now, was really secondary to the appeal which his massive privacy, his innerness, had for her. Had his life been unhappy? Yes, she was certain it had.

He was looking at her intently, with cool eyes which at this stage of his life were beyond all expression save heavy seriousness. "You must be well versed in your music history," he said, "to know that Couperin played for Mme de Pompadour. Have you had much of a musical education? I assume yes." He rattled the ice around in his glass unselfconsciously, and then took a large swallow.

"Not really. I took piano lessons when I was a child, but they didn't work. I really got to know music through Mort's Great Aunt Anna, the one I went to the opera with for so many deadly years. I mean," she amended quickly, "deadly performances. Then too, I went to the Philharmonic every Friday afternoon with another music lover, Mort's sister, Christina. For years we did that. Every Friday afternoon. And she drummed music into me. I've been exposed to music."

"Force feeding."

"Yes. But it took. I mean, in spite of the automatic-ness, I mean the unspontaneity of going those thousands of afternoons to listen to music—I wouldn't have gone on my own, you know—in spite of the horse being led to water, the horse did drink. I got to like music. I have to admit, though, I find Mozart and Bach hard, though Bach less so than Mozart. Anyway, I guess with certain exceptions I listen to music more with my head than with anything else."

"How very interesting," Cabe said with great attentiveness. After a moment he said, "How did you feel about the Chopin?"

"The Chopin?" Celeste hesitated. She was suddenly acknowledging the suppressed eagerness here—Cabe's, hers. "The Chopin?" she faltered, with a strange little laugh of inexperience and elation. And suddenly she had no way of going on, there was a spinning blankness in her head, she was speechless. Be careful, she warned herself in the midst of cautious elation, be careful. "Oh the thing was," she at last managed to say lightly, "really, to be honest with you, I didn't entirely listen." Now she smiled capably. "I'm afraid I *heard* your Chopin, but I was *listening* to mine, oh years and years ago. Never mind. Your Chopin was lovely, in spite of my drifting away from it."

"Yes." Quietly. "I see. Yes. Music can do that. But somehow, particularly Chopin."

They were both quiet now. Outside, the wind whistled across snow-flat fields and then roared away into the woods, raging softly there, like distant surf. Which was it, wind or surf, or both, that, off there beyond the fields, was an insistence of surging sound under a darkening sky? Here, in the warmth and light of this benevolent interior, the fire sounded softly, as insistent in its way as the surf.

Winds shaking the old house, distant surf sounding, and in here the fire—sustaining, solicitous. Cabe felt comfort. He felt a kind of thankfulness. He felt excitement and peace and a love of the ways of this earth.

He rose. "I need another drink. How about you?"

"Oh I'd love another. Thanks."

Cabe put the glass in Celeste's hands reaching up for it, and he looked steadily down at her, noticing intensely the pleasantness of her expression. Sunny, he thought, her face could be called sunny. And strangely innocent, though it was not a childish face, it was a woman's face. It was as though strength and reasonableness and boundless good humor had approved of innocence and wanted never to lose it, knowing that it, and maturity, were a successful amalgam. And the lines in it went up, not down; he noticed the regularity of fine lines running straight up from her jaw to her cheekbones, radiating up and out to skin pulled tight over their prominence. And the corners of her mouth went up, too, but tensely, as though with effort, betraying that when off-guard they tightened. He thought of her flippancy and made up his mind to disregard it.

He went back to the couch and sat down, rather heavily. It was unbelievable to him that a woman, a beautiful spirited woman, was sitting beside his fire with him. The room seemed brighter than it ever had, and he wondered whether it had something to do with the voltage. He watched the silver moon rising and falling quite perceptibly on her breast, catching the light of the fire as it moved. Construing this rapid breathing as emotional, he was complacently pleased. And he was excited too. He could feel excitement making his breath come short as he talked, and it bothered him one moment, and the next moment not.

Cabe had no sense of ownership of this place, he had never had any sense of ownership about the places he had lived in, perhaps because Catsy's had been so skewed, and yet having Celeste here in this room with him, with the snapping fire declaring this an occasion, gave him a feeling of the importance of fireside that he was unfamiliar with, but liked. Perhaps for the first time he was feeling comfortable in this room. And the excitement in his chest, this was exhilaratingly comfortable too, because it was a way he had never felt before but was at home with, as though innate but unused capacities for a new dimension of feeling were being revealed to him.

"You mentioned Christina Hunter. I remember Christina," Cabe said. "I remember her very well."

"Oh? Really. She was my roommate at Cloverly."

Celeste lifted her glass to her lips. Cabe lifted his glass to his lips. Another silence. Comfortable now. Broken again by Cabe. "My wife went there."

"Oh? What was her name?"

"Catsy Turnbull."

"*Catsy!* Oh, good heavens. Not Catsy Turnbull. I didn't know her well because she was a year ahead of me, but I worshiped her. Everyone worshiped Catsy. She was such a, such a, *good egg.*"

"She was that."

"I'm sorry to know," Celeste said quietly, "that Catsy Turnbull is dead."

"She died of cancer," Cabe said. "Four years ago." There was nothing more he wanted to say about Catsy. He didn't want commiserating looks. He didn't want hypocrisy. And yet, in Celeste's pained silence, he found himself saying, "I admired her spirit. It was splendid. Always. Even dying." Why am I saying this? he wondered. But unable to stop himself he went on, "It was her spirit I was bowled over by, from the first."

"Oh I remember it well. She'd stand up to anybody. Even the teachers. How did you meet? Probably at some prom, I'll bet. Catsy didn't miss any of them. We were all jealous of her. Where did you go to college?"

"Harvard," said Cabe. "And yes, it was at a prom. She was my roommate's date. The senior prom. How pretty she was. And peppy, as we said then. Nothing flirtatious about her. That big friendly grin. Where did she get all her confidence, I wonder?" What am I doing? he worried. And then,

"The next day I took her to lunch and afterward to meet my mother."

"Did you always take girls to meet your mother?" Celeste asked sweetly, acidly.

Startled, Cabe gave her a keen look. "Mother *hoped* I would," he said. Then, looking at her through distances, for it was unreal now, he said quietly, "You remember my taking *you* to meet Mother, I see."

"Yes. I do."

Cabe narrowed his eyes. Celeste was tantalizingly off there behind veils, like a dream. And his mother's disapproval of her was there, too, powerful as the earth beneath his feet. "Wasn't she lovely, Mother?" "Very. But I don't know anything about her, do you?"

Oh yes, between Christina and his mother, he had been warned off, and stayed off. And, truth to tell, he had soon pretty much forgotten Celeste, although from time to time in his life he had thought about her with a stirring of his blood and with a faint wistfulness, as if for something lost. The thought of his mother made him feel suddenly uncertain, unanchored.

He looked down into his glass. But then he looked up again, slowly, and threw a glance at Celeste which was cold and arrowlike and intense. And he saw that her face was lit from within, like a strong steady lamp. It was like alabaster, white and translucent and glowing from within. She doesn't eat herself up, he thought, she has a kind of ease of spirit, an emotional temperance. It was an inspiriting thing to be with because it was uncomplicated. He found himself remembering her stride.

"Well, Catsy was a great girl," Celeste said in the heavy silence. So, it was Catsy Turnbull he chose. Did he kiss her on the side of the neck, at that prom? Did she like being kissed on the side of the neck? No. Catsy Turnbull was not a girl to be turned into rivers of sweetness by a kiss.

"Yes. A great girl. Spunky. How seldom you see spirit like that. She threw the pope's nose at me across my mother's Thanksgiving dinner table, the first time she was there for dinner."

"Why, how absolutely wonderful." Celeste began to laugh helplessly. "I can just see her. Was your mother amused?"

"Mother was not amused."

"No, I don't suppose she was." The dark arid pomp of that Beacon Street house came into Celeste for a moment like shadow. She remembered that the house had looked brown and felt brown and smelled brown, like the halls of Grandma's orphanage. And Mrs. Kingsley—a darkness, like the house; a blur of tall stiff black, inscrutable with power. Was Catsy intimidated by Mrs. Kingsley, in spite of her confidence and spunk? "I think Catsy got a great bang out of being daring, don't you?" she said. "It must be a heady feeling to know *not* only that you're naturally daring, but that you can get away with it. That people love it. Envy it." Then, more seriously, "Which is not in any way to diminish Catsy's fineness."

"Catsy was the salt of the earth," Cabe muttered. The memory of Catsy's fineness settled over his face soberly, even gently.

"I was thinking 'all wool and a yard wide,' but I think both of us are being a little unimaginative, don't you?"

"Excessively. Can't we do better than that?"

They both laughed, excessively too.

"Grandma would have called her 'a tartar.' Or 'a live wire.' Today's jargonese would call her 'a fine human being,' god forbid."

157

"Were you close to your grandmother? I seem to remember something about you and your grandmother." Cabe leaned forward intently, put his elbows on his spread knees and thrust his head toward Celeste. In his two hands he held his glass, revolving it slowly with a sound of slipping ice.

"I lived with her. My parents both died when I was tiny. I lived with Grandma." For a moment Grandma was vivid—"Now, Celesty," with the hushed intense voice, the big piercing eye an inch from hers, the chalky pushing fragrance of Djer Kiss sachet, "just realize they have nothing and you have everything, sssweetie. Try to count your blesssings."

A gust of wind boxed the house, and could be heard hollowly in the chimney. Another gust came wailing around the roof, tossing violently the snow-weighted pine trees below it. Grandma's ghost? Hello, Grandma, you funny lady.

"I see," he said. But he didn't, of course. What must it have been like to be brought up by an old lady? Good? Bad? "Do you have any children?" he asked her suddenly.

"No. No." Celeste said this lightly, too lightly, Cabe thought. And she looked away from Cabe, toward the fire. The light of the flames danced dazzling in her eyes, making them incandescent and seemingly expressionless.

Since this was clearly, painfully all she was going to say about no children, Cabe helped her out by launching into another Catsy story—the one about Catsy swatting a Saks shoe salesman with a box lid because he'd insulted her by telling her he didn't have a larger size, and that the next size was the box. "She did have big feet, and it was a sore point," Cabe said.

"Catsy must have been fun to live with," Celeste murmured, wholeheartedly though perhaps wistfully.

"Yes. She was fun to live with. But her fire wasn't all cheerful mischief by a long shot. She could be as furious as anyone I've ever seen. There was an incident with my mother. Mother was absolutely despicable, I'm sorry to say. Unforgivably so," almost pridefully. "But Catsy faced up to her. Very few people faced up to Mother." His voice had risen.

Was spiritedness being extolled here? Or was a parent being denounced for inhibiting it? "Good for Catsy," Celeste murmured thinly. She did not want to hear this sort of thing. She thought it far too intimate. She hated it. She hated the look on his face of weakness and of spite. She lifted her glass and hid behind it for a moment as she drank from it.

"Yes. I don't think Catsy was afraid of anything," said Cabe, regretting his indiscretion, regretting his disloyalty to his mother. Suddenly he felt exposed. What in hell had he been doing, telling this unknown woman such private things? He felt heavily back against the pillows. "Well." He cleared his throat so violently that the loose skin of it quivered. "I'm afraid I've taken your friendship for Catsy as carte blanche to say anything that comes into my head. Forgive me."

They sat in a silence now that pounded with embarrassment. Ice seemed to rattle accusingly in their glasses, and the snap of the fire sounded like rebuke.

Celeste gave her head a little shake, trying to look pleasant.

And Cabe? What's done is done and there's nothing so bad about it, he said reassuringly to himself. He put his glass down on the table. Then he spread his knees again and put his elbows on them, following down with a tensely, attentively held head, fingers locked and drumming. "This concert," he said. "Will you tell me about details—where it will be, the piano, the audience you expect, or hope to have. The piano's of course what I do have to know about. But I'm sure you wouldn't go ahead with any performance without the solid ground of a good piano."

Suddenly Celeste was sorry for him. She felt strength, and something that wasn't strength—that heaviness again. He was heavy with lack. He was heavy with something he wanted to have supplied. But she saw nevertheless that for a moment something very real had broken out of Cabe Kingsley's massive reserve. It felt like a warm, a very alive flow from him to her, and she opened up and let it come into her. "The piano's not the greatest," she said. "I think you'll find it good enough. We'll go and see. Right away we'll go and you'll play on it, before I start all this in motion."

Cabe unlocked his hands and sat back. "Yes," he said. And in a minute, "Very good," he said. He heard the wind roar softly to itself in the valley below the High Road. A log collapsed and sent up sparks. He looked at her with a faint smile around his expressionless eyes.

"I should be going," Celeste said. She had declined a third drink. She was suddenly tired. She had been here a long time. She looked at the clock on the mantelpiece, which said ten minutes to one, and which was making no sound, no movement. Its glass was opaque with dust. The clock declared neglect. It depressed her, even angered her. Suddenly she thought that she hadn't another word in her, as though her voice had gone. She was spent. She must leave. But she wanted to be careful not to rupture something. She must be sure not to cut back this vulnerable man. She looked pointedly at the mute clock. "It's getting late, I think," she exclaimed. "It must be close to six. I hope I haven't kept you from something." She rose, picked her handbag up from the floor, held out her hand decisively while smiling with such sincerity that she did not seem impetuous to Cabe, only straightforward.

Not ready for this at all, Cabe rose too, slowly, in surprise.

Disappointment flickered at the corners of his mouth. "Well," he said quickly, "I'm sorry you have to go. I've liked this very much, Mrs. Hunter."

"Celeste."

He took her hand. "Celeste."

"Goodbye, Cabe Kingsley."

"Cabe." Standing in the encasement of his aging, and the sorrowful rigidity of years, Cabe suddenly felt himself loosen from within. He felt a helpless softening trying to push out of him through armor-tightness. Then he felt a flood of tears coming up into his throat. He wanted to say something about this, he wanted to tell her about the way he was feeling. She had done this and he must tell her so. He was bursting, cracking. He could not speak.

"Goodbye, Cabe," she was saying, "and thank you for the splendid, splendid music. I'll be in touch with you about details. I've enjoyed our talk, too. Very much."

She turned suavely away, gracefully hitching her bag up onto her shoulder. "Oh, Gaudy *Welsh*," she cried airily. "Grandma's passion."

Holding a flashlight, Cabe walked out to Celeste's car with her. The night was crisp and cold and starlit. He opened the door for her and helped her in.

"Heavens. Such chivalry."

They shook hands again. Plumes of breath swirled from smiling mouths. Goodbye . . . Goodbye.

Cabe stood in the dark night, watching Celeste's red taillight growing smaller down the road, then disappearing around a curve. He looked up at the sky, full of stars. The immensity and the serenity of it, its calm, clear beauty, was there to behold and to marvel at. He pushed his arms up high over his head, then let them drop heavily. "Well," he said aloud, to the darkness.

He turned and plunged back to the house, and closed the door and stood in the front hall. After a minute he said, "Well, well," emphatically. Then he went back into the living room and sat down again on the couch, and picked up his drink, slowly shaking his head in disbelief. He looked over at the piano, and a jubilant sense of alliance with it softened his eyes, and the lines of his face. Good performance. Amazing. . . . But it had been Lidi who had really felt it, he admitted to himself now. Not Celeste. Lidi had gotten it, *felt* it. Celeste had only appraised it, ". . . listen to music more with my head than anything else."

Dumbfounded, elated, perplexed, he sipped, and ruminated, and moved his lips occasionally with words he had remembered speaking. ". . . feel about the Chopin?" ". . . Mother was absolutely despicable, I'm sorry to say." A strange thing to say to Celeste Hunter, a perfect stranger. Bad performance. One good performance, one bad performance. Par for the course, he thought. Success canceled out by failure. "It never fails," he declaimed mockingly, with a kind of weary relish, "failure never fails."

He drew a great sigh and flung up his hands. "Oh well," he said heavily. He closed his eyes, he brought his hands tiredly, tidily together across his lap.

He yawned, enormously.

The distant sound of surf.

The steady seething of the fire.

The whiffle of small snores.

Part Five

I

EVERYTHING was ready, the coffee, the grapefruit, Freddy would be here in a minute, glittering snow was piled deep and soft over everything, thick smooth curves of it on bush and branch and fence rail. Oh, tomorrow! . . . Lidi picked up her coffee cup with an elated hand that shook from the assault of a sleepless night.

Smiling at everything, and at the launching this sudden new white world was giving tomorrow's trip, she had the shock of seeing one and then another cardinal fly down to light on the platform of Freddy's birdhouse, two vivid spots of red under the soft thick rounded thatch of snow which swelled on its little roof. "Oh, how incredible," she rejoiced aloud. And when the birds as suddenly darted up and shot off, "Oh, why wasn't Freddy here to see them," she mourned. Some of her joy fell away. Freddy, you just missed two cardinals, breathtakingly red against all this white. . . .

Just then Freddy strode into the kitchen, caressing his shave, his gaunt dark-skinned face scrubbed and satin smooth. He wore his new mail-order L.L. Bean red and black checked wool shirt, tucked into his new mail-order Eddie Bauer melton-lined field pants. "What do you think of this," he exulted, "how's this for a winter wonderland! This is what their 'snow flurries' turned into. If you want to be sure of the weather, plan on its being just the opposite from what those guys say it will be."

"Just as long as it was today and not tomorrow," Lidi said. "You know how usually I hate snow. It's too, oh, I guess too shrouding. But today, somehow, it's exciting. It's like a present, a magic present." Then she shook her head. "My, if you don't look the picture."

"It's a good warm shirt," Freddy said meekly, proudly, running testing fingers up one sleeve. "Feel."

Lidi had an indulgent, faintly scornful smile for her big boy. Patronizingly, she felt the shirt. "Um," she murmured. She picked up her coffee cup. "You just missed two cardinals," she said, trying to say this to him as rousingly as she had in her imagination, "breathtakingly red against all this white," she effervesced, feeling anticlimactic, futile. She turned accusing, stone-black eyes up to Freddy over the cup she held in two hands, elbows on the table, her arms rising wigwam-wise to the shaky support of it.

But Freddy was turning away, used to these detonations, even deaf to them. Sauntering across to the dishwasher, he opened its door, peered in. "Were the dishes wet again this morning?"

"Yes," flatly.

He got down on his knees, pulling out the trays and putting them on the floor and sticking his head into the machine.

"Why don't we just call the service man?" Lidi asked.

"He doesn't know anything and he'll charge me an arm and a leg."

"But *you* can't fix a dishwashing machine. What do you know about dishwashing machines?"

"I *like* doing it myself. I bet I can figure it out."

"Well, perhaps you can. I wouldn't put it past you. But come and eat breakfast first."

"I probably should." He backed out of the machine and set the trays back in and stood up and closed the door.

"How did you sleep, old boy?"

"Like a log," Freddy said forcefully, turning one palm up and striking down on it with the other.

"Well, good," Lidi murmured.

"How did *you* sleep?"

"Sketchily. Hardly at all, to tell you the truth. It's the excitement. I'm journey proud."

"I don't for one minute like the idea of your driving on those slippery roads."

"Dear," exasperatedly, "they'll be *plowed* by tomorrow on the mainland, for goodness' sakes. It's a wet snow. See, you can tell it's a wet snow. Half of it'll be gone by this afternoon. Oh, I'm so excited. Finally, tomorrow's almost here."

"Now tell me again where this poetry reading's going to be."

"At the Friends of the Arts Gallery. I'll leave a complete list for you, addresses, telephone numbers, what boat I'm getting back on. Things like that. I think the reading's at two in the afternoon. We're each allowed ten minutes, but I'm not going to take that long. I'm only going to read 'Dawn Departure' and two other short ones, 'Moment of the Rose,' and 'Seagull.' I'm scared. I've been practicing in front of the mirror, and my *face* looks frightened."

"Just think of the words. Don't think of the audience."

"Yes, but it's the words I'm nervous about. Whether they're

any good. Whether everyone else's will be much better."

"That's not the way to go into this, Lidi. What you've got there to read is your best. There *you* are and there is your *poem* that's the best of *you*. There is that fact. There's nothing beyond it. Stick to it. What's the use of worrying about what is a fact? Just peel off all the nonsense and let the fact stand there."

"That's an intelligent way to look at it, Freddy, but what you're forgetting is that I don't believe those poems are my best. I can't get next to my best. I've never gotten next to my best."

"You never give yourself any peace, do you, Lidi?"

"No. And why should I?"

Freddy sighed and turned away.

In some part of himself he is looking forward to the peace of being alone for the next three days. Seventy-five years old, is Freddy. Retired from his happy little booming business for three years now, content that his nephew has taken it over, glad to have given it up, eager for new ventures. Freddy will always make something happen. And there is always adventure for a large heart like Freddy's. But. Freddy is tightening. He is alone now, on this island, with this frantic little woman whom he still adores. She is worth adoring, he knows. He knows the whole of Lidi. Yet he is tightening. He is beginning to be strung tighter and tighter. He is trying valiantly not to let the disappointment and the burden of this frantic woman pinch his outlook, swamp his optimism. He thinks he can still give her everything in himself, but sometimes, now, he doesn't even hear her, doesn't even see her. He wonders often, with a nervousness that he pushes instantly away, why he has been obliged to spend his life alongside such starvation. Little white starving hands, clawing at him, always clawing at him—feed me, feed me.

He sighed again, uncomfortably, turning to pull back the muslin curtain and to peer out. Then he cried, "Look at that," pointing down the driveway to the road. "Can you beat it. Look at the mailbox. Snow certainly plays funny tricks."

Lidi turned to look. There, indeed, was a funny trick; the mailbox had on top of it an exactly duplicated mailbox of snow, a rounded, smooth, perfect white loaf.

"That's not funny," Lidi said after a moment.

"Why do you say that?"

"Because it's a mockery," she said, "nature piling absurdity on absurdity, literally."

"I don't understand." But he did. He knew her obsession with the mailbox.

Now she laughed a little, but her face was expressionless. "Nature laying it on thick. Literally."

Freddy smiled. "Touché."

Nature is ridiculing me, Lidi thought, it is warning me. And she felt a surge of relief at the thought that for three days, beginning tomorrow, she would be freed from the tyranny of having to go out to the mailbox. "What I don't know won't hurt me," she murmured, scarcely moving her lips.

Now she looked at Freddy. Was it possible to exist anywhere else but inside oneself? What would it be like, she wondered, to exist, as Freddy did, outside of oneself, to exist in plans, things, people, events? . . . And without a second thought she concluded disparagingly that it would be unrewarding and limiting, that living so exteriorly would be a shallow existence for her. Which just goes to show that ours is a mismatched marriage, she said to herself. She knew that this was really so.

She looked away from Freddy. She saw a blue jay come

rocketing down to alight on Freddy's birdhouse. Freddy makes birdhouses that are little copies of Swiss chalets, she thinks. He makes little men in little rowboats whose fluttering oars are wind indicators. Freddy plays tennis. He sails. He jogs. He watches sports on television. Freddy takes old ladies to the Blood Pressure Clinic. Freddy reads the Sears Roebuck catalogue. Freddy falls asleep at the Boston Symphony. Freddy thinks he can repair a dishwashing machine. He wants to repair it, he wants to do everything himself. He needs to do everything himself. He needs to plow the snow away himself. He needs his new tractor. Man and machine. Freddy can hardly wait to get up in the morning to go into his workshop and make toy wind indicators. He could hardly wait to get up this morning to go out and plow with his new tractor. That's Freddy. . . . There it all is, or almost all, she thought. That's him. That tractor spells out Freddy.

Triumphantly this was her summary now of Freddy. And yet uneasily she also knew that it was a limited and biased version of Freddy, and that if this was all she saw in him, it was because this was all she wanted to see in him. At this moment, anyway. Yet she cried, "Your tractor, Freddy. I've just realized. You can use your new snowplow attachment, finally."

"Don't think I'm not going to," Freddy said. He dropped the curtain and came back to his chair, letting himself down into it with a long, exhaled "Aaaaaahhh," which protested and scorned the suggestion of possible arthritic pain. He passed a hand all over his face slowly and with it scrunched his eyes together, bunched up his mouth. But then he took his hand away and smiled at Lidi. "The day has come," he said with mock solemnity.

Lidi looked at him with sudden disdain. Why must she be married to a gadgeteer? Why must she be stuck for life with a man whose favorite reading matter was catalogues? For a moment everything was flat, she felt a sudden emptiness in this kitchen, and she thought: He is the last person on earth I should have chosen to spend my life with.

"I'm going to plow out Turck's driveway," Freddy was saying. "I'm going to surprise him. Betcha he'll be out there shoveling."

"If ever there was a candidate for a heart attack it's Turck."

"He'll be out there, shoveling away. And Tilly inside having a quiet fit."

"Exactly."

"Speaking of Tilly. Cabe and Celeste seem to be getting thick as thieves."

"What makes you say that?" Sharply.

"I've seen them together twice now walking the beach. Talking sixty to the dozen. And Tilly said she and Turck ran into them at the Harbor House having lunch."

"Well, that's only three times that you know of. That doesn't mean they're getting thick," Lidi cried indignantly. She didn't want this news to come to her today, spoiling perfection. For a moment the joy of tomorrow drained away, leaving anger with Celeste, reproach for Cabe.

His music had been singing in her continually since hearing it last week. Together, Cabe and music, the one now inseparable from the other, had grown in her; it was her secret; it was a longing that was taking her over. It was there to lighten her days, it was there as a promise, something always singing, promising, at her center. Cabe was there just for her, his mouth was just for her. Not for kissing. No. She had no fantasies of kissing that sensuous mouth. It was more that the whole man attracted her—mouth and music and the bleak seriousness of his eyes, all of which seemed one thing to her. He was not so much a compelling man, as he was the promise of what she could become with a compelling man. She did not want to imagine making love with him. No, she imagined reading her poems to him, and having him be moved by them as she had been moved by his music. She imagined walking on the beach with him, both of them pouring out their hearts. She imagined herself filling his deepest needs, just as he would fill hers. Soul mates, people would call them. And Freddy would not mind. He would only be glad for the fulfillment she and Cabe were bringing each other. Platonic, people would say of their friendship.

But here was Freddy, shocking this deeply held longing out of her, shattering it.

"In a little place like this island, everything anyone does is noticed, and misinterpreted," she cried, "and gossiped about. I don't think they're getting thick. Celeste hasn't said a word about him to *me*. Anyway," she said hectically now, "they have all the concert arrangements to make together. I should think they *would* have to be together, now and then. After *all!*"

"My, what a diatribe," Freddy said mildly.

"Oh, for*get* it." And then, penitently, "I'm sorry, I didn't sleep."

Freddy sighed and looked away. Then uneasily he poked out a cheek with his tongue, shifting sideways in his chair and crossing his legs.

"Listen. For heaven's sakes call the service man," Lidi said. And then, penitently again, "I'm going to get veal today and make a stew so you can heat it up and have it for dinner tomorrow night."

"That's nice of you, dear."

"Well, why is it *nice*. Naturally, you have to *eat*."

"Still, it's nice."

～～ II ～～

"Now you will not go out and shovel snow, Turck."

"I will."

"That's very foolish of you, dear."

"No it isn't. I need the exercise. I love it. Uses my muscles."

"Did you ever discuss it with Dr. Ratisbone? No. I know the answer is no."

"The answer is no."

Tilly now sank back in her armchair in the sunny bay window. She did not sigh. Other women would have. Other women would have protested longer, not given up so soon, would have dominated the thing, somehow. She put her elbows on the arms of the chair and brought her hands together and laced her fingers, shakily. Her eyes were worried, but her mouth was complacent and showed only a good-natured resignation. Eyebrow pencil applied in the dim light of the bathroom was crudely black on her sparse white eyebrows, rouge was sketchy and too strongly pink on her pillow-soft, white wrinkled cheeks.

"Well then, dear, remember, for goodness' sakes, not to hold your breath. That's what's bad. To hold your breath."

There was a visible pulling together now of all Tilly's forces.

Purpose settled in her shoulders, in the forbearance of her eyes that shifted away from Turck, toward the window. She looked at the splurge of red geraniums on the table in the sun, and let it, for the moment, be everything. She had learned to live for the sake of the day itself, not for what it would lead to, nor for what it promised. Leads to? Promises? The end of the road leads nowhere. She knew that. And why, anyway, should the road have to lead somewhere else? And why should one need to be carried along by promises? Why look toward future enjoyments? Wasn't it enough simply to sit still, unconcerned with past, unconcerned with future, and, in the very present moment, enjoy what there was to enjoy? She was an old woman, she'd come a long way, and she'd reached her destination and a wisdom that let her present moments be eternities. Her destination—being profoundly in love with a man, more so perhaps than she had been with her long dead husband though she had loved him well—her destination, arrived at, was loving Turck. She knew how lucky she was, to be, at eighty, physically, emotionally, and intellectually inseparable from a fine man. She was aware of her unusual good fortune in waking up every morning, at this late age, in the arms of a man she loved completely, and who loved her in the same thorough way.

So for the moment she summoned all her strengths to deal with the fact that Turck could die shoveling snow, just as, day after day, she summoned her strengths to deal with the fact that he could die making love. And then she looked away from what could be, to what was—Turck standing there alive and vital, and by the window a blaze of red flowers in the sun—and was able to take joy from both.

The clasp of her hands shook, their polished nails flashed in the sun. Now she drew her hands apart and brought one set of spread fingers up to her cheek, and they fluttered there, as she looked at Turck with the sudden sweetness of her smile. "Dear," she said, "I really think it's the most perfectly beautiful sight, this snow. I don't think I dread snow, like most old people. It's so wonderfully pure. I don't like it when it gets dirty, I like it now, the first day of it. The purity of it." It was on the tip of her tongue to add, "Now for mercy's sakes don't do more than the path to the turnaround," but instead she pressed her lips together.

Turck's face was bunching and frowning toward a quip. He looked at Tilly with his twitching lips suppressing a smile. Then he sniffed up, raised his shoulders, and said slyly, delightedly, "Pure as the driven snow. That's not us, Til, old girl." He chuckled. "No. That's not this old pair of fornicators." He came over and bent down and kissed her on the lips, slowly. They tolerated all the tastes of this kiss, stale coffee, old breath; every taste was a knowledge of the body of the other, and tolerated, yes even loved, for its existence in that body. Kissing was their constant joy. "Half past kissing time, time to kiss again," Turck would bark, pretending to look at his watch, bending down with his lips ready.

They had first kissed ten years ago. At a wedding. After enough champagne. Then, it had been a kiss quickly, almost playfully started, which had surprised both of them by lingering. Ten years ago—Turck a young-looking seventy-two, tall and bony and fierce, Tilly at seventy still with a tennis-playing slimness and a fading beauty and a vigorous straight-shouldered vivacity, Turck only recently a widower, Tilly a long-time widow, and from the first ridiculously, for a sensible woman, jealous of the wife whose house she found herself in.

"Filthy," she would hiss to Turck, discovering in the back

of a cupboard drawer a tangle of string and grocery store slips and sunflower seeds hoarded there by mice. And, "Who'd ever use a kitchen stool but Beryl," she would say to Turck with an edge to her voice, giving the stool a little shove. "It's in my way."

Beryl was in her way for a long time. But as kisses grew deeper, Beryl grew more indistinct. And now she was only a ghost rubbed smooth, a part of the walls but without prominences, faint and secondary and finished as an echo.

Their lips nibbled happily. And the sun warm on Tilly's shoulders, along with the warmth of the kiss, drenched her with a radiant contentment. Turck took his lips away. Their eyes held together, deeply, seriously.

Then he straightened up. "So, my dear," he said, "to work, to work." He pulled on his red wool cap with the pompom on top, he hunched himself into his old sheepskin-lined leather jacket, he thrust his hands shakily into leather-palmed mittens and clapped them against his sides. "Can't wait!" he shouted. "Love it!" And really not to Tilly. It was his separateness, and his pride in it, that he was declaring, his stubborn determination to do what man must do and what this invincible man had always done and to hell with the consequences, and this was no part of him and Tilly together. It was separateness. Separate, man shoulders the world. First and foremost, before love, even before life, this was what he believed he was for and he gloried in still being able, at the age of eighty-two, to do it.

ᨳᨳ III ᨳᨳ

ENTHRONED on his shining new tractor, Freddy pulled out
from the driveway he had just plowed and set off down the
road toward Tate's store and the bridge. The town plow
had been through, leaving walls of freshly turned snow along
the sides of the road, and the great wheels of the tractor
squeaked and crunched on the slick-packed surface of it.
Freddy was exalted. The sky above him was a marvelous
immensity of blue, not one cloud. He drew in deep breaths
of air, saying to himself aloud, "Oh boy, oh boy," prayer-
fully.

He sat proudly there at the wheel of his new toy, jouncing
as his great machine worked along, his heart pounding pleasantly from the exertion of shifting gears and tugging round
the wheel. His face was purple-red from the cold, his eyes
streaming, but the sun was climbing and he knew that soon
he would be warmer.

The morning was clear and breezy, the grinding persistence of the tractor dominating it. This was the part of the
road Freddy liked best, the rocky stream burbling along
beside it, the woods on one side, and on the other side, the
flatness of Great Meadow, with the cold blue sea in the
distance. The stream was almost entirely frozen over except
for an occasional black hole in the whiteness, deep, inky
pools which would be faintly murmurous in the snow stillness. Freddy stopped the tractor just to listen to the soft

sound of the water, but only for a moment, he wanted to get on to Turck's. The wind rose, blowing a stinging spray of snow across his face. But he liked it. He began to whistle "Ah Sweet Mystery of Life," his vibrating lips creating a sound clear and sweet as a bird's song, his eyes traveling off into the woods. The white floor made the woods a simple thing to see into for some distance.

Suddenly he saw a cardinal. Lidi's everlasting cardinal. Perhaps because of her, and because he hadn't shown interest in her cardinals this morning, he looked intently at this one now. The shocking simplicity of the scene, everything red and black and white, only that! He liked looking at the cardinal like this, in his own way, not in Lidi's. A red bird on a black branch lined with white snow—how simple it was, Freddy thought peacefully. Red and black and white. Primacy. Without putting the emotion into words, he felt nevertheless that he had just been explained to himself.

In the woods to his left a gust of wind soughed, bending the trees and sending up a cloud of glittering snow. Soon, Tate's cow pasture appeared on his right, and then there was the crossroads at the bridge, and Tate's store, organized and cleared, the parking area plowed, the steps swept, all snow dusted from the gas pumps. Smoke rose straight in a windless moment from the chimney in the back wing, and a strident pinkish glow beyond the misted windowpanes showed that the neon ceiling lights were on, the store open for early morning trade. A soft continuous roar, that was Judas Rip coming in from the sea, active beneath a layer of ice and snow. The spans of the little bridge were trimmed with thick ropes of snow, the black stream poured noisily between glazed hummocks upon which the sun danced crazily.

A delivery truck was parked in front of the store. The driver was lifting out a carton of baked goods, preoccupied, his face a red spot in a white world.

"*Good* morning," trumpeted Freddy, waving a comradely arm. "Quite a snowfall, eh?"

"Real blizzard."

"Any trouble getting through?" Freddy stopped the tractor and let it idle. "Roads bad?"

"Plow's been all the way through," hoisting up the large carton and trotting toward the store. He had work to do. "Bit slippery on the High Road," he called back.

"Take it easy," Freddy sang out. A great well-being held him here, bundled up in fleece-lined leather, gloved hands inert on the wheel, tears oozing from the corners of squinting eyes which felt weak and unequal to the glare of the snow.

But he had work to do, too. He set his machine in motion again, and wheeled out enormously into the road and continued on, his chin jutting out in a tensed, alerted way. Soon he was in sight of the Turckman driveway which even at this distance he could see had not been plowed. And there was Turck, as he had predicted, up by the house bent over his shovel, working in precious little cleared area, Freddy saw.

Relief and excitement seized him. The tractor all at once seemed too slow. But at last, impatiently, he was there, high, important, thundering, above Turck. And Turck stood down there, the proud old militant, undiminished by this might, even feeling akin to it, his stern eagle face as red as his cap. Freddy loomed high over him, bending down, smiling, rejoicing, "Say, boy, put that shovel away."

Turck said nothing. He leaned forward and set both mittened hands on his shovel, panting heavily. In a second he brought one hand up and touched his forehead in a smart salute, then brought it back to his shovel and shook his head slowly, incredulously.

Tilly opened the door. She stood in the brittle cold, her hands hugging a sweater across her chest. "Freddy, are *you* the angel of *mercy!*" she called out. "Come in, darling, and get warm. Have some coffee. Oh, it's freezing, I'm going back in."

Freddy came stiffly down out of his high tractor seat and began to stamp on the snow to warm himself, flapping his arms across his chest, doing a kind of dancing step on his icy toes. And now Turck stabbed his shovel into the deep snow and began to rock from front foot to back foot, his eyes sparkling under the cliffs of his brows. On both their faces was a look of getting ready for something.

Now they looked full and deliberately at each other, the overture to their ceremony, and Freddy whispered, "Son of a gun," and licked his lips, and then they began to edge toward one another with the sly look of getting ready to pounce, curving their arms up into fending positions, both grinning. Next they commenced to take little prancing sideways steps, preparatory steps. And then Freddy stopped and stood where he was on the hard-packed snow and began a rocking, dancing motion from his forward foot to his back foot, quick and smart, punching the air toward Turck, but with a kind of gentle tentativeness. This was the signal to lunge; and as Freddy had intended, it was Turck who lunged, grabbed Freddy's right arm, swiftly but carefully bent it, twisted it down and around and behind Freddy's back, and pinned it there while Freddy made one halfhearted squirming effort to twist himself out of the hold. They stayed locked like this for a moment, grinning and panting and wordless, and then Turck dropped Freddy's arm and stepped away, and Freddy let out a little laugh and said, "Say, how about that," and shrugged his jacket up into place on his shoulders, and Turck chuckled, and they walked toward the house, their smiles easy and amused and satisfied. At the bottom of the steps Freddy clapped Turck on the back, and then Turck clapped Freddy on the back, and with their hands resting like that, not looking at one another, they went in silence up the short flight to the door.

Tilly stood at the window, watching them, unsurprised and grave.

∿∿ IV ∿∿

AT six-thirty that evening, Lidi turned on the weather report once again. She had listened to it in the morning and at noon—it would be fair, the meteorologist promised—and now again she must turn it on, for reassurance. In order to sleep soundly, she told herself. What she heard now did reassure her, or to put it in her way of reacting, the outlook, partly sunny, breezy and cold, gave her no cause for concern. She wished the "breezy" weren't there, but still, breezy probably really meant just that, nothing stronger. And there wasn't a breath of wind now.

Looking out at the winter evening she saw a mournful, still beauty. Everything was gray—the sky, the snow in the dusk. Ducks were like unmoving brown rocks in the pale flat silver water of the pond. The sea, over there beyond the dunes, was a sorrowful straight line of metal gray. She saw that it was all desolate, and yet she thought it was incredibly beautiful. "All pure still silveriness," she said aloud.

She switched off the television and went to the bar table to make her drink. Pouring bourbon into a glass was like a new experience, every facet of it was penetratingly pleasurable, vivid, immediate. And as she walked from the living room down the hall to the kitchen with her drink in her hand, sipping once as she walked, she realized that her walk was swift and that it was proclaiming joy. It knew exactly where it was taking her, and why; she could feel the movement of her legs fired with the energy of anticipation and promise. Self-determination was in the sure planting of one foot in front of the other, in the upward tilt of her pointed little chin. She was not exuberant, she was simply normal, she was feeling the substantial bliss of being without negativism and with promise. Normalcy. Uneventful, superb normalcy. Normalcy feels quiet, she thought.

She was so silently happy that she knew she would sleep well. Even when she woke at four, she didn't allow herself to worry that she might not fall asleep again. The alarm is set for six, rely on that. Regular but sibilant breathing from the other bed told her that Freddy was deeply asleep; from all that outdoor exercise, she thought envelopingly. She fell asleep again lightly but peacefully until almost six, and then, seeing edges of light around the shades, she got up. She got up in a glow of normal, unemphatic joy. She threw back the blankets with a practical elation, with the vigor of an independent, a self-determining woman, a woman about to go forth into the promise of what she could shape.

Freddy's bed was empty. She could hear him in the bathroom, whistling, turning on the water tap. Hurry, she warned herself, the boat's at eight-thirty. Leave here at seven-thirty.

The light around the shades was not sharp. She knew this gradually. And at the same time, even as she began to raise a shade, she heard a soft dripping. And yes, the shade raised, there was wetness on the windows, and beyond, grayness.

She wasn't concerned. But she was surprised, and a little sorry. Sun would have been so much better for the hallelujah of departure. The weather reports had made no mention of rain. But that's the quixotism of January, she thought. The January thaw. One day a blizzard. The next day rain. It was faintly disturbing to her that nature could be so contrary. "It's not supposed to be raining," she said to Freddy who was brushing his teeth. "It said 'partly sunny.'"

"Guess this is the other part," Freddy said bubblingly through water and suds.

There was so much to do but she did it all in a decisive and organized way—bathing, dressing, snapping her suitcase shut, feeding the birds, fixing egg salad for Freddy's lunch, making a chicken sandwich for herself and packing the lunchbox with little cans of juices and a small mason jar of pickles, paper napkins, a plastic fork for the pickles, a little cardboard salt shaker. So much to remember, so much to do. Ten more minutes and I should leave.

"Have fun!"

"I will!" She sang. Then she thought it would be nice to kiss Freddy goodbye, really to kiss him. On the mouth. She put down her suitcase and turned to him, where he stood quietly and uncomfortably in this unfamiliarity, at the center of the hall rug, his usually determined hands hanging uselessly at his sides. She gave him a short, full kiss, and for a second kissing was faintly, surprisingly reincarnated. Freddy looked embarrassed and pleased. She gave a little nervous hoot, and picked up her suitcase and opened the door.

Out of the house she walked, away from the carapace of

no self-determination, toward her car which led to the boat and the sea and the mainland, and from there to the initiation of self-determination. Out into the world she went, almost skipping along in the melting snow which felt like the springing ground of promise, out into a world that was hers alone, to be determined by her.

Overnight, all the snow had been washed from the road by the rain. Lidi drove carefully upon the gray gleam of its early morning wetness, planning as she went along what topics she would spend her driving hours thinking about. She lowered the window for a breath of the damp sea-smelling air she loved.

The whistling sound she began to hear meant nothing. But to shut it out, to deny that it was a sound of wind, she rolled the window up. There had been very little wind in her part of the island. The pond had been just slightly ruffled. Thus, persuading herself that it couldn't be wind she was hearing because no trees were bending and tossing or even moving, she said to herself, "No trees are seething" as though to someone at the poetry reading who would be impressed by the word "seething." However, now she began to watch trees.

She drove into Seahaven, heading for the dock. Here, there was a stronger whine of wind, and the trees above the old winding street were leaning and tossing. But she refused to admit concern. In a second, around the next curve, she thought, I will see the waterfront and the sea. She drove down Park Street, past the laundromat, past the post office, turned right into Main Street, where now trees indeed were whipping and bending wildly. She turned the corner and came out onto the waterfront.

It is a strange process of the mind's unwillingness to accept, that it can allow a person to see something obviously threatening and yet disbelieve it. Lidi saw. And she refused what she saw. She simply could not and would not believe what she saw. The sea was wild, heaving, racing with white-caps. There was no line of cars. There was no boat. There was only the space of raging sea, and the deserted wharf which had the look of a Sunday morning street. She was so stunned that for a moment all she could think of was the color of that expanse of sea—pale green, milky dull, racing and cresting with white. Great waves were mounting, piling, crashing into the dock and flinging spray high above the dolphins. And it was toward her it was coming. Nothing existed but herself, and the sea perpetually, enormously on-coming, at her, against her.

Still she could not believe it. She told herself that the boat was late, that all the cars that were to take it, were late getting here. And though she already knew what the sea was telling her, she didn't. Credulous and yet determinedly incredulous, she drove to the curb and stopped the car and stepped out into the brutality of wind and spray and roar. Pushing against it, wading into it, she got to the ticket office and inside. A line of people at the ticket window meant something, she comforted herself. They were buying tickets for the boat that was late. But in the next minute she heard the word "canceled."

She waited two hours in her car, going into the ticket office at intervals to ask whether there were any reports that the wind would abate and the boat would get here from the mainland. She called the airport to see whether she could get on a plane, but the morning flight had left and the after-noon one would be too late for the poetry reading. Booked full anyway, with all those people who had hurried from the deserted wharf to the airport.

Sitting stone-still in her car, she kept despair well hidden from herself, while this afternoon's poetry reading expanded and grew in her like the promise of the Holy Grail. Haloed, luminous, it held everything in life for her. With every minute of her long waiting here in this cold car by this stormy sea, the poetry reading grew more entire for her; it was the great achievement, even the solution, of her life. There it was, and here she was. Between it and her was the crazy cruel sea with the appearance of forbidding it. But she would not bow to that sea. She would be at the poetry reading this afternoon. Self-determination was the power, the sea was not the power.

She said to herself, "I won't."

Finally they told her at the ticket office to go home.

She drove into her driveway and stopped the car and got out and took out the suitcase, the lunchbox. She carried the defeated suitcase and the expectant lunchbox into the house and set them down in the center of the hall rug. Freddy came up from the cellar, his face astonished, caught out in a disbelief and disappointment he could not conceal. "Lidi, what on earth?"

"The boat isn't running."

He was suddenly, overwhelmingly sorry for her. He could have wept for her.

"I don't really believe I can bear it," she said. She turned, with her suitcase in her hand.

"Well, dear," he called jocularly, helpfully he thought, to her back as she walked with mechanical steps toward the bedroom with the suitcase, "at least you don't have to cook dinner tonight. We have the veal stew."

She absolutely could not bear this.

She stood in the center of the bedroom. She would not take off her coat. She would not unpack. While the suitcase was still closed, it was as it had been early this morning, there to be used, ready, on its way.

During the next half hour, she moved only twice from this spot in the center of the bedroom, once to go to the bathroom, and once to go into her cubicle. She stood there saying to herself, "I won't." She stood facing a wildly lashing white-streaked sea coming straight at her from out there. From an endless horizon of heaving white-flecked pale green it came at her and she stood facing it. Canceled. . . .

Finally something gave in her and she went over to the suitcase and unlocked it and began to unpack it. With a kind of angry agony she took the carefully folded, tissue-paper-stuffed dresses out, which said to her as she hung them back in the closet, "Nothing happened to us."

Nothing happens. I cannot make anything happen. Freddy can. My self does not determine what I do. Freddy determines what he does, but I do not. Everything out there determines me.

She took off her boots, but now with a sense of dead capitulation. Everything comes at me from out there.

The last thing she did was to take off her suit skirt. She hung it back in the closet and she felt an unendurable pain and she said again, aloud, "I won't."

All during that long, numbed afternoon, she saw the sea. There was nothing in her but the picture of milky gray-green water mountainously heaving and frothing with white. Coming at her. That was its sole purpose, that was its existence. To come at her. And yet she kept thinking, "I won't." And never once said, "I can't."

At four o'clock, sitting numbly in her chair in her cubicle, suddenly, Lidi remembered the mail. A spark of aliveness flared in her and she jumped up immediately and hurried out to the hall and got into her coat. "I'm going for the mail," she called out to Freddy, who was in his shop hammering. She called out to him in a voice that was sharp and sad but that lifted a little with the promise of the mailbox.

Struggling impatiently into her boots, she had the growing sense that a letter from *Viewpoints* accepting "Dawn Departeur" would totally reverse this day. Ho and to hell with the poetry reading, she thought. Triumph was not to be in the reading of her unpublished poem, triumph was to be in the news of the publication of her poem. She might be saved, after all, from this awful day. She had a strange, sure presentiment that the letter would be there.

The air was soft and moist. It was good to get out of that prison house, into this air that led out to the mailbox. Her boots sucked at the mud as she trotted along. Spring was in the air. A chickadee called from a tree over her head, and she could smile slightly at it because she was on her way, perhaps, to salvation. She let a slim volume of poetry stand behind her eyes, vellum with gold lettering, *Collected Poems of Lydia Pratt Luhin*. She would dedicate the book to Freddy. On the stiff white frontispiece it would say in black letters: *To Freddy, the Truest of Them All*.

She arrived at the road. She crossed it very slowly, very carefully, as she always did, because traffic dazed her and she did not want to slip or trip on this busy thoroughfare. She opened the mailbox, her head elated and sure, though hammering. She fished out the pile of catalogues and newspapers, with the pile of letters on top. She hugged the whole thing tight to her chest, and closed the mailbox, and looking carefully both ways, dizzily, she recrossed the road. And then, safely across it, she took the pile away from her chest, and began to leaf through the letters.

It was there. The small white envelope with *Viewpoints* in the upper left corner.

She thrust the pile of mail under one arm, and tore at the back of the envelope with such force that the slippery cataloges and bulky newspapers slithered out from the grip of her elbow and flapped down into the slush. Let them. She ripped the envelope open.

It was a card. Not a letter.

It was a form.

Thank you for allowing us to see this material. After careful consideration, we have found it unsuited to our needs.

The Editors

They had had the veal stew. Their trays were pushed aside. No surcease from the wind. All the noise was outdoors. In this room the lamps were alight, the fire glowed, but in stillness.

Freddy was hidden behind his newspaper, which he was unable to read because of the fearful silence in this room and because of the taunting wind out there. And Lidi sat rigid across from him like a small ancient carving, eyes set in her face like two black beads. She seemed for hours not to have made the slightest move, even though she had brought her fork to her mouth with pieces of veal on it, and had brought her wineglass up to her lips and then set it back down on the tray. There was an electric stillness about her that Freddy thought awful. He told himself that she was in shock. Although he couldn't conceive of why, nevertheless he knew that the rejection of her poem on top of the poetry reading being denied her, was a shock of profound consequence. He also knew that she would get over it. "You'll bounce back," he wanted to say to her, though realizing sensitively that it was absolutely the wrong thing to say. But he wanted to say something. The silence seemed awful, and the longer it went on the more awful, even absurd, it became. He thought that his silence was only endorsing Lidi's, and he felt unnatural, frustrated, in seeming to agree with it. But silence was the law here, abide with it he must.

He wanted to go to bed. Yet he didn't want to seem to be deserting Lidi, "in her hour of need," he said to himself. However, to bed he would go. And put an end to this wearisome and bitter nonsense. Yes. He really did think, at bottom, that it was nonsense. He folded his paper and put it down and stood up. "I'll do the dishes, dear," he said to her. *This* could be said, without intrusion. "You go on to bed when you're ready. I'll finish up here."

Sudden wind panted down the chimney, sending a balloon of smoke into the room, then gave one crazy shriek and dwindled off, whistling lonesomely.

Lidi nodded her head up and down, once, slightly. Then she spoke. "Thank you," she said, in a voice that seemed to come out in one straight tiny line from her carved lips.

She got up then, too. The wad of her paper napkin fell from her lap to the floor and she didn't even know it. Freddy leaned over gently to pick it up.

She lay in her bed, in the dark. Tears had begun to pour steadily out of the corners of her eyes and down along her temples and into her ears. This cool smooth wetness, this sorrowing flood of her inner self pouring down over her outer self, was in a melancholy way, soothing; slippery and smooth and soothing as a cool ointment. Something was being done. The tears were for perfect hopelessness, the perfection, the absoluteness of hopelessness. The tears spoke. They were real, alive. They were hopelessness rising to a flood in her, and pouring out of her to tell her so. Believe it now, they said to her, and their wetness was believable, it was real. Sluicing sorrowfully down her temples, over her cheeks, her self spoke to her self with a kind of elegiac, maudlin comfort.

Freddy, in the other bed, wide awake with impatience and concern, heard the soft rhythm of sobbing. He lay tense, fighting between a hunger to do something, a fear that he couldn't, he mustn't, and a strong desire to go to sleep and forget it all.

For a long time he lay tight with struggle, eyes wide open in the dark. But then suddenly he ripped off his blanket, staggered up, and made a dive for Lidi's bed. In a hurry, he lifted her covers and climbed in under them, shoving her over with a nervous defiant roughness that made no bones about doing so—here he was and he meant to stay and that was that, like it or not. He burrowed one arm under her and flung the other arm over her, and he pulled her tight. He held her tight.

With relief and triumphantly, he felt the stiffness of her body begin to slacken. Then all at once she turned in his arms and put hers around him. He felt her small bony wet face settle on his shoulder.

She began to retch with sobs, making a great shivering noise against him. He had never seen Lidi cry like this. Never. He was appalled and humbled. Soon she grew quieter. He put a still kiss on her wet cheek. Salty. He even smiled a little.

She clung to Freddy. She held onto the refuge of Freddy for dear life. This was a goodness she had forgotten all about. She was astonished to find it still here. All along it had been here, and neither of them had remembered about it. It was like the kiss this morning, reincarnating closeness for a moment.

They lay in each others' arms. Freddy sharp-thin, his white tousled hair raked over his forehead, his face relieved, and Lidi all skin and bones, tear-soaked hair strewn over the pillow, her stiff little face fighting relief. They lay breast to breast, locked together, though neither of them was aroused by this touch of their bodies all along each other, by arms breasts legs genitals intertwined. Lidi felt Freddy's sex pressed against her. In repose. And so was her own sex. Unalive. Their bodies were sealed together with a furnace of feeling that was not libidinous at all. And the feel of Freddy's maleness against her was only a memory, fond and benign. And the feel of Lidi's little breasts and the softness of her small thighs was only a mild sweet comfort to Freddy, only that. But that was all right, they both knew. That's what it had become, which wasn't to say that it was sexless. It was still a woman lying against a man. Freddy could not lie here and not be aware that in this body he had, for so many years, rapturously planted such useless seeds. And Lidi could not lie here without remembering what this embrace had once been for. The echo of it sounded sweetly, faintly around them but not in them.

Only echoes of fullness. This was their old age. And yet to feel this and to know it, as Lidi found herself doing now, was a kind of fullness in itself.

A drained, sad peace settled over her. She let finality enclose her like another skin. Hopelessness now seemed more complete than it had been a while ago. Were there no boundaries to hopelessness? Lidi felt hopelessness honed to the finest point, stinging like a needle. But, just as it can happen that when one puts one's mind to pain, pain can go away, so Lidi, finding herself dragged into the pain of terminal hopelessness, felt the discomfort of it begin to lessen. In putting her mind to hopelessness, in dwelling on it, gradually she began to feel, for a while, a melancholy compliance.

They fell asleep this way.

Part Six

～ I ～

CABE let three days pass, for the sake of decorum, and in order not to seem overeager, before calling Celeste. There had been no doubt in his mind, after the day of his recital, that he wanted to see her again. And again. But he decided that dignity and circumspection should prevail, and so he waited.

He called her early, too early he worried, on Saturday morning, and asked her if she would go rowing with him that afternoon on Great Pond; he did this frequently in the winter whenever a mild day permitted, he assured her. She agreed with heart-lifting alacrity, yes, eagerness, he felt, and he hung up the phone absolutely elated, dazed, his hands shaking. He went and stood by his piano and looked out of the window, scattered, bemused, unable for a while even to sit down and practice. When he did sit down to play, he was too distracted to play well, and hearing nothing that was musical, he switched to Bach's Inventions, exercises that required no emotional concentration, and raced up and down the keyboard, mechanically, for a stretch of hours that seemed to him endless. Finally he gave up, and ate lunch. And then, after an interminable post-lunch hour at his desk, he set out in his jeep to call for Celeste.

The afternoon was gentle, with a pale sun shining occasionally through softly massed gray clouds. Cabe rowed with strong, long strokes, effortlessly. There was very little wind on the pond but the air was cold, and Celeste lay bundled in her old fur cape in the stern, her wool cap pulled over her ears and down to her eyebrows, one hand trailing in the icy water. Soon after starting off, she found her airy-talk mechanism inactive. Trying to gear herself up to it, she failed. And after a short while it became perfectly all right not to talk. Cabe's quiet was the mandate here, and the rhythmic dip of the oars, and the small liquid sound of water rippling along the hull. A V of geese came barking and croaking low over their heads. Once, three startled ducks took off in a splatter of water and an airborne rush. And a single swan flew over them, with its pumping rush of air and its long white neck stretched out.

Cabe felt completely at ease, though he had expected not to, after the uneasiness of the long unprofitable morning. It was being outdoors, on the water, rowing, and also somehow being in charge, that gave him this almost single-minded contentment, he thought. He rowed as though alone in this world of boat and water and birds. His head in the navy skullcap was thrust forward as it was when he walked, or played. His lips, usually mobile, were partly open and quiet. And his eyes were quiet, gazing over the water and along the shore.

He had taken off his gloves in order to have a better grip on the oars, and Celeste watched the large long strength of his fingers as they lay firmly and competently on the handles.

She was attracted to those hands that played the piano so powerfully and rowed so powerfully. She remembered "My bare hands froze to the oars . . ." and she began to laugh.

"What's funny?"

"Oh nothing much. I was just remembering."

"Your laugh is a perfectly wonderful sound," he said comfortably.

"That's a nice thing to say. Your saying it made a nice sound too." He was a different man, here on the water, she thought. At the piano, and here on the water, he became someone else, or rather, he was without something, he was without that weight of insufficiency. He seemed strong and separate, not requiring anything from anybody, here in his own kingdom. She brought her icy fingers, dripping, up to her cheek and held them there, startled by chill, smiling with the sensation of it. She felt peace easing her spine, making a pleasant, loose sensation there. "Cabe," she said, "I love this."

"I do too."

They came to the narrow sand dune that separated the pond from the sea, and beached the boat and walked across to the shore, meeting there a sudden, wildly different world of water—great waves whopping thunderously, and the unending spread of heaving gray-green sea. They stood watching the awesome incoming power of these hurling tons of water, and then set off down the beach, elated, invigorated, the pond mood gone. Celeste's cape swirled behind her in the wind, Cabe plowed along, swinging his arms, his face sober with rapture. There was no talk, there couldn't be, with the roar of the sea and their rousing striding mindless absorption in it and in themselves.

Celeste was wildly excited, she loved it, she gloried in it. "I love this," she called to Cabe, above the roar of the water, walking with long eager steps, her cheeks faintly pink with exertion and her eyes remote with inner joy.

"It's great," he yelled back. He thought he had never in his life felt so perfectly, purely happy. He watched Celeste striding along with her wide rapt smile, her cape straight out behind her in the wind. That stride was the fullest, most vigorously optimistic human motion he'd ever seen. And here, with her, he felt his own stride going along evenly and equally with it, keeping up, feeling to him the way her stride felt to him. Like marching in unison, he thought.

They raced along, sometimes dashing sideways automatically and expertly to dodge the sudden silver-pool spread of water up across the beach when an oversize wave broke, running desperately sometimes to race a wave's collapse and sometimes not escaping, Celeste laughing, shrieking, "Gotcha, Cabe! Watch out, here comes another one!"

How crazy wonderful it all was. Nothing but the sea, booming with the even strenuous thud of breaking waves on smooth cold sand; gulls soaring; flocks of terns running at the water's edge, their tiny legs blurred by speed; miles of ocher-colored shore curving to distant headlands soft and gray and misted with spray cast up by the surf; miles of green-dark sea with crests ridging it and surf blowing back from them in streaming white manes; way off on the horizon a thread of bright silver—the sun coming through the clouds.

They walked until Celeste began to get tired, and said she thought they should turn back. The sky and the sea were darker now, thickening with the grayness of dusk. The wind had strengthened, and they were walking into it, not with it, so that the going was hard. Her head bent, her cape slashing out, Celeste plowed into the wind, and Cabe was slowed down too, curved almost U-shape as he struggled along. They were grateful when they got back to the pond and the boat.

Celeste climbed into the stern and lay back with a long exhalation of relief and exhaustion. "This is when I realize I'm no longer young."

Cabe's eyes were streaming from the wind, his hands were clumsy-numb as he fumbled with the oarlocks then fitted the oars into them and began stiffly to row. In a moment, though, his stroking was looser, stronger. He was dazed, tired from the excitement and exhilaration of the beach, and he said to her in a quiet, distanced voice, "You seem young to me. I don't know how old you are, but numbers wouldn't be significant. You're young."

"I'm sixty-five." Amazing, how readily this had come out. Yet she regretted it. Not for its disclosure, but because it sounded intimate.

"I'm sixty-six," he said with a resonant satisfaction, elated to find that they were almost the same age.

"Well. We're both at that time of life when it's a major topic of conversation either to skirt around the subject of one's age, or lie about it, or else confess," she said, hectically. "In either case, I guess it's the seriousness of the condition that makes it topic number one." She did a little something with her mouth that passed for a smile.

"Yes. I guess it's topic number one," he said, almost disinterestedly. Bending, pushing out the oars, leaning back, pulling them in, he rowed with a powerful rhythmic assurance.

The pond was silver-dark now. Celeste shivered. "It's getting cold," she said. "It's lovely though, this quiet dusk."

"Yes. Better now than that menacing sea."

"It was menacing, wasn't it." She shivered again.

"Here we are," he said. He rowed silently into the sudden twilight gloom of the forest-shaded inlet, darkly, mysteriously quiet, the only sound the rustle of the oars, and the tiny runnel of water along the hull. The steady rhythm of Cabe's rowing slowed, and then with short scoops of the oars he turned the boat around and headed it for the shore. Scrunch on the stony shallows. Sudden stop. Absolute silence—still water, still forest.

Celeste was suddenly, extravagantly glad it was all over. Shore, home, lights, that was hers—known, safe. Back there the sea seemed mighty and dark and terrifying. The pond, too, out there, belonged now to darkness, to evening, to itself. I'm too old for such adventure, she told herself, unsurely. She felt disgruntled all at once, lost, anticlimactic. It seemed now that there had been a kind of treachery out there on the pond—she being borne along by Cabe's powerful assured oarsmanship, something she had loved, but why? It felt unsafe to her that she had loved it. And the peace of the pond had been sorcerous, too, softening her, allowing intimacies. She drew a large, restorative sigh. She was back here now, in a harbor, back in herself.

Cabe was making tiny metallic sounds of busyness that echoed in the silence and darkness, removing the oars from the oarlocks, taking the oarlocks out of their fittings. In the dusk his face was blurred, absorbed. He stood up, and then made a long leap to the shore, a movement, she thought, of comely and strong masculinity, and she allowed herself a second of admiration.

Easily then, with Celeste's weight in the stern, Cabe hauled the boat up onto the shore, and stood there with his hand stretched out to help her.

"Well, *now* let's see if *I* can make it," she cried brightly, to disperse the silence and the gloom. Standing up, then bending over, stiff with cold she began to scramble clumsily toward the bow, holding onto both sides of the boat, which lurched. She lurched too, and almost fell, laughed shrilly, angered at her ineptness, her secondariness, here in this ridiculous element not hers. But now her hand was firmly in Cabe's outstretched hand, strong and supporting, and she stepped safely over the bow onto the shore.

She began to shiver convulsively. "Heavens, I'm really chilled," she stammered, through chattering teeth. But it was a chill reinforced by nervousness. She laughed again, in shrill spurts, unjoyously, not feeling at all like laughter but unable to stop. "I've gotten some sort of silly chill," she gasped, in apology.

"You need a drink. I wish I had something with me."

"A drink is *exactly* what I need!"

They walked single file up the dark little steep path, to the jeep, Cabe carrying the oars, which he put in the back of it. Then he came around and opened the door Celeste was struggling to open with numbed fingers, and with a strong heave under her elbows, helped her to climb up into the high seat. "*There* we are," he said. He closed her door and went around to his and got in. "Where to now, for that drink," he asked, "your house or mine?"

The wonderful unexpectedness of this, the unpredictability of it, simply bowled Celeste over. There was no darkness now, there was no cold, no peril. She turned to Cabe with a vivid smile. "Why don't we go to my house," she cried. "It's my turn, now."

II

THEY began to walk together every afternoon. Having drinks together afterward was the inevitable development of the walks. And on one of those evenings—they were at Celeste's house—she asked him to stay to dinner. After that it was an afternoon walk, then drinks and then dinner, every day. Cabe practiced in the mornings. Celeste, in the mornings, did housework, paperwork, read the daily New York *Times* from front to back, lingering over the financial section—the little girl who had seen a simple solution for keeping track of her money by looking in her purse, now at sixty-five was knowledgeable, even shrewd about investments—did her errands, went once a week to her Yoga class, met in committee about such things as nuclear disarmament, conservation, local politics. Always busy, busy. But at three o'clock, Cabe would come racketing into her driveway in his jeep, or she would pull into his driveway and beep the horn twice, to announce herself, and they would walk toward each other with the most transparent, the most intemperate delight.

Cabe was enormously attractive to her. Celeste openly admitted this to herself, one day as they were walking together on the beach. It was late afternoon, a beautiful soft afternoon, not wintry, one of those mild days that often surprise Islanders in late January. The sand was gray-gold in the afternoon light. Long low smooth waves curved and fell with a tranquil soft explosion, ran placidly up the sloping sand, hissed away. She was mesmerized by this calmness and beauty. As she walked she began to feel easy, soft, fluid, she was without the tightness in her upper spine, she was without the tightness in her mind, she felt vulnerable but didn't care. She wanted to drift along, listening to the rustle and slap of quiet water, feeling the scrunch of mussel shells under her boots, breathing the sharp pure air of the sea, and all of this quickened by the presence of Cabe at her side.

She strode carelessly, Cabe plunging along beside her with his long-legged lope, his head jerked forward. She kept turning to look at him. They were facing the low sun which flushed his face and kindled his eyes. Cold, his eyes, but majestic, she thought, because by now she knew the man behind them. And suddenly Cabe stopped. Leaned to pick up a stone. Examined it. Then flung it with a great twist of his body, off into the sea.

This sudden explosion of virility seemed to her a powerful, manly movement. Again she was astonished and even thrilled, as she had been that first evening on the pond, when he had leapt from the boat to the shore. She felt male force. She thought of it as youthful. For the first time, she allowed herself to have a complete sense of this man, who could play the piano so delicately, and hurl a stone so powerfully. She saw that the sudden beautiful movement had burst from a man who had both a spiritual and a muscular vigor, and that it seemed to moderate, even to transcend, his weakness.

She looked at him in an entirely new way, sensing the whole man, but now particularly his body, responding to this sudden contortion of it, and feeling it related to her own body. He was the Discus Thrower, naked and muscular and powerfully phallic. Her femaleness was elated. Her sexuality was uncovered now. She felt it. Loved it.

"Oh, Cabe," she cried, "you have an elegant vigor. You strike me as young, young."

From that moment on, she lived with the discomfort and the rapture of physical longing. She wanted Cabe. She wanted the boy who had kissed the side of her neck, and, how could she help it when her body told her so, she wanted the man. She thought constantly about how it would be to make love with Cabe, and lying in her bed, she would spread her legs wide, and thrash her head in a frenzy of physical aching.

And she knew he wanted her. There were innumerable signs, which she luxuriated in, but was at the same time deeply, nervously distressed about. She could imagine that marriage was in his mind. It was in hers, too, but only as something she knew she didn't want. They were two imperfect, obviously wounded people, and it was a horror to her to think of a union of imperfections for the second time in her life. There was something in Cabe, not in what he did, or said, but something signaled—subtle yet deep and evident, a kind of sycophant demand, a tugging at her sleeve—which reminded her of Lidi, and she was determined not to succumb to it. Lidi expected everything to happen to her, she seemed doomed not to make anything happen out of her own efforts. And didn't this smack of Cabe? She thought of Mort, and was resolved never to repeat a supply and demand that passed for a marriage. It was not a way she wanted ever again to be with a man. She didn't want Cabe's sadness. She didn't want to nurse his sense of failure, she didn't want to be his support, no matter how subtly. Mort had asked her to supply something outrageous instead of her own self. She would not fall into that trap again. If she should ever fall in love, and she sincerely doubted that she would, she wanted that man to want her for herself, not to use her for himself. And that, she thought fairly, would have to work both ways, for she knew at last that she had been guilty of using Mort for herself and of wanting him for something other than himself. In innocence, she had committed the crime of her life. There would be no second offense.

So. There it was, and she would stick to it. There would be no marriage (or substitute marriage, for conventional weddings were anathema to her). And there would be no sleeping with Cabe, either. No, not without love. Even though it was a temptation to settle for just sex, should this be proposed to her, she thought she would not want it without love. Sex, she told herself, ought to be the foundation of love, but not the house built on top of it. The more she grew to appreciate the potency and quality and quiet of Cabe's worth, the more unthinkable it was to her to contemplate sleeping with him without wanting union with that, too. If their two bodies were ever to make love, it would have to be love, entire, it would have to be the whole man and the whole woman. She was certain that it was too late in life for either of them to have any satisfaction from sharing less than that. She assured herself that it was too late to trifle, too late not to keep trying, over and over and over, to get where she wanted to go, wherever that was. All her voices of self-doubt, in the silence of this sea-existence, told her that that was all there was left to her, or to any aging person—the pursuit of what had been lost, the attempt to find it. I am sixty-five, she would say to herself over and over again. Cabe is sixty-six.

They had been rowing on Great Pond in weather too blustery for it. Back at Cabe's house, he lighted a fire in the living room and collapsed on the couch beside it, while Celeste bustled about in his disorderly and unclean kitchen, making drinks and putting cheese and crackers on a tray.

They were quieted, even drowsy from all the air of the afternoon, and Cabe was bone tired. They drank, wolfed the cheese and crackers, smiled contentedly at each other, yawned. They talked some. Not much. Cabe finished his drink and then stretched out on the couch, while Celeste told him Dearie stories—he loved to hear them. She told him the one about the night she and Mort came back from a charity ball, both rather drunk, and announced to Dearie that they had danced past the Duke and Duchess of Windsor, "near enough to touch them, though of course we didn't, Dearie." And Dearie, sozzled too (he drank secretly, when they weren't there), pumped his paw down and said in his most scornful voice, "Who cares about the Douche and Duckess of Windsor?" "We alway pretended to blame that tongue-slipping on Dearie," she said. "I can't begin to tell you how hilarious we thought that was."

"Which one of you said it?"

"*I* did. Mort laughed so hard he got hiccups."

"What ever became of Dearie? It must have been hard to get rid of him. I hope he died a natural death."

"He's in the bottom drawer of my living room chest. The other day I simply marched into the bedroom and picked him up, just like that, without very much emotion really, and put him in a box and put the box in the bottom drawer of the chest. I didn't say goodbye to Dearie, and Dearie didn't say goodbye to me. Sometimes, though, I think about him lying in a dark box in a dark drawer, and it feels sad and wrong. I have this faint sadness, thinking about him."

She got up suddenly, brushing cracker crumbs from her lap. "I'm going to make us some supper, Cabe. I'm starving, and I'll bet you are."

"I'm ravenous."

She made scrambled eggs for them and some toast. They sat on by the fire, eating, talking, until she yawned too many times and said she must go. At the door, as she was surrounding herself with the warmth of her cape, Cabe said, looking piercingly at her, "I wish you could stay. And stay." There was a beseeching revelation in his eyes which instantly made connection with a delicate, tingling expectancy in herself. His look probed and sought and it pled, while a spreading pulsing heat in her stomach responded. She didn't say anything. Couldn't. Helplessly she simply stared at him. There wasn't a word in her, only stillness, and a spinning. She staggered a little as she opened the door.

She drove slowly home along the snow-walled black road, churning, groping for something to stabilize herself. Desire for Cabe was like a pump inside of her, pushing a flow through her whole body, from the delirium in her head, down through the dilation of her heart, to the swelling rapturous discomfort of her loins. She gripped the wheel as though to anchor herself to it, for it felt concrete to her. She was desperate for an anchor, for something to keep her from being swept away and drowned. It was the wheel of her car and she was controlling it, she was feeling, doing something tangible, which could anchor her.

When she got home she went straight to the kitchen without even taking off her cape—from the anchor of the steering wheel directly to the anchor of the bottle—and poured herself a long dark drink of bourbon with shaking hands. Then she sat down at the kitchen table, still in her cape, and began to drink the bourbon in long, greedy gulps, trying now to find something in herself that was an anchor, searching, as though compelled, as though looking through a card index, for a word she knew was there, and which would steady her, bring her to her senses. INDEPENDENCE. Hah! There

it was! INDEPENDENCE. "I prize it," she said aloud. "Yes."
And then she came upon another word, a brain-numbed
faint word, NONATTACHMENT. And then after a while,
into her dazed mind there flashed another word, CONVIC-
TIONS. "I do have convictions, you know," she said aloud,
to herself and to Cabe, but the success of the anesthesizing
bourbon brought it out as "convisions." Where were convictions? For that matter, what were they? Ah. SELF-CON-
TAINMENT. There, that was a conviction. The most
important one. But where had the stillness, the safety, of
self-containment gone? She sensed, sitting here in this whirl-
wind of big black taunting words, that where she had once
had a smooth surface of something covering her that felt
invulnerable, there was now a worn-out surface of something that felt cracked, unprotective, open to invasion. All
over myself I feel like old, cracked leather, she thought. And
laughed.

"Heavens!" she said, and flung the last of the bourbon
down her throat, and then hung up her cape and went un-
steadily into the bedroom to undress.

After she had gotten into her nightgown, she stood in
front of the long mirror in the dressing room, thinking about
her body, trying to see it through Cabe's eyes. Lifting her
arms up and out sideways, she saw that the soft flesh of her
arms swayed like white hammocks. Ugh! Was there any
exercise, she wondered, that could tighten them? Look into
it.

"Oblivion." She said this aloud, suddenly. "So. What's
the matter with oblivion?" Then she began to laugh. "Everything," she said. "Everything's the matter with oblivion."
Obli-yon was how she said it.

Boldly then, she pulled up her nightgown. She liked what

she saw. I'll do. I'll do very well, she thought. After all, I'm only sixty-five. Sixty-five isn't old. Even seventy doesn't seem old to me anymore. I certainly don't in the least feel old. Maybe eighty doesn't even feel old to Tilly. Are they lovers? Oh, of course they are.

She saw a mole which needed close inspection, and so she went for her glasses, and put them on, and came back to the mirror and pulled up her nightgown again. She scrutinized the mole, then looking up she saw the woman in the mirror—white hair hanging down her back, loose flesh of her upper arms hanging, glasses on her nose. Glasses! She began to laugh at this absurd white-haired woman with her pulpy arms and her nightgown so tensely pulled up. In an intoxicated, detached way she saw herself clearly. The thing she was looking at was unseemly. It was even pathetic. "You are grotesque," she said with sad disgust to the woman in the mirror.

But I know that old flesh doesn't matter, she reassured herself quickly, letting her nightgown drop. I. Am. Being. *Silly.* I. Am. A. Little. Drunk.

Then in the next breath she told herself that she was very very glad her body was still all right. And wondered just how she would feel if it weren't. She made a pig-snout face at this shilly-shallying woman in the mirror. Would she be awfully unconfident about making love with Cabe if she had a quilted old body, she worried. Did it matter to Turck that Tilly's body was that way? No. Positively she knew it oughtn't to matter.

Sixty-five. Seventy-five. Eighty. Oblivion. She looked at her shoulders and said to herself: They are nice white non-old-appearing shoulders, under what I regard as an elegant nightgown. And she congratulated herself on still having the interest and the energy to go out and buy new nightgowns. The nightgown told of confidence in the endlessness of these non-old-appearing shoulders.

She felt an enormous surge of joy and relief looking at this seeming nontransience. Here I am, not seeing anything that looks like sixty-five, except these arms, she gloated. Maybe I'm drunk, but all I feel at this moment is confidence. Why feel anything else? There's no evidence, except for these arms, that I should feel old. That's a miraculous picture I'm looking at, the here-and-now of my still not puckered body, and my optimistic nightgown over it.

When she got into bed and turned off the light, she lay listening to the thrash and scuttle of the waves on her stony winter beach and she was full of the marvelous importance of her body.

And then she realized that there was no separateness in her sensing of it. Thus she understood that she had lost the safe separateness of self-containment, had grown away from boundaries and was overflowing them, pouring out to Cabe in an absolutely mindless but absolutely essential way. Lying here in a fever of flesh consciousness, she knew that it was unbearable to think that their two bodies would never come together.

But. What about her determination not to sleep with Cabe without love? What about the whole man and the whole woman? And something still unfound?

She wondered. She sighed. She shook her head helplessly, knowing that it was no longer her mind that ruled.

⮜⮜⮜ III ⮞⮞⮞

THE days went wonderfully, swiftly by. To both of them time seemed to be racing along, whereas before—"BC" Cabe called the years before Celeste—time had moved ponderously, and often, particularly in the evenings, had seemed not to be moving at all. They rowed, they walked, they dined out, they watched the evening news on television, they went to the movies. They did not go to parties because Cabe detested them. And Celeste soon realized that she was giving up nothing that really mattered to her. She would far rather be alone with Cabe, in his living room, by his fire, listening to him play, she told him. And of course, for Cabe, this was the entirety of satisfaction.

Of course Cabe knew that he was falling in love with her. And when desire first moved in him, as he lay in his bed one morning after waking up, he fully understood what was happening to him. Almost more than anything else, this arousal invigorated and rejoiced his spirit, though it also caused him the wildest alarm about whether it was here to stay, and whether, if put to the test, it would be confident.

But underneath this happiness, there was one serious, nagging doubt about Celeste, and about Celeste and himself together. Why, he worried, could they not talk about themselves? His reticence forbade it, he knew, and her flippancy, her opposition to intimacy, forbade it too. This seemed wrong to Cabe. He felt a holding-back between them that was a

213

sort of deadness. He thought that if only she would open up, he could dare to, too. But he doubted that he could ever take the initiative.

More than this, he was perplexed and even disturbed about her seeming inconsistencies. Why was she strong and open, and yet at the same time closed and flippantly opposed to serious feeling; outgoing, and yet nervously private; passionate, and yet locked-up? She enjoyed everything so obviously, so fervently—flowers, birds, the sea, people, cooking, even doing laundry, because, she had told him with one of her innocent smiles, she loved the smell of it. He understood that flippancy was a way of disregarding deep feeling, and that there *was* deep feeling there, under the mockery of it. He appreciated Celeste's essential nature. But sometimes he was discontented with her and confused and greatly cooled off in his emotions about her.

One day, in despair over this evasive privacy, which felt always to him like a door being slammed in his face, he made the sudden, astonishing decision to break and enter. And without preamble he said to her, "Celeste, I've never met anyone so happy as you. But you were divorced. You never remarried. You're obviously reticent about having no children. It seems hard for me to understand how *any*one, under these circumstances, could be happy. What's your secret?"

They were sitting in her living room. Outside, snow was falling steadily, veiling the sea.

She turned a white shocked face to him, eyes wide with pain and with the effrontery of this. Then she turned away and said casually, "Oh, I love life, I guess."

"That's a very simplistic way of saying it." Such daring was not as difficult as he had thought it would be. Nevertheless, his heart was pounding. "Is it that simple?"

"Yes I think it is," she said now unguardedly, almost eagerly. "Even when I'm depressed, as I sometimes am, I can bounce back. I have almost an idiot's ability not to stay depressed. I'm like Tilly. I enjoy. Honestly. I get up in the morning and go out onto my deck, and the shock of contrast between smothering indoors and sad sleep, and then that sun and the way the air *smells*, sea and grass and pure air, *pure*, it simply elates me like nothing human. And after all, what else is first? Aren't sun and air *first*? Well maybe not," she was warming to her feelings, "maybe what comes first is good health. A good body. Mine has always been such a nice reliable body. A very very strong body. It must have been, not to be ruined by all that endless drinking."

"For god's sake, Celeste. You? When?"

"Oh, for all the years with Mort, except toward the end, when I rebelled, after I started working. We drank like fishes."

"We all did in those days."

"I know. The so sad unserious 'thirties. A very bad time for the young. Beginning to emerge, but only in our inner rebellions. No outer rebellions. I always wanted something nice and clean."

"What wasn't nice and clean, Celeste?"

"Parts of my life."

"What about having no children?" he asked quietly, for he was feeling safer now, surer of the validity of insistence.

"I had a premature stillborn daughter. Did you ever see a stiff white tiny dead baby? Almost small enough to hold in the palm of your hand." She stopped. "I didn't mean it to sound so dramatic."

Cabe was quiet for a moment, looking out at the whiteness of snow which was coming down intense and still. Then he said, really only to help her out, "I saw a three-year-old dead boy. My son."

"Oh *Cabe*. Dearest Cabe. I've thought so often about that."

"But it never got to me, Celeste. So spare your very dear concern. I could never love the child. And I've never wasted any time feeling guilty about it. It was for Catsy and her mother that I grieved. And for my mother."

"You were very close to your mother, weren't you?"

"As close as a helpless victim in the embrace of an octopus." A look of surprise, of triumph lighted his face. "My goodness," he said quietly. He felt excitement tickling his spine. "No. It wasn't that simple," he said. "Nothing is really simple with one's mother, I suspect." His eyes were cold and comprehending.

"Did Catsy get along with your mother? You make it sound as though your mother would have been quite a formidable mother-in-law. She would have been for me," Celeste said, and blushed wildly.

Cabe looked at her. For a long moment they looked at each other without reserve, with an identical biding breathlessness, Cabe's eyes steady, Celeste's wide and shocked and transparent with confession.

Then, impulsively, in the way things were happening to him right now, Cabe said to her, "I can imagine how hard it was for you to lose your child. I'm not a child lover," he said quietly, "but I think you are. I can see what it must have meant to you to lose a child. Hard."

"I suppose it was. I don't feel much now. It was so long ago. Oh but yes, of course it was awful, awful. Not to have that child. *And,*" she said scornfully, "to have a womb that was a tomb."

And now she flung out her hands and cried, "One, two, button my shoe, three four, shut the door. Do forgive me Cabe, for spilling over so, I don't know what got into me."

"I do. Five six, pick up sticks, seven eight, lay them straight."

"Oh yeah? Well, nine ten, the big fat hen," she lilted, with a wild smile.

So it seemed that his daring had come to nothing, after all. And now he was more concerned than ever about her flippancy, even frightened of it. Wouldn't she ever stay with the sincerity of her feelings? Would she, with such withholding, ever be able to love him? He knew she liked him. He was well aware of her growing interest in him, even her growing affection. She would put her hand on him, often, impulsively. She called him "Dear Cabe," more and more. And there was an occasional spontaneous opening up, as with that revelation about her stillborn child. But. Would she ever love him?

Recently he had begun to think that there were as many kinds of love as there were people and that the only statement that could be made about what love was, was that it was simply being oneself, staying wholly with one's essential nature. If this were so, and he believed it was, then there was very little hope that Celeste, who was continually repressing her feelings, could ever love him. He had understood, after the revelation about the child, and the clear implications of unhappiness with Mort, that this was cause enough for a heart to be locked. And he suspected that way back, the abundant naturalness and bestowal of her true nature had come up against some pretty awful obstacle, and stopped dead. Why, with such a life, hadn't she grown bitter? he wondered. Perhaps because bitterness was alien to a personality like hers. Instead of becoming embittered she had become enraged. Rage was purer than bitterness, which was a corrosive. Rage was volatile. He understood Celeste's rage, and approved of it. But nevertheless he was uneasy about such an exaggerated evasion of feeling. In a way he distrusted this thing in her, and wondered whether a woman who was both jubilantly natural and furtively unnatural could ever truly love.

But in spite of these concerns, he knew he was in love with her. Ardent in his bed, astonished and relieved though prudishly embarrassed, he daydreamed of her, feeling a life in those seedless loins he had thought was gone forever. Doubting that daydreams predicated performance, should it ever come to that, still he rejoiced in what was happening to him, and thought how absolutely miraculous it was, after such a long lack, to move and grow and tighten with yearning for a woman, this woman.

IV

HE liked to drive his jeep to Wampanoag Beach in the early afternoon before meeting Celeste, and sit there doing nothing, looking at the spread of the sea. Some days he took a notebook out of the glove compartment and composed. Amazing successions of notes came into his head and he would put what seemed to him little treasures of melody into that notebook. Later, when he looked at them, he was incredulous. Was he beginning to be a composer, he wondered, with a feeling of expanse in himself that was like the sea he was looking at.

Other days he would sit, and be willing prey to an endless train of seemingly unrelated thoughts: Celeste in a long sarong-like yellow silk skirt tight across her small buttocks which jounced from side to side as she walked out of the room; Mrs. Elgin, who did his laundry and gave private lessons in Greek and had a cat named Anwar; Celeste's fury, her black cursing rage, when Anwar Sadat was assassinated. Anwar Sadat, his halting, laboring passionate talk, his utterly convinced eyes; Celeste's white face in candlelight; the white pheasant in his russet fields, like a ghost pheasant, or like the silver pheasants on his mother's dining room table; the lack of profit for tour buses on foggy days with only a handful of passengers and a forty-mile round trip; Lidi Luhin's sensitivity, behind her mask face.

He liked the purposelessness, the entertainment of just sitting and thinking, or rather, of floating along without plan on this river of what he thought of as "mumbo-jumbo." It rested him.

But sometimes, as he sat watching the smooth high waves of an incoming tide crashing, breaking white, receding, crashing, his thoughts would be attracted, compasslike, to whole sections of his past. Episode after episode would spring into his mind, would blossom there with a vividness as of color, then recede like the waves. And sometimes an encapsulation of his entire life was there, both visible and explained, and he would sit mesmerized by this phenomenon.

The episode with his mother, which he had hinted at to Celeste the day she came to hear him play, stood in his mind in such a way as he sat one afternoon, looking out over the immensity of the sea. Sun filled the jeep. Waves thrashed the shore with a mighty monotony. He was warm, detached, drowsy.

And then there it was, not only the entire scope of the episode swiftly and vividly replayed, but the meaning of it, and the reasons for having remembered it as profoundly and as significantly as he had ever remembered anything that had happened in his life.

He was astonished. There everything was, brought out into the light—piercingly clear and awful. He was shaken and sickened, and yet at the same time at peace. There was even comfort, even sustenance, in seeing this nasty business with such shattering accuracy and finality.

A few days later he invited Tilly to have lunch with him at the Harbor House, and no sooner had they ordered their food than he found himself pouring out the whole story to her. He had invited her because Turck was in Boston seeing his lawyer and Cabe knew she loved, as she said, to "eat out," but also because, quite unconsciously, he had wanted to be alone with her in order to tell her that story.

They had a small table by the window. Glasses and silver and white tablecloth sparkled in the sun. Beyond lay the empty blue harbor which the withdrawal of summering yachts had given back to nature, only a few scalloping boats swinging at anchor there, the docks long and empty and silver-gray in the sun.

They had ordered their drinks: Tilly a Scotch on the rocks, and Cabe a small straight bourbon, which he didn't want in the middle of the day and would only toy with to keep Tilly company. Tilly sipped and studied the menu. Decisive about almost everything, it seemed to Cabe she was maddeningly slow about deciding what she wanted to eat. It appeared that she loved the idea of choices, and liked to browse through Appetizers, Soups, Sandwiches, Entrees, Salads, Cold Plates, just to bask in the luxury of possibilities.

"I'll have the Roast Beef au Jus," she said finally to the menu, folding it, then looking up at the impatient waitress with a smile of flashing sweetness.

"There's a baked potato comes with it," the waitress said. "And your choice of buttered beets or spinach gratinée. Our salad dressings are Russian, French, Italian, Blue Cheese, and the House Dressing."

A whole new spectrum of choices opened up for Tilly. Cabe sipped his bourbon resignedly, while Tilly pondered. Finally she decided on spinach gratinée. "Now what's the House Dressing?" she wanted to know. But then she said, "I don't think I really want the salad. Thank you, dear." She handed the menu up to the waitress. And now, freed from the long lovely challenge of choices, and ready to realize that she was here with Cabe, another new and promising interest, she sat up straight and shrugged her coat from her shoulders, letting it drop over the back of the chair, and smiled across at him. "My, this is just lovely, Cabe. You were so dear to do this. And look here. These are *fresh* flowers. In January." She poked the little vase around, then lifted it up to her nose and sniffed. She set it back with a look of satisfaction.

Cabe felt a rush of tenderness for her, and for little things, little satisfactions, and for the strength, the optimism it took to be supported, even enthused by little satisfactions. He had no little satisfactions, only the one big one, or rather now, with Celeste, the two big ones. Would it ever be otherwise? And did it matter? "I was thinking about Catsy yesterday, Aunt Tilly," he said musingly, pursing his full lips and pouring a little bourbon between them. "I was thinking about her rather amazingly."

"Really, dear. I somehow thought you were quite reconciled."

"Oh, I am. Indeed I am. It was in another way that I was thinking about her."

"Well, you're better off without her," Tilly said firmly.

"Which does not mean that I wanted that fine woman to die." She had begun to say this to Cabe, frequently and deliberately, a year after Catsy's death, and everytime she said it, Cabe loved it. Tilly was absolutely right, he was better off without Catsy. But, unlike Tilly, he knew that because Catsy's death had been the promise of liberation for him, in some base part of himself he had been glad of her death. He thought it was the worst kind of cowardice to be grateful that death had accomplished what intelligence and courage could have accomplished instead—the necessary ending of a wrong marriage. And yet, there was the undeniable fact, which Tilly was aware of: he was better off without Catsy. Subtract guilt, accept fact, he had commanded himself.

"I wasn't thinking about Catsy painfully, Aunt Tilly," he said. "Nor even in relation to me. But I was remembering an episode which so clearly showed me why I wanted to marry her, and most particularly, told me the story of my mother and myself."

Tilly put down her drink. Her dark eyes grew still. She held her white trembling fingers loosely around her glass, and looked at Cabe with sympathy, with curiosity. "I know the story of you and your mother, dear. I know it well."

"You *do?*"

"Yes, dear. Can you imagine I wouldn't?"

He hesitated, looking down into his glass, thinking that perhaps Tilly had saved him from the splurge of a confessional. He felt a certain healthy relief. And yet in the next second he said, "Be that as it may, Aunt Tilly, I have good reason to want to pursue this subject, so if you'll give me leave to hold the floor for a while." He looked up unwillingly at the waitress, who had arrived with their order. "It's very *hot,*" she was saying, putting in front of them plates that were noisy with sound and heat and steam. "So take care."

"My," Tilly said, lifting up her hands and holding them high and still on either side of her plate, as though blessing it. Her downward smile was concentrated, frankly gluttonous. She had forgotten Cabe.

Cabe sighed, and began to eat his Seafood au Gratin. The first bite was brutally hot, and he said, "Damn," explosively, painfully, lunging for his water and flinging its coldness into his mouth.

"Goodness gracious, dear!" Alarmed and laughing, Tilly shook her head. "Mine looks perfectly delicious. And done just right, just the way I like it. Dr. Ratisbone scolded me about using salt; he tells me I'll get to like the natural taste of things without salt, but I don't believe that for one minute. Anyway," she reached for the salt shaker, "today I'm going to throw caution to the winds."

"How about some red wine with it, Aunt Tilly? C'm on. You shouldn't have roast beef without red wine." He had decided to give up the story.

"Why, *wouldn't* that be nice. I believe I will."

Cabe called the waitress and ordered the wine. The wine would drag this lunch out interminably, he knew, but he would be patient. He had asked Aunt Tilly out to lunch, and he would be patient. At the same time he felt impatient with old age—the fussing, the procrastination, the doddering. He wanted to be with Celeste at this moment, he wanted to be practicing, he wanted to be walking on the beach, he did not want to be chained to a table in an overheated, smoke-filled restaurant in the middle of the day, drinking liquor he didn't want, listening. Only listening. That was the trouble with old people, he thought, they talked, but they didn't listen. He flung back his head and drank down the last of his bourbon.

The wine was brought, and Tilly, her eyes gleaming, picked it up at once, and held it out toward Cabe. "Cheers, dear. My. This is lovely." She sipped it. She set it down. She placed one shaking blue-veined hand, with fingers spread, lightly upon her breast, picked up her fork with the other and dipped into the spinach gratinée. Suddenly she put the fork down. "Cabe! You were beginning to tell me something important when the waitress came. Forgive me, dear, and do go on."

"It's quite long," he said, eagerly.

"Never mind. I'll eat while you talk. But don't you stop eating to talk."

"I won't." An ease passed over his face. He sat up straighter and leaned forward. "This story. Well. Catsy and I always called it the 'Incident of the Step-ins.' Today, no one'd know what step-ins were."

"Oh, *I* would," she said, her voice muffled with munching. "I know all about step-ins, my dear man. Why I remember the place on Newbury Street where I used to buy mine, the nicest little shop only a hop skip and a jump from the old museum on the corner of, of, oh fudge, what's the name of that street. It begins with a B. Bre, Bel . . ."

"Berkeley," Cabe said patiently.

"That's it. Berkeley. Imagine forgetting that. I've walked that street possibly a thousand times on my way . . ."

But Cabe cut in. "Since you know what step-ins are, Aunt Tilly, then the story will be more, uh, visible. Well, anyway. To begin," he said darkly. "It all started with my asking Catsy to give me one of her silk step-ins so that I could sleep with it beside my face, back home that summer she was abroad with her mother buying her trousseau for the wedding. It didn't seem at all an odd thing to want, at the time. The step-ins were crumpled and creased from being worn, which was the way I wanted it. Because that way it smelled of her. Closer than that to Catsy's, um, skin, I didn't get. While we were engaged. Well, she was agreeable to giving me the step-ins, but embarrassed because they weren't a nice fresh pair, not immediately getting the point of it all. Ah, the suppressions of a conventional young couple in the thirties."

Cabe flung himself back against the chair with a loud sigh, staring at nothing with wide light eyes. "Reluctantly, then, after more explanation, she went into the downstairs lavatory and took them off, and came out and handed them to me. They were pink, with a little white monogram in one corner. I put them in the drawer of the table next to my bed. At night I'd take them out and put them on my pillow." And bury my nose in them with what you might say was erective enjoyment. Ah yes, he thought with shame, erective enjoyment, a nicer way of putting it than what it actually was.

"Well, while we were on our wedding trip Miss Stoat found it there. As you probaby realized, she was already jealous of Catsy. She still had a great possessiveness about me, as you also know well. And she'd gotten to be a real snoop after Catsy came into the picture. At the moment I'm probably not telling you anything you don't know, Aunt Tilly."

"No you're not, Cabe. *Why* your mother kept that impossible old woman on I don't know. Oh, of course I do know. The poor old soul had no place to go. No family of her own. Your mother had no choice. She was Scotch, wasn't she, Miss Stoat?"

"Yes, Scottish without the poetry. Really in some ways a mean little woman. She'd barge into the living room where Catsy and I were futiley necking, not knocking; she'd open the door and walk in and then pretend to be surprised to find us there, though of course she'd known we were there. Peeping Miss Stoat. Frustrated spinsterhood. And of course, eventually, she found the step-ins in my table drawer. I wouldn't be surprised if not-so-unsophisticated old maid Miss Stoat wasn't looking for contraceptives."

"I wouldn't be at all surprised." Tilly nodded, all concentrated interest now.

"Anyway, she promptly took them and showed them to Mother, with all possible innuendo you can be sure. Reconstructing what happened, I can imagine that Mother was scandalized and delighted to be so, thinking I'm sure that the step-ins had been removed by Catsy in that bedroom for one of the purposes that step-ins are removed. She had Miss Stoat launder it, *launder* it, and then she *mailed* it, now this is the unforgivable part, she mailed it to Catsy's mother with a note saying that the step-ins had been found in my bedroom and that she had had them *laundered, Christ,* and was returning them to Mrs. Turnbull. No accusations spelled out, mind you. Later I saw the letter of course. Just the unspoken insinuation that Mrs. Turnbull's daughter was a tramp. Hell, it was more than an insinuation, the accusation in that letter was absolutely clear."

Cabe's eyes were cold and stunned. "I could never forgive Mother for that," he whispered with a kind of savage enjoyment, "it was simply one of the lowest, cruelest, most arrogantly nasty performances I have ever known of. As you see, I could never forgive her for it. Neither could Catsy. When her mother showed her the letter, after we were back from Bermuda, she flew into a rage the likes of which I'd never seen, disclaiming any shenanigans, of course. And her mother, who trusted her, believed her."

"Of course," Tilly said indignantly. "Catsy was utterly

to be trusted. Why Cabe, honestly, I'm astonished at your mother, if anyone else had told me this about her I wouldn't have believed them, I'd . . ."

Cabe held up his hand. "But wait, Aunt Tilly. Now comes the splendor. The splendor! I'd gone the next day to see Mother, planning to have it out with her. I was sitting there in the library with her, having tea, trying to work up to the right way of putting it to her, thinking I'd start in after we'd finished the tea, when suddenly the door burst open and in marched Catsy. She had the step-ins in her hand. She came right up to Mother, close enough to touch her, and she said. You know what she *said?* To *Mother?* She said 'Damn you,' quietly, scornfully. Then she tossed the step-ins down into Mother's lap and turned and walked out of the room."

"I'm not one bit surprised," Tilly whispered, "that's just what I would have expected of Catsy."

"And I just sat there, Aunt Tilly. I didn't say anything. I didn't say one word. I just sat there. Appeasing my mother because she had insulted my wife and my wife's parents." He looked down at his hands. "I suppose that's no blacker a spot than all the less 'overt' ones, as they say these days, no blacker than the years full of an infinity of small and large impotences. But it's the one I remember the most vividly and painfully because of the outrageous behavior of Mother. Oh, I suppose it was the most outrageous of my impotences, too. I don't know which was worse, cringing passivity, or arrogant nastiness? What a pair we were!"

He looked searchingly at Tilly. Then he sighed and looked away from her. He felt better, purged. He had put into words, finally, what had been for all the years of his life a fermentation of humiliation and rage. He had removed it from himself and in so doing given it a form, a life of its own, and he felt lighter. Yet now, in the silence coming strongly across to him from Tilly, he felt exposed and awkward. He bent to his cold food and began to eat self-consciously.

Tilly put her knife and her fork side by side in the middle of her empty plate, carefully. Then she looked across at Cabe. "My dearest man." He loved the kindness and the sternness in her eyes. She reached over and put a hand on his. She said no more.

"Thank you, Aunt Tilly." There was a fullness of tears in his throat, which he cleared noisily away.

"You know," she said now briskly, looking down at her napkin and snapping it neatly across her lap, then looking up at Cabe. "I'm really happy to see that you and Celeste have gotten to be such good friends. If I may be so bold."

"You may be so bold. I adore her, Aunt Tilly."

Her smile, he thought, was absolutely heavenly. "Well, Celeste's the woman for you," she said in her decisive, no-nonsense way. "Catsy never was. Any more than you were the man for Catsy. I'm perfectly thrilled to see what's going on."

Now there was a climate surrounding this table that had not been here before. It was no longer he sitting here, Tilly sitting there, he eating, she eating, he talking, she talking. It was himself on the brink of love, and Tilly deep in it. They were fused, they were one single emotion. And in realizing this, Cabe looked at her, thinking of her and Turck, searching for whatever it was in an old woman that could arouse an old man. He was in a sea of sexual awareness for a moment, and thoughts of Celeste, of her breasts, her thighs, spread out to Tilly. He was dismayed. Helplessly, he tried not to see Tilly as sexual, desperately, he tried not to see her as a woman who made love. Yet there was no denying the universality of the fact of breasts and thighs and erections that was the climate of this table, now. A complicity of sexuality was here. Or, was it more than sexuality?

He dared to look fully at Tilly. And as he did so, she turned her head to look out at the harbor. The turn was slow, it was elegant in its dignity. The curve of her lips in profile was full. Suddenly, vividly, her quiet was eloquent. More than that. In that turning of her head, in her lips, and in her quiet, he saw a potent femininity—or was it just the color pink of the scarf around her throat? Then he saw that all these things, and the mind behind them—oh yes, that of course was what was important in this woman, the temperance and devotion and strength of her mind—all this made the picture of her lying naked under Turck an absolutely natural one.

"Thank you, Aunt Tilly," he said again. And now he knew that he was not ashamed of himself for pouring out to her. On the contrary, something destined had taken place fully. He had had to speak that story in order to make knowledge of it final. Like an earthquake, recognition of the truth of it had strewn everything all over, in pieces, but now that he had spoken it, solid ground could be felt, underneath the wreckage. He had at last arrived somewhere.

He turned and looked out at the harbor, and he saw the docility and ruggedness of work boats floating on calm waters, the ceaselessness of waves slapping on an empty shore. Everything was tranquil and ageless—water, boats, winter, two aging people together. He felt the torrent slowed down, the quiet place reached, which was acceptable because loving had made it so. Briefly, he felt immensity and unison: the water on which those scalloping boats were slowly swinging, the blue winter sky empty of clouds, the communion of maleness and femaleness and, yes, agelessness, between Tilly and himself, which had come about simply because they were both in love.

V

So be it, he said to himself one day. He was driving along Great Pond Road behind the usual car with the two white heads, one high, one low, motionless. The road was shining wet in bright thawing sun. And suddenly he compared himself to the melting snow along the sides of the road. He saw snow melting, pouring across the road in rivers, and he found a feeling in himself that was just like that. So be it, he thought.

It was in this way that he recognized a change in himself. He understood, with relief and interest, that his panic about those two white heads had now been tempered with reason. He no longer felt panic. Dignity, emotional balance had reasserted itself, and he did not repudiate those two white heads. Celeste was in all this like the sun melting the snow. And the telling of the story to Aunt Tilly. And the passage of time. And the slow subliminal process of seeing more in those two white heads than he had imagined he saw. The obsession with old flesh was gone. He recognized this with enormous relief. And it was because of Celeste. Or mostly because of her. The process of taking from her was like a transfusion of her blood enabling his to flow. Her strong and cheerul personality was a contagion that poured into him and seemed to jog the dormancy of his spirit. He had known from the beginning that he aspired to something she had which seemed to make living a happier thing for her than it was for him. He envied something in her. And now—oh, Mother, this is your son—he wondered whether he dared admit that whatever it was, it had rubbed off on him in a way that could perhaps reveal his own strength to himself and to encourage it. He felt now a feeble conviction about the possibility of a kind of success, though alternating with a counteracting conviction of the more than likely possibility of familiar failure. His old friend failure.

But at this moment, looking at the car ahead of him, and at the dazzling snow melting down into the road, he raised his shoulders way up to his ears in an awkward shrug and said to himself: There *I* am. *I* am that white head. *I* am that old geezer in his silly swimming trunks. Or will be soon. So be it.

Cabe was a man of depth, which provided lots of room for creativity but also for torment. Seeing the two white heads, but now without an angry anxiety, seeing them and knowing them, he felt like shouting with relief, and he felt all the spaces of himself filled up with a buoyant well-being.

He began to hum "Jesu Joy of Man's Desiring," which he planned to use in his concert as an encore, if indeed an encore was demanded. Singing in his strange cracked wisp of a deep voice, he fell to thinking about Celeste. The truth is, he thought about her all the time now, even when he was at the piano. The pressing of a legato tenderness down into the keys was really the tenderness of himself making of the music a palpable tenderness with which he was caressing Celeste. The joy and splash of the Arensky Waltz was Celeste striding along the beach on a wild gold afternoon, the sea all whitecaps. The music was inseparable from Celeste and from himself pouring it into her.

Suddenly he remembered the man in the subway. And he knew right away all about the man, and himself, and why he had resigned from the firm that afternoon. At last it was clear. He had seen and immediately understood with sensibility if not with sense, that he was looking at a man who owned himself unquestioningly and uniquely. Very beautiful and powerful that man had been, with the sureness and the immutability of being in command of himself. And now Cabe saw clearly that it had all begun there, this new and necessary road. And for a moment he had a sense of having come quite a long way on it.

Part Seven

"TURCK died last night."

A light snow is falling, spaced, fine flakes drifting straight down. The effect is of gentleness, a continuous peaceful gentle presence out there in the grayness of the morning. But perhaps soon there will imperceptibly be no more specks of snow in the air. It could be. When such a small snowfall stops, you're not aware of it right away.

"He died in his sleep."

You know it is snowing because everything has a fuzziness—the car is blurred, for instance. If you were sitting behind the windshield, you couldn't see out of it because it is lightly powdered. It is the third of February and it is snowing.

"Freddy just called me."

And Cabe calls *me*. Right away. *I* am the one he calls first. Celeste turned away from the window and switched on the floor lamp beside her desk. "Come live with me and be my love," she said aggressively, as a declaration of something, or just as a declaration, just to hear a voice, a sound to break the grip of this thing, like a pebble being dropped into still water. She sank against the back of the desk chair with a small sound that was a helpless sigh coming from between tightened lips. "What in heaven's name is Tilly to do now?"

What did Celeste feel? If asked she wouldn't have been able to explain. Except that around a shocked center, there was a warm nimbus that was Cabe's voice on the telephone, calling *her* first, turning straightaway to *her*.

She looked at her watch, and then got up and went to the closet for her jacket and her boots. She looked at her watch again, five minutes before Cabe would arrive to pick her up to take her to Tilly's. Just Tilly's now. Not Tilly and Turck's.

"I can't grasp it," she said in a loud, exasperated voice. She went into the bedroom and put on pale pink lipstick. Then she pulled down low over her forehead a white knitted cap which made a straight bulky line just above her eyebrows, so that her astonished and angry gray eyes seemed enormous and the only thing in all the whiteness of cap and face.

She heard Cabe's jeep arriving and hurried out to it. She didn't smile, or wave to him, it seemed inappropriate to this snow-shrouded morning of death and to the way she felt. She was enormously agitated, torn between a hesitant tenderness about Cabe's concern for Tilly which both flustered and excited her, and an awful anxiety at having this thing thrust upon her, demanding that she give something which everyone else would be wonderfully capable of but which she wouldn't. Agitated, really deeply fearful, she hurried along to the car. And all at once she said to herself: Here it is. There's an empty space. Turck's gone. With someone you see all the time, in a small place like this, it gets to you. In a row of little tin soldiers, you see one little tin soldier knocked down, leaving an empty space.

Cabe watched Celeste striding down the path toward him. A heavy ache and a disorientedness that was centered in his chest softened for a second into something else, more endurable. She walks toward the car like she danced last night, cutting through all those people like a sword, he thought, wistfully, admiringly, almost with pain.

He heard the surf roaring and pounding beyond the dune. The sea was very endless and steely gray and dreary beyond this fine net of snow falling. Just last night they had been square dancing, of all things. It seemed unbelievable now. He felt a kind of helpless resentment which he admitted, and a fear which he did not. He was well aware that he was shocked and saddened by the unthinkable predicament Aunt Tilly was in now. He had been fond of Turck, very, though in truth he regretted the old tartar's death principally for Aunt Tilly's sake. But, mingled with genuine grief was the resentment he felt at having death, that menacing presence, intrude on the way things were beginning for him now, each day new. But this is one day spoiled, he thought. And maybe many more. Would he have to bring Aunt Tilly back to her own house, now, to look after her? The thought dismayed him. Just when he was beginning to wake up every day with a feeling of wanting to live it, this blow had been struck. Failure, he thought wearily, it never fails. And death, he thought with a clutch of fear, that never fails either.

But. The thought of last night's joy was uppermost in him now, he knew, more so even than today's mournfulness. Last night we were dancing. A little wild, he'd been. Clumsy, of course. The fun of it, unbelievable now. She had moved, flashing, in and out, with a stern happy concentrated look, her white face turned pink. Wine by her fire afterward. They had talked about why she had come here, and she had opened herself to him again—another confidence, minuscule, but a confidence—"I think I needed the bare bones of beach and sea. My life there, my city life, felt stuffed. Overfed artificially, like a capon, my life felt to me in New York City. I was born near the sea, and to the sea I must needs, as they say, return." That spoofing again. The minute she exposes herself, she regrets it, he had thought. And he had had a queer frightened moment of wondering whether the constant repression of a naturally outgoing nature like hers would eventually warp it badly; and then had had one of his moments of being really cooled off about her.

He opened his door to get out, but before he could, Celeste had the other door open and was climbing up into the seat beside him. "Morning, Cabe," she said quietly, not looking at him, clicking the seat belt in place across her lap. She stared straight ahead, and tightened that strong white jaw.

"Good morning," he said carefully. They were both quiet. Embarrassed. How were they supposed to deal with sudden death, when in them and between them there was new life?

"Poor Tilly," Celeste said resentfully. "Damn, why couldn't they have died together?" She was really furious, and not surprised at her fury. She hated death—grim, dreary, black—she hated the whole aura of it, the brutality of its suddenness, and besides its obvious threat to her, she hated what it did to the people it touched. "I would have liked it to be other than this," she said, dispensing with it in her loud, positive way.

But then, impulsively, still not looking at Cabe, she put a hand on his knee. She was compelled to leave it there because she felt her fingers putting something into the warm bones beneath the cloth—there was a faint connecting sensation in her fingertips—and she felt her fingers, too, taking something from the warm bones, which traveled up into her and softened her shoulders.

"Freddy's still there," Cabe said. His knee tingled. For a minute there was no sadness in the world. None at all. "He called me again a minute ago. Lidi's on her way over."

"Poor Freddy." She took her hand away from his knees. "It must have been very hard on Freddy."

"He said he walked into the bedroom—he'd gone into the house after knocking for a while and getting no response, and immediately sensed something was wrong because it was nine o'clock and no coffee on the stove, no sound in the house. He walked into the bedroom and found Tilly lying in bed beside Turck, with her eyes closed. At first he thought they were both dead. But then Tilly opened her eyes. Turck didn't. Freddy said she only looked at him, didn't say a word. He couldn't tell me any more than that because he broke down and cried."

"Oh dearest Freddy. Of all people how fortunate that he was the one to be there first. How fortunate."

"Yes. I'm glad it wasn't me."

They drove through the mesh of simple snow, along the road with the grayness of winter trees bordering it, not talking, jogging in their seats from the bounce of the jeep. Still as statues. Lined faces, white hair stating a condition that dominated. Now the feeling grew, in this rackety little jeep with its frenzied windshield wipers, that they were the only two people in the world. The absence of talking was letting this be felt. It was a feeling defined by a sense of the enormousness of each of them. It was a single sensation because each of them felt it, but it was a unified sensation, too, simply because it was the unity of it that was creating the singleness of it. It was an incredible feeling they were experiencing and sharing, incredible because of the sensation of being so enormous and of having this enormousness blot out everyone else.

They were on their way to death and undertakers, and responsibilities neither one wanted and both dreaded, but for the moment they weren't giving any of that a thought because they were so satisfied and safe and huge and bonded and there was nothing else but this.

As they turned into Turck's driveway, Cabe said, "Celeste." She turned quickly to look at him, full and responsive. "Shall I bring Aunt Tilly back to my house now that Turck is gone, do you think?"

"Oh, Cabe, no! You wouldn't be able to practice!"

"I could go somewhere else and practice. I could move the piano."

"No, Cabe!"

"I would do it for Aunt Tilly," he said, "reluctantly of course, not happily. But I'd do it."

"The concert's next month, Cabe."

"Don't I know it."

"Well I don't think Tilly will want to. I don't think it will come to that. I think Tilly'll want to stay at Turck's. In that same bed."

"And alone with Beryl's kitchen stool?"

Celeste began to laugh, rather hysterically. Finally she said, blowing her nose, "Oh dear, it's so awful, Cabe, isn't it. Anyway," she then said strongly, "Tilly will decide. She will decide."

"I'm glad you're here, Celeste," Cabe said with great force and directness, keeping his eyes on the road.

"So am I," she spoke with such quick sincerity that he turned for a second to look at her. And it seemed to her that it was the very bleakness of that cold and noble eye that made him, and his words, so powerfully warm. Their eyes held. Then Cabe turned back to watch the road again. And Celeste looked away, satisfied, huge.

But in the next second, customary caution seized her, swept it all away. Why shouldn't she doubt this feeling? She should! She should be careful! She made a sudden sound with her mouth. "Dear god," she exclaimed, "look! There's that gruesome ambulance!"

Part Eight

∽∽ 1 ∽∽

L ATE February. The sun is hot today. A redwing sings
his song of arrival from the top of a swamp maple,
and in the warm blue space of sky above this island,
gulls soar, serene and searching. "What a day," Freddy says
ecstatically but wistfully, as though it were not for him. He
is sitting in an old canvas captain's chair beside Tilly's couch,
holding her uncaring hand in his. Lidi, with her hesitant
step, is moving about in a tight little red sweater and slacks,
watering the red geraniums. The clatter of dishes and the
sound of splashing water comes from the kitchen where
Celeste is busy cleaning up. And Cabe sits in Tilly's old
armchair by the bay window, reading D.H. Lawrence.

Turck has been dead three weeks, and these four have
spent an increasing amount of time, separately and together,
with Tilly, who wants to die and is managing to. In Turck's
house, not her own. "No, my dear, this is my home." Her
answer to Cabe's suggestion that she move in with him. She
will not go to the hospital, and Dr. Ratisbone has been

persuaded by the faithful four to let her be taken care of at home.

"Listen to this," Cabe says to everyone. "It's so remarkable, I feel obliged to make you all listen to it." He knew that he was not including Tilly, that she was far away from everybody, and that listening was gone from her. " 'She saw in the rainbow the earth's new architecture,' " he read, " 'the old brittle corruption of houses and factories swept away, the world built up in a living fabric of Truth, fitting to the over-arching heaven.' "

Lidi had stopped pouring, and was standing with the watering can in her hand. "I think that's fan*ta*stic," she burst out, after Cabe had stopped reading and was looking, yes, at her, she was certain he was looking at her because he saw that she would be the only one here to understand this! "It's so marvelously hopeful, isn't it?" Why couldn't she, when she wanted so much to, say more than this to Cabe, words that meant something, not just meaningless adjectives? Why did she flounder and sputter with this absurd emotional eager helplessness? She felt demeaned.

Cabe said he thought that's just what the paragraph was. Hopeful. That's why he had read it aloud. "No writer today would end a novel on such an apocalyptic note, unfortunately. I'm glad to find it somewhere in fiction. I like to be inspired."

Lidi put down the watering can. She brought her dry little rejoicing hands tight together across her chest, clasped them so that her knuckles showed white. "Yes. So do I. Wonderful to end the book on that hopeful note. I remember it. I think he's absolutely superb," she raved, "he was the first one ever to give me a feeling that physicality was good, not bad. Oh, he's, he's fan*ta*stic!"

"Tilly dear," Freddy said gently, "I want you to eat something."

Tilly lay on the couch propped up by three pillows, her white head absolutely still. There was no color in her face now because there was no rouge on it, no lipstick, no eyebrow pencil. Her hair was flat, because she would not let the hairdresser come. "Why?" she asked dully, when Lidi suggested it.

They all knew that Tilly wanted to die, and that she would. No one of them was insensitive enough to try to cheer her up or to cajole her into doing what she didn't want to do. Except sometimes Freddy, who could not bear it that she ate almost nothing. He would bring her a cup of broth, with the steam rising so encouragingly from it, and eagerly watch her begin to sip it but with no expression on her face, her eyes seeking nothing. Then she would put the cup down and push it away with faint disgust, as though it were an impertinence, and his heart would sink. But shouldn't he understand this? Shouldn't he know she had nothing to live for and that it was up to him, to all of them, not to help her to live, but to help her die?

And yet this was somehow impossible for Freddy. One of the things he had loved most about Tilly was her composed and jubilant immediacy, her love of being right at the center, not behind it or ahead of it. Vaguely he sensed that he himself was this way, that he lived for the day, for the moment, thinking very little about the past and not at all about the future. But to see Tilly without this marvelous core was appalling to him. Had Tilly's love of life—and that included the friends she loved so staunchly—been wholly dependent on one man? And shouldn't love of life be dependent, fundamentally, on oneself? Tilly no longer seemed interested in people. She was intent on the little things—her feet were dry; she wanted more pillows, then fewer pillows; she wanted the shades up, then down. Her mind wandered a great deal. She almost never mentioned Turck. Freddy was horrified to see a once full love reduced to this husk, to see the verity of undying love disproved. Sometimes it left him with nothing to hold on to.

"I'm going out to the kitchen and ask Celeste to heat up some broth," he said to Tilly's unyielding face with its sunken cheeks. "Or maybe you'd like a nice hot cup of tea, dear Til."

"Not now," she said tonelessly. "Thank you."

He sat up in the old captain's chair and pushed nervous fingers through his wild white hair, and sighed, and looked away from Tilly, out toward the blue and sparkling sea. He wished Turck were here. He missed him every day. It was strange and flat not to have Turck anymore. He thought that a breeze might be coming up—the meadow grasses were moving—and that when he and Lidi left, he'd go for a sail. But not with Turck. No more racing companion. Who could he get now to sail with him this summer? Who'd ever begin to replace dear old Turck?

Celeste swept into the room, wiping her hands on a kitchen towel, which she then began to fold neatly. She was all in black, slacks and jacket, and pinned to her lapel was a long-stemmed yellow daffodil. The effect of the long pale green tube of stem and the sunny blaze of the flower cup was astonishingly, wonderfully blatant. But it was as much a woman's uninhibited purpose and delight—the naturalness of the long stem, the idea of not cutting it short—as it was the yellow of the spring daffodil against black, that made it all so remarkable.

She was smiling. "I can't stop myself in someone else's

kitchen," she cried. "The night nurse is rather slapdash if you ask me. She left a white film, a sort of deposit of something, all around the inside of the stainless steel sink. So I've been at it. We need Ajax, Lidi, and I'll get it tomorrow. I've used the last of it."

Cabe closed his book. "You've restrained yourself in *my* kitchen," he said.

"There was no restraint involved, my dear Cabe. I wouldn't know where to begin, and even if I did, I don't think I could face it." She gave Cabe a wide smile that was just for him. She went across to the bay window and sat down on a straw hassock next to Cabe's chair and leaned her elbow on the arm of it. "What are you reading?" she asked intimately. "Still *The Rainbow*? I thought you'd finished it."

"I have. I've been rereading the last few pages."

"Oh, he read the last paragraph aloud," Lidi cried. "It's su*perb!*" And that flower flaunts, Lidi thought. It is insensitive here. It is in flamboyant disregard of Tilly, it is too loud, too happy, for Tilly. Like Celeste herself. Lidi drew her mouth tight. She could not bear the growing confidence of Celeste's soft blazing cheerfulness, and the way she sailed through the days reflecting some radiant power. She felt it was brazen of Celeste to be so unrestrainedly happy when no one else was. No one besides Cabe, that is. For he too was full of something, though it was held in. It seemed to Lidi that he was full of indrawn breath, full of joy sucked in and held, an expressiveness turned inward, seething there and only revealed by an occasional distention of his nostrils or a sudden loosening of his mouth.

"My," Lidi said, "that's quite a flower, Celeste. *Primavera*," she said a little tauntingly but also to show that she knew a thing or two about art.

Celeste ducked her nose into the daffodil. "Ummm. You should smell it."

"I will." Cabe leaned down and put his head to the flower. It seemed clear to Lidi that he would have liked to keep his head there, upon the flower, upon the breast it was pinned to. There was a moment for her, watching Celeste's sudden ardent look bent down on the gray head which was there under hers, of a sadness so deep that it was not characterized by any emotion, only by a word—unfairness. Unfairness was the name and the color and the size of herself standing in the emptiness that was the part of the room she was in. Fullness over there. Emptiness here, a sovereign, irreversible unfairness.

"I'm about to go," Cabe said, drawing his head away from the daffodil and standing up, closing his book. "The fellow's coming to tune my piano at three and I've got to be there. To let him in, anyway. Are you ready to go, Celeste?"

"Someone's got to stay with Tilly." Lidi pounced before Celeste could speak. "Freddy and I have to leave too. Wthin minutes. And Mrs. Smith's not coming until three-thirty."

"Well of course I'll stay," Celeste said unwillingly. She was startled. She had not once had to stay alone with Tilly, because always when she had been here, either Cabe, or the Luhins, or the cleaning woman or the night nurse had been here, too. Little chills of resistance ran across her shoulders. She would not be forced. "Maybe you and I should arrange all this beforehand," she said to Lidi in a loud, spaced voice. "I'm up to my ears these days with the concert—today was the printers about the programs, tomorrow tacking up posters all over the place, committee meeting at the hall the next day. What have you. So really we ought to get our schedules talked over ahead of time, don't you think so Lidi?"

Lidi's nostrils flared. "All right," she said shortly.

"You could come back and pick me up, couldn't you, Cabe? Or I could walk over after Mrs. Smith comes. That's another half hour. Too bad I didn't bring my own car. Are we going for our walk," she cried with a cheer she did not feel, standing there trapped, with her bold joyous flower quivering slightly on her breast, and her face unable to match it. Actually the daffodil was a declaration, because of the joyous motivation Celeste had had for putting it there, of how much more difficult it was now for her to contemplate staying alone with Tilly than it would ordinarily have been. She felt a small dismay she would not encourage. She set her jaw. "Do let's have our walk, Cabe, if it doesn't get to be too late. On this beautiful day."

"Absolutely. I'll come back for you. In half an hour if not before." Cabe went over to Tilly. He leaned down and put his mouth on her forehead. "I'll see you tomorrow, Aunt Tilly," he said, straightening up. "Do what the nurse says, my dear. At least take your sleeping pills."

Tilly's smile was no less sweet for being automatic. She lifted a hand slightly and then let it drop. "I don't need pills to sleep," she said with a trace of her old vigor. "All I *do* is sleep."

Cabe looked at her closely for a moment. Then he sighed and slapped his book against his leg, and swung away.

Celeste came over to the couch. She stood beside Freddy. She thought she could actually feel vibrations of concern emanating from Freddy. She felt that she was standing beside a pillar of concentrated concern, generated totally in itself and held within itself so that it was constantly being renewed there. She thought that Freddy did not need to do or say anything in order to convey how much he cared. It was there in him, needing no demonstration. It was the man himself.

Celeste absolutely felt this, and was awed. She was shaken. She felt a sort of panic. She wished Freddy wouldn't go.

~~~ II ~~~

"I really don't see why you stay, Celeste," Tilly said. She turned her head with difficulty on the pillow and looked up with dark swimming eyes that seemed to be looking through Celeste to something way beyond her. "I don't need all these people," she fussed.

"Would you rather be alone, Tilly? There's more to do in the kitchen if you'd like to just lie here alone. Do say, Tilly."

"No don't go and clatter around in the kitchen, dear. Sit down a minute here beside me. It must be almost time for the mail."

"Oh. Would you like me to go out and get the mail?"

"No. Turck always gets the mail."

This was the first time in days that Tilly had mentioned Turck. She spoke with such conviction that for a moment Turck was here. Celeste looked around the room with surprise, alertly. She saw the two old brown plush chairs by the fireplace, where he and Tilly must have sat every evening, opposite each other, their drinks in their hands and the fire lighting their two peaceful faces. And then, still vividly, she sensed Turck in other parts of the house, in his den, in the bedroom. She looked curiously at the hall leading to the bedroom, and imagined there the big fourposter bed, with the two white heads lying side by side on the pillows.

But Turck was not here. The sudden vividness of his past presence made his absence emphatically clear.

And she was staggered, suddenly, by the emptiness of this place. She had never felt such emptiness in her life. The clock on the mantelpiece ticked, the sun struck the geranium into a blaze of living red. And yet nothing lived here, not even the movement of the clock nor the flamboyance of the geraniums. It was death here. Turck was dead, and Tilly was already dead, and so the clock ticked for no ears and the geraniums blazed for no eyes.

Some of Celeste's omnipresent happiness faded down, and the sureness of it faltered. "Can I get you anything, Tilly? Can I make you more comfortable? Here, let me plump up your pillows."

"Oh, for mercy's sakes no. My pillows are all right. It's my feet that aren't. They bother me. They're so dry. They're so scratchy."

"Shall I rub them with lotion? Would you like that?"

"Yes, I would." A pause for breath, which came short. Tilly panted for a second, her eyes intent and distant with the strange treachery of pain and disorientation. "It's in the bathroom," she finally said, "on the shelf over the tub."

Celeste felt that she had a job to do and she would do it well. Fighting resentment and distaste, she found the bottle of lotion and brought it back to Tilly on the couch, and folded the blanket back from the white sticks that were legs, and took the knitted bed socks from the icy, soft feet. "Oh, Tilly, they're so cold. Why didn't you say? We could have gotten you a hot water bottle. I will, as soon as I've used this lotion. Here. Let me get some circulation going."

A cold, scaly foot lay docile in Celeste's hands. She felt the warmth of her hands, soft warm skin against cold rough skin, and she saw that there was some kind of declaration here. Thus an unwanted task became, faintly, something of interest. Whatever the declaration was, it eluded her, although it was providing some purpose to the task. Next she felt a flair of irritation at the supineness of this foot, at the demand of its supineness.

She began to smooth the lotion over the toes and in between them, attentive to the ticking of the clock, which spoke of ongoingness. And then the attentiveness of her ears caught the distant muffled sound of surf. Then she had a quick strange hallucination—this couch with Tilly on it and herself sitting beside it in this captain's chair, were on an island which was the size only of a large rock. And all around them was the sea.

She began to smooth the lotion into the foot to the rhythm of the clock.

Then she felt a foot, for the first time. In her hands, she felt the bones and joints of toes under her fingers, and she recognized that she was holding a woman's foot in her two hands. She saw that she had never *felt* a foot before this, or felt, even known what a foot was for. And now it was *for* nothing! It was terrible to her that it was useless, that it was ending. It had come flailing out of a womb, it had stood and walked and run and danced through eighty years of life, and here it was, ending—dry and ancient and cold. And with the feel and the vision of this poignantly personal part of an old woman, Celeste again had the sense of some sort of declaration which she couldn't name but which expanded her.

Now she sensed, with interest bordering on pleasure, that

her hands were slowing and flowing into this foot as she rubbed and pressed and kneaded it. She almost felt that the foot was responding. She saw that she was soothing the foot. She looked up at Tilly, whose eyes were closed, her mouth partly open as though she were abandoning herself to being soothed. But Celeste really felt as though it were herself who was being soothed. This was in one way the sensuous pleasure of self-soothing.

Now the techniques of soothing seemed endless. She began to like to stroke this foot that was growing warmer, less rough, she felt she could endlessly rub balm into this needy, receiving foot. She finished with it and put the bed sock back on, and took up the other foot. It occurred to her that when she had finished with both feet, she would be sorry.

Tilly spoke. "That feels so good."

"I'm glad."

"You do it better than Mrs. Smith. She's just a lick and a promise."

"Could I rub your back, Tilly?" Daringly. How far did she really want to go? Feet were one thing. But a naked back, and the heart beating under it, did she really want to spread herself that far? She hoped Tilly would say no.

"No. Thank you, dear. Mrs. Smith will do that. I've got to occupy her. She's so costly."

"Would you like a cup of tea now, Tilly? Hot tea might be nice."

"No." And in a moment, after another struggle with breathing, "but what I *would* like is a small glass of port." And before Celeste could move she murmured, "Yesterday when I was in Australia, I saw a book in that living room with the gold brocade couch. It said *Where We Are* on the jacket but I couldn't read it very well because it was blurred in with the pictures. And I went ahead and took it on myself to send the gold pebbles to Agnes, but Hy was furious with me. I stole them."

Celeste felt a very faint stir of sympathy, very faint, very far away, and it drew her face into a concentration of grieving concern. She folded the blanket back over Tilly's legs. And then she picked up Tilly's hand, light as dust. How beautiful it was, dead white, with its coils of purple vein, and its lovely long unchangeable shape. To hold and feel a hand—immediately this again was something new. She felt that Tilly was quietly and willingly letting her hand be held. Not supinely, but willingly. So. There was self in Tilly still. There was will in her, and life. She thought that Tilly was letting her hand be comforted, and through it her confused and detached and helpless heart.

For only a second, and very faintly, Celeste was out from under the restraints of her life. Just a little bit. She felt no resentments, no demands, she felt a tiny spark of free will, centered in her chest and expanding there. And she felt as though she should pat herself on the back. She felt as though something had just freed her. She wanted to hold onto this. And the sense of Cabe wove in and out. She wished she could hold onto this feeling of having "made it." If only she could define it better, learn it, keep it. She liked it. It was a new feeling and yet it wasn't. She loved holding this old dying hand. Her fingers felt the way they had the day she touched Cabe's knee in the jeep, the same faint connecting sensation. There was a power here that transcended self-service.

She rose and picked up the bottle of lotion and put the cap on it, standing very still in her black suit with the wild spring yellowness of the flower on it, here on her little island with an old woman.

~~ III ~~

THERE was not enough wind for Freddy to sail. Driving along the High Road with Lidi at his side, he exclaimed about this, rather passionately, like a disappointed child. "I thought there'd be a breeze, but there isn't. It's died down."

"Oh? You wanted to sail?"

"I sure did. I wanted very much to sail. Get the cobwebs out of my head."

"You seem *down*, Freddy. *Are* you down?"

"No, I'm not *down*." Defensively. "I do find it hard to see dear Tilly the way she is, though. Don't you?"

"Well, it's awful," Lidi said, but shutting it out.

"What gets me is that she doesn't want anything, anymore. I mean, *want*. When you stop wanting, what is there that's left?"

"Oh god, I presume nothing, when stamina runs out, physical and emotional stamina. It takes energy to care about living. I think old age is a sort of dreadful laziness that takes over. *I* know, because more and more there's so much that doesn't seem worth the effort to *me*. So I know. Unfortunately. Yes, I think it's a sort of stamina thing. A sort of deterioration of stamina, arteries, brain, what have you." Well put, she thought. If only I could talk like that to Cabe.

"As though you had an eggbeater inside of you that kept whipping you up, and then it stops, you mean?" Freddy had never felt that way.

257

"Good analogy, Freddy. So what *is* that eggbeater?"

"I don't know. I wouldn't know."

They drove along in silence for a while, the two white heads, once startling a flock of hundreds of starlings lining the telephone wires along the road in side-by-side exactitude like a lengthy string of close-packed identical thick black beads. Clouds of them flew up at the sound of the approaching car, the air was suddenly full of falling sweeping particles of black rising as one in a great upward swirl, then dropping separately like scattering leaves toward the ground, to be lifted again and carried and dispersed. Even above the noise of the car Lidi and Freddy could hear the dense vibration of wings and chirping.

It was a far-spread palpitant mass of sound which stirred Freddy. "That's splendid," he said. He was excited. He felt happy again. "That's really something, isn't it." In a minute he said, "I think I'll chop some wood when I get home."

But Lidi's mind was on something else. "I do think it was very tasteless of Celeste to come in flaunting that flower," she said. "She seems to have no regard for Tilly at all."

"Why should Tilly mind?" asked Freddy casually, perhaps wearily.

"Well, because it's such a declaration. Of life, somehow. It spreads vibrant life all over the place."

"I don't suppose Tilly noticed. Or if she did, cared. And if she had cared, she would probably have loved it. I thought it was great."

"Actually I wish Celeste and Cabe wouldn't be quite so *obvious*. In front of Tilly, I mean. It's perfectly clear," she said spitefully, "that they have a thing about each other. Don't you think so?" She wanted to be told that she was wrong, that nothing was going on between Cabe and Celeste. "Don't you see it?"

"How could you miss it?" Freddy said shortly. He was so tired of this.

"Yes. Well, I think it's terribly inconsiderate of both of them."

"Goodness, I don't see why. I think it's wonderful," he said longingly, "just wonderful."

Lidi wanted to get somewhere in this. What did she want? She wanted to castigate Freddy for his approval. She wanted to turn Freddy against them, and she wanted him to side with her in denouncing them. And also she was made to feel a tight-lipped helpless anger by the liberating thing that it was for Freddy to feel happy for their happiness. She had a momentary feeling of Freddy as being like the starlings, free in the sky, flying. He was in motion and she was bound in chains. She hated his motion, and wanted it. She hated her chains, and wanted them.

"Actually, I don't think they're really right for each other," she said, "Celeste's an extrovert. Cabe's much too inward for her. *I* think."

"Lidi, for goodness' sakes, why does it *matter* so much."

"Heavens, it doesn't *matter*. How absurd." But of course it did matter, crushingly. It was getting more and more intolerable for her to see what was happening to Cabe. Cabe was hers, he was the promise of her becoming. She had never stopped believing that one day he would look at her, and see her, and hear her, and that then their marvelous friendship would begin. In spite of all the evidence to the contrary, she still clung to this belief.

And the freshness of Cabe and Celeste together was having another undermining effect on her, it was emphasizing the staleness of herself and Freddy together. As she watched the radiance expand around those two, she was made more and more aware of the silence and the lifelessness that em-

anated from herself and Freddy. There was a tightness about
her and Freddy together that was like a dead weight. Whereas
there was a radiance and a flow about Cabe and Celeste
together which created an effulgence that tormented Lidi
and seemed to her to disavow everything she and Freddy
had ever been to each other. Lidi couldn't feel close to Celeste anymore because of this. She was ragingly jealous of
Celeste. But at the same time she said to herself: I must give
up this thing about Cabe.

"You know what I like," Freddy said suddenly. "I like
that sign." He pointed to a neat gray clapboard house set
back from the road, with long black shutters folded away
from the windows, and above the little porch roof, a black
sign lettered in gold, *Island Coal Company*. "I like the house
too. It's nice and simple."

At once Lidi saw how beautiful this building was, with
its clean gray paint and its sharp black trim. She had passed
it a thousand times and never noticed it. She was astonished
at Freddy. "It *is* beautiful," she said. Who was Freddy? She
looked at him. How everything about Freddy deceived her
into thinking him incapable of esthetic sensitivity! She looked
at his clothes: beige corduroy jacket with leather elbow
patches, brass-buttoned red flannel vest, tight-fitting, brand-
new, prefaded jeans. And on his feet, the red and blue argyle
socks Tilly had knitted for him. A careful dresser, Freddy.
Even a flashy dresser. A sucker for the latest thing. And yet.
There was the pure and beautiful little building. And un-
Freddy-like, he loved it.

She felt a flat desolation. She was a million miles from
Freddy. She felt the crime of mismating—how it laid waste,
how it diminished and how it devoured—declaring itself to

her. And she said to herself: Marriage is an institution for the propagation of waste.

Suddenly she felt very tired. She thought she would take a nap when she got home. She looked down at her hands, which were puckered and glazed, like polished, grained leather, and rough, old. My hands look older than any other part of me.

She drew a long denying breath and opened her purse and took out a pad and pencil. She began to write.

> *There is a heaven,*
> *It was being young.*

Just like that. The words had popped into her head and she had written them down.

"Freddo," she cried. "I've written a poem. It's *good.*"

"You've written a poem? When? Now?"

"Yes. We were driving along and there it was, in my head."

"Let's hear it."

" 'There is a heaven/ it was being young,' " she declaimed with nervous triumph.

"Is that the whole thing?" Freddy asked after a minute. He was frowning attentively and considerately.

"Why, *yes.*" Her voice rose.

"Shouldn't it be 'is being young'?"

"Oh for heaven's sake, Freddy. That's what's good about it, the 'was.' Don't try to be pragmatic about poetry. I can't tell you precisely what it means, but I feel that it says something profound, *that way.* With the 'was.' It's the 'was' that does it. Otherwise the poem's nothing, nothing."

"I still don't see why you can't simply say 'there was a

heaven, it was being young.' Or even 'it's heaven to be young.' "

She tossed her head, her flat white hair swinging away from her shoulders. "Dear god," she murmured scathingly.

His face blurred. But then he straightened up. And in his usual way of rescuing them both, he said jocularly, "Well, I guess there's only one poet in this family, and it isn't me."

And so they drove along, and arrived home, and had some tea together, and Freddy went out to chop wood, and Lidi prepared their breaded bay scallops and fresh asparagus to cook later, and then went into her cubicle to type the poem she would send tomorrow to *Viewpoints*.

The western sky above the bare low hills along the sea was spread grandly with broad rose rivers and lavender streaks. Lidi stood watching the sky as it throbbed into vaster flamingo-rose pastures and deeper purple streams. And with something rilling along her spine that could bring tears, she suddenly thought: Oh, before it is too late how I want something to jell, to formulate, to arrive at a place recognized, instead of this formless mass moving out, like a river moving out into a sea and being lost in it. How I want to put a stop to this endless flow outward that somehow can't be encircled, be called by some name, *be* something. It's all flux, nonarrival. An unending flowing away.

It was mostly Lidi who put the records on, after the fire was lighted and the drinks had been poured. Lately she had begun to want music, instead of a book at this hour, "to *feel*," she said to Freddy, "instead of *thinking* all the time." She said she hoped it would be all right with him to play a classical record or two occasionally, before the six-thirty news came on.

It was all right with Freddy. He even enjoyed the background music as he read his spring catalogues, or his noisily turned newspapers. And once, to Lidi's surprise, *he* went to put the record on before she could get there, murmuring, "Nice tune," as he stood with a look of timid curiosity on his dark tense face, listening to the opening notes of a Beethoven piano concerto.

And again tonight, while she was pouring her drink, suddenly there was Freddy, sliding a record out of its envelope, settling it down onto the turntable, pushing over the switch.

Music burst forth, the suave velvety sweep of *My Fair Lady*. Boldly sudden, super-sweet, it sprang into this settled room, into Lidi—"I have often walked, down this street before." Shocking. For a second she was rigid with opposition to this glossy flouting of esthetics. She whirled around with her glass in her hand, hard black eyes accusing.

But then she was smiling. It was a smile that grew entirely by itself, taking her over. How astonishing of Freddy to have put this on!

She looked at him now. She saw him standing there, saying nothing, just standing stock-still in front of the record player as though he had been shocked into immobility by this cascade of sound. She saw—Freddy. He was young. He was the tall young man she had first danced with on the deck of the *Mauretania*. He hadn't changed. The dark-haired man was there, inside the white-haired man. The music made them the same man, so that a Feddy of all time stood there. And at the same instant the music had swept her out of an encasement and over to this Freddy who was both Freddies. And she wasn't this Lidi standing here, either. She was young and loose, like something cracked open and pouring out. She was touching Freddy all down the front of her body, very lightly, and sweeping across the floor with him on this romantic river of music.

The delicacy. The points of her breasts and the bones of her hips under the chiffon, chaste, delicate along the front of Freddy. They moved to the music coming from the ballroom as lightly as though they were the air itself. They were gossamer against each other in the dark. Withheld, but the delicacy getting finer, sharper and sharper. Chiffon floated out. A soft night, the hiss of the sea slashing against the sides of the rushing vessel, stars, millions of them, all over the sky. How could a man's body be so delicate, like fine wire? Freddy, withholding himself tensely and chivalrously, and her chasteness questioning itself, turning electric.

Standing beside the bar table in her tight red slacks and sweater, gripping her glass in both unsteady hands, she kept on smiling in a fatuous wide dreamy way, imagining herself gliding across to Freddy and holding her arms out and dancing away with him, back to there, back to them, there. "I could have danced all night, I could have danced all night."

Faint chills swept over her skin. She was there, putting her ageless self against the delicacy and decent vigor of this ageless Freddy and sliding away with him on glissades of music.

The fire spat and crackled in a fury of combustion. But in front of it the iron Hessians stood stopped in their strides— Onward christian soldiers, marching as to war. And on the calico-papered walls, Audubon birds in curly maple frames were stopped on branches and in flight or with a beak poised to snatch a berry. And Freddy stood stopped. And Lidi. Only the loud shaft of fire was in motion. And the music. And the faint presence on the air of asparagus cooking in the distant kitchen.

All the inanimate parts of this room were made to seem more powerfully inanimate by the motionlessness of the man and woman in it. And the very perfection of the room, its strict neatness, its museum-like adherence to correctness, reinforced this aura of inactivity, of life stopped at the level of antique andirons and the long wordless habit of drinks and a fire and the evening meal cooking.

Lidi stood as stiff and still as a mannequin in a store window. But inside herself she was wonderfully alive. She had been brought back to a happy light center where the promise of love goes on forever, and she was dancing. She stood there with an enormous unguarded smile on her face, in her withered hand a glass that caught the light of the fire. And over there in front of the record player was Freddy, stock-still, looking at her. But she was dancing with him. Immaculately, she was waltzing off with him on the sweep of this caressing music, full of the absoluteness, the never-ending-ness, of the promise of loving him.

She thought of her poem. And saw what it meant.

All this had happened in only seconds. And now Freddy moved. He crossed over to his chair by the fireplace. He threw her a furtive look, gentle, searching, embarrassed. He smiled.

She was still smiling. Freddy hadn't seen her face like this in years—exposed, quite sweet, unsure. Their smiles grew. Neither of them spoke.

⤚⤙ IV ⤚⤙

THERE were too many people. So confusing to have this house so full of people. This wasn't what the house was for. There was no sense to any of this, it was like a stilted joyless party repeated over and over again, every day. And in addition, she couldn't make out the pictures all over the jacket of the book in Australia with that nice title *Where We Are*. But it was very clear to her that there were lots of people here all the time and that it was an unnatural way to treat her home. I'm glad Freddy comes, Tilly thought inconsistently. And dear Cabe. I like men, she thought without interest. And I don't blame Hy for being furious about the gold pebbles.

There's no earthly sense in my going on like this, Tilly thought now with sudden lucidity. It's eating up money I want Albert and Mary and the children to have. And dear Cabe, I see Cabe and Celeste growing so happy, and I want them to be free of this dead house. Every day, every day they have to come here. Stuff and nonsense.

Dear Cabe. And now a miraculous thing happened to Tilly. She moved her head a little and in doing so she saw the bottle of sleeping pills on her bedside table. As though for the first time, she saw a little plastic bottle, and, in it, many many sleeping pills. And simultaneously she heard Cabe's voice, "Do what the nurse says, my dear. At least take your sleeping pills."

"All I *do* is sleep." It was such a miraculous and at the same time such a simple solution that Tilly almost laughed. Though suddenly cagey, she did not allow herself to laugh. Mrs. Smith was in the living room with the TV turned down low. She must not let Mrs. Smith hear a laugh.

It was unexpected and reassuring to Tilly to have this faint familiar sense of doing what was best and what was sensible, which had been the core of her life. For a moment she felt tiredly, unwillingly alive, alive as she had used to be, weeks ago, before Turck died. But how unwanted this feeling was. She hadn't the strength of body or of will to handle it. And yet she had a flicker of something like satisfaction, as though she had tasted all of her life in one bite and had found that it was good.

She listened to the clock, which in this house had ticked off the best hours of her life. She heard it as she had then, with Turck, and she realized momentarily and vividly that it was unbearable to have the safe cocooned process of dying be arrested and to let in for a second the glaring and impossibly strong light of living. Listening to the clock had brought Turck back, and so she knew, again with that faint sense of reassurance, why she had wanted to die, and now would.

She wished she didn't have to hear the television going on and on with its charged life, saccharine music, gunshots, and she sensed wearily that that hodgepodge of obscene noise she had once enjoyed now represented everything in this world that was well worth leaving. Above its drone, the clock struck five. Five clear, conclusive strokes. The voice of order and of time.

Tilly sat up. She hesitated a second, feeling a faint sweep of alarm. And then, as practically and as hungrily as though she were eating handfuls of peanuts, she began to swallow the sleeping pills and to wash them down with water. When she had swallowed them all, she turned out the light and lay back on the pillow. Beside her Turck said, "That's my Til. Enjoy." She smiled comfortably and crossed her hands over her chest and went to sleep.

⚶ V ⚶

AROUND ten o'clock, Cabe looked up from his book, Walt Whitman's *Sundown Papers,* and had the clear idea that he wanted to walk over, on this night that was perhaps starry, and look in on Tilly. The walk would do him good, and he had an uneasy feeling, anyway, about Mrs. Smith, who seemed always either to be watching television or to be asleep when he dropped in.

He yawned. But the yawn echoed a richly benign saturation of everything he was filled with, not a finished kind of tiredness. It was a full world he lived in now. All the spaces of himself were filling up yet seemed endlessly to accommodate more influx. Expansion seemed endless, no limitations to his body or to his spirit. He felt absolutely immense all the time, bewilderingly blown up, incredulous with expansion.

He looked at the pages open across his knees. " 'Nobody, I hope,' " he read aloud, " 'will accuse me of conceit in these opinions of mine own capacity for doing great things.' " He pushed out his full lips in a smacking sound of approval. Then he clapped the book shut and stood up and put the screen in front of the fire and went out to get his jacket.

He swung along the creek road at a good pace, for the night was intensely cold. Above him, the sky was brilliant with stars, the moon serene and pure in its fullness. No wind stirred, and the clarity of the night had a sharpness as of sound. In the stillness, the creek, the narrow, deep thread of it which was not frozen, curled along with a tiny sound. He walked swiftly, happily, and in a few minutes he reached Tilly's house, which was dark.

꿈ᄼᄼᄼ VI ᄼᄼ

CABE felt very calm. He felt a little sick, but nevertheless he felt amazingly calm. Spread out. It seemed to him that hours had passed since he had walked into the living room and found Mrs. Smith asleep in front of the television, and had then walked into Tilly's bedroom and found her dead.

Actually, no more than fifteen minutes had passed. The ambulance, which against all his instincts he had allowed an hysterical Mrs. Smith to call, was on its way.

And now he sat on the edge of Tilly's bed. He had tried gently and unsuccessfully to close the black gap of her open mouth, and repelled, had given up. Then he had taken a comb from his pocket and with it had awkwardly tidied her unkempt hair, thinking that she would have wanted him to. With a practicality that he was somehow ashamed of, he had taken pains not to touch the empty pill bottle, or the glass, or the carafe, and had warned Mrs. Smith, more vulnerable than he to suspicion, not to touch them either. But he had only thought for a second of this possibility and then dispensed with it. Tilly claimed him.

He loved what Tilly had done. He thought it made perfect sense and he couldn't even remotely see why taking one's life, in a case like this, could be regarded as a cop-out. He thought it marvelous that she had had the lucidity and the common sense and the spunk to do it. He could only feel glad for her, and for everyone.

But more than that, it was as though she had simplified everything, for herself and for him. She had never been one to sit back and let the substance of her life develop without her say-so. She had made the substance of her life happen. And so, she had not waited for death to come to her, she had gone to death. It was an action of such spirit and such resolve that he could not see it as having brought about an ending. No. Tilly, lying here as white and still as marble, nevertheless seemed to him to be electric with aliveness. He thought, reverently, that Catsy had had a lot of her Aunt Tilly in her.

He felt everything in his life explained.

Far down the road he heard the growing wail of the ambulance siren. He sighed heavily, dreading its energetic, crisislike intrusion. But for another minute he was here alone with reason and peace. He spoke to Tilly. "I never underestimate *your* capacity for doing great things, Aunt Tilly," he said to her quietly. Then he leaned over and with tenderness put his lips to her cold still cheek and kissed her goodbye.

Part Nine

I T has been a long afternoon, here on Cabe's living room floor, going through cartons and old suitcases brought down from the attic in search of memorabilia and documents and photographs which Tilly's son, Albert Bernhard, wants sent to him in Australia.

"I don't see how we can select," Celeste said, "I have the feeling he should have everything that's here."

"I agree. But we can at least eliminate the duplicates. How many of his cousin Catsy playing tennis, for heaven's sakes, does Albert need? One, I'd say."

Celeste is tired. Her bones ache from sitting cross-legged for such a long time. She and Cabe, surrounded by a sea of paper, are side by side on the worn rose and blue oriental rug that smells of dust and centuries. Penning them in, cartons and suitcases emptied of their valuables look looted and betrayed and temporarily helpless, as though waiting only to be refilled and closed again. It is getting on toward five o'clock. Down the road, the clock in the white steeple of the Congregational Church will soon strike the hour, leaving ripples of silence on the country air.

"I've just about decided to send the lot to him," Cabe says, sighing and casting a jealous look toward the piano, "and to hell with the cost."

The front of Tilly's mahogany breakfront is splashed with a deep winey light from paths of late sun slanting through west windows. Motes of dust spin and glitter in it. There is a quiet here, of time, of the past, of two hearts distracted and subdued. The sea sounds, way off across the fields. The sun makes two gold moons of Celeste's glasses which she is wearing on a cord around her neck. "When you begin to wear your glasses around your neck, you know you've admtted something to yourself," she had laughed to Cabe, earlier, when she had taken them out of her purse and put them on. She has just pulled them away from her face, leaving a small pink indented crescent over the bridge of her white nose.

In her lap is an enlargement of a photograph of Tilly and her husband, Augustus Bernhard. They are standing in front of a long, low-roofed stucco house half concealed by billows of globularly clipped shrubbery. Tilly is young, perhaps thirty, and slim and incisive as an arrow, in a straight beltless dress ending at her knees, and with a cloche hat that sits on her ardent head like a mushroom. She has the look of simmering contentment and interest that Celeste remembers as being so characteristic of her. Augustus Bernhard is tall, broad, blond and complacent, wearing a dark suit and tie, and clamping a white straw hat against one leg. An unlikely man for Tilly, Celeste thinks, but he had the air of possessing Tilly. They seemed to possess one anoher. They seemed fitted together as tightly, as neatly, if perhaps as predictably, as a picture puzzle.

"Do you think I could ask Albert for this picture?" Celeste says. "Or rather, couldn't I ask him if I might have a copy made? I would very much like to have this picture."

"I should certainly think so. Or just go ahead and have it copied without asking. Why ask? Of course he'll say yes." The sun is making of his longish gray hair a dusty, silvery light in the dim room. He has had no chance to get his hair cut since Tilly's death a week ago, and he badly needed one even then. Uncomfortable, he plucks constantly at sideburns grown thick and grizzly.

"I'll do that," Celeste says. "Because I do want a picture of Tilly. I miss her." I need her.

Tilly's death had been a blow to Celeste. She felt an irreplaceable loss. Tilly had gone, and with her had gone what Tilly had shown her. Or, what she had shown herself through Tilly. She felt that something begun had been capriciously stopped. Having experienced through Tilly a trace of longed for, welcome, but disbelieved-in unrestraint, she was sure that a repetition of this feeling was only possible through Tilly. She was even, at times, enraged with Tilly for deserting her, for taking away with her this secret of herself. She felt as though Tilly had absconded with whatever hope there was for her, as though it were Tilly who held the secret of how to unleash it, not herself. Tilly had taken the best part of her, and now she would never know what it was. When she had seen Tilly lying still as stone in her coffin, a primitive helplessness had made her think, for a horrified second, that she would strike her.

"I miss Aunt Tilly too," Cabe said. "More than I would ever have thought possible. She became something absolutely splendid to me by dying that way. She always was splendid, but she topped everything by that act, as far as I'm concerned."

"I know you feel that way. I wish I could see it your way. I don't. And it was so strange to me how a loving person like Tilly could fade out so in terms of loving. I mean, toward the end she really didn't seem to be thinking much about Turck. Or her family. Or anyone, for that matter."

"To me her suicide was a supreme act of love," Cabe said quietly. "She had told me repeatedly that she felt she was being a burden to us. And that she dreaded seeing her money going for round-the-clock nursing instead of to Albert. I think she did it for love of us, as well of course as having the common sense to know that it was utterly pointless to go on living."

Celeste found agreement softening some of her resentment, her deprivation. "Yes," she said. She felt little pinchings in her nostrils that were tears. "Yes, I see, somehow, that even though she wasn't behaving lovingly, I knew all about her anyway."

Down the road the church clock began to strike, pure resonant bells spaced in stately pronouncement. There was a peace about five o'clock, in an old room full of old things, and outside the sun getting lower, and firing and gilding everything with its reddish light. Celeste had the comfortable feeling of two people in this room together in a past and together in a present, and with an ancient sun giving them a blazing benediction.

She sighed noisily, and blew her nose, thus dispensing with the imminence of tears. She felt rather more peaceful. Yawning, she shifted her stiffened legs, and thrust them out straight in front of her, and leaned back against the arm of the couch. "I do think you are saying something very wise," she said gently.

"I think it's time we stopped for today, and had a drink," Cabe said. He was tired. He felt detached from himself, even from Celeste. He was in the nowhere of memory, that tenebrous land, so drawn back into its unaliveness that the present was unalive, too. He had lost himself. He was neutralized, he was out of his body, and in a still life of the past which had saddened him with its hopelessness. Not Tilly's, but his own, the Turnbulls', Catsy's. There had been many photographs of Catsy in Tilly's albums. And photographs of Mr. and Mrs. Turnbull—a mountainous Mrs. Turnbull overflowing a straw peacock chair on a summer veranda, a reserved, stoic-looking Mr. Turnbull standing with an arm around the tiny waist of his sister Tilly, on a beach, probably here on the island. Cabe's heart was sore with a rediscovery of love for the Turnbulls, the defeated dominating giantess, and the contained, gentle man. And there was picture after picture of the lovely decent grinning girl, their daughter, his wife. And himself. Growing older. Growing soberer, reserved, like Mr. Turnbull. No wonder he had had an affinity for the man.

"Here's one of Catsy at Cloverly," Cabe said, picking up a cracked, faded sepia photograph of a semicircle of piously important-looking girls in white blazers.

"Oh, let's see," pounced Celeste.

As she took the photograph from Cabe, the soft pad on the side of her hand touched his fingers. Electric, hot, the touch swept up her arm and through her chest and down into her loins. "Oh, it's the hockey team," she cried nervously, "and here's Christina, for goodness' sakes."

She felt vigorously alive all at once, sitting here amid these piles of old paper lives, old cardboard sorrows. And with an elation that was quite specific she saw that what this evidence of the sadness and insufficiency of the past was doing was miraculously to expose the happiness and completion of the present. She saw that this was a revelation. The past was the very opposite of the present, the past was tragic and the present was not tragic at all, the past was full of hopelessness and the present was loud with hope. And she said to herself: It is unbelievable, it is instant magic that cannot last, to be sixty-five and all at once to see the present, and even the future, as being so infinitely better than the past.

"Whatever became of Christina?" Cabe was asking.

"She lives in France. She married a nice fat Frenchman and they live in a little chateau with a vineyard. She had so many children I lost count. She turned Catholic."

"She was always a decisive female," Cabe said, drily.

"Oh she was, she was," Celeste sang. Christina seemed light years away.

Suddenly it came over Cabe that he was glutted with photographs, and that he had been stupefyingly tranced by this documentation of long-gone sorrows and half-lives, irresolvable lives. He had the feeling of coming suddenly out of bewitchment, out of a dusty haunting unreality he had allowed himself to be taken in by. He was not wholly there, nor wholly here, he was nowhere, and with sorrow lying heavily in his stomach like a weight. He looked at the clamor of photographs, their somehow senseless claim, and desperately wanted, not so much to forget them as not to be seduced by them, deluded by them into something that wasn't himself, now. It felt unreal to wallow in the past like this. The present moment seemed brilliant to him, absolutely immediate and absolutely alive.

He began to shuffle the piles of photographs together, helter-skelter, and to dump them into an open suitcase. He filled it to the top, and then he closed the cracked brown leather lid, and decisively snapped the old brass locks. "There," he said loudly, trying to finish with this, to get out of it, wanting to be helped out of it.

On the floor next to the suitcase, the toe of Celeste's black patent leather espadrille was ashine in a last faded patch of sun. He straightened up and turned to look at her. It seemed to him that neither of them had been here and now suddenly they were. In the dusk her face was a whitish blur. Pensiveness sharpened the fineness of the bones, giving her face a spectral beauty. He saw her glasses rising and falling on her black sweater. On her breasts. He imagined her breasts, not for the first time. They must be very white, like her face and throat. They must be very white and smooth, like the smoothness of her face.

The present struck Cabe with a wonderful force. He felt a great relieved surge of rejuvenation. Then in his head was exactly what he wanted to say, and he said it. "Celeste, we've never talked about the night we met."

"No." She gave him a frightened smile.

"Well, let's talk about it."

"All right." Her eyes were startled. This was not Cabe.

"I kissed you. Do you remember that?"

There was utter silence in this room. Off there, over the sea, the complaining squawk of a gull insisted. And then the sound of a little plane grew, came slowly across and died away, leaving a greater silence. These noises were prominent because they were believable. Cabe's words, the nearest sound, were unbelievable. They hung in the air like soap bubbles about to burst.

Celeste began to laugh, wonderfully. "*Do* I remember. But frankly I'm surprised to know *you* remember. I'd thought you hadn't."

Cabe dropped his elbows to his spread knees and tensed his head toward her. "And I thought *you* hadn't," he said after a minute.

Celeste's face lit up with an instant, guileless responsiveness. She felt a joy akin to prayer. "Do you mean that it meant something to you, that night?"

"Meant something. That's certainly a mild word for it. Yes, it meant something. You would have had me on your trail if it hadn't been for Christina."

"*Christina?* What did *Christina* have to do with it?" There was something new in Cabe, a decisiveness, a direction, a force. It thrilled her. It opened her and softened her and invited her. She began to look at him with an honest searching fervor he had never seen.

"Christina warned me off," Cabe said tightly. He drew a long, rather hissing breath, and then with his jaws locked, held it, contained it, until he exhaled and spoke again. "She told me to keep hands off because you and Mort were engaged. The day after we had lunch. Remember, we had lunch? She told me to lay off. And Mother. Mother wasn't interested."

"No. I can see that she wouldn't have been. And I can also understand Christina's doing that—her loyalty to Mort was total."

"You and I would probably have done the same thing," he said appeasingly. "That was the code then. And we were above all creatures of the code. Oh my yes."

Sudden fury shook Celeste. "How could you," she blazed out, "let *Christina* tell you what to do about *me?* And your mother," she shouted, "my god, your mother!"

Cabe looked surprised the way a man looks first of all surprised when he has been slapped. Then his face froze. And a bleak, judicial eye stared her down. Deliberately composed, nevertheless he was shattered. Yet he was tuned up, intense, on the edge of something. Between them there was something flaring up that was no longer cautious, muffled, oblique.

"I can't take this in, Cabe. I simply can *not* register it. In other words. If you hadn't listened to Christina that day . . ." She stopped. She felt so preposterously helpless. She was enraged beyond rage, to the point almost of acquiescence; and so stunned by the paradoxes of existence that she grew calm quite suddenly, knowing that what this had added up to simply had to be assimilated, and accepted, and borne. She closed her eyes for a moment, whispering, "Well, what's done is done." Then she opened them and looked full at Cabe. "So *that's* why I never saw you again," she said in a soft, appalled voice.

"I'm afraid so." He looked down at his hands, which were trembling. "But does it matter that much? Did it?" Failure had fallen over him like a familiar heavy gray cloak, almost welcome, as though an essential part of him that had temporarily gone away had now returned. Sickened, he felt like himself again, rather proudly, not humbly. Yet oddly, though he was back in the refuge of not expecting anything, in the next second he was tuned up, keen. Failure/hope was violently at war in him, he was jittery with it, on edge.

Celeste's face was intense and open and sad, but reconciled. "Yes, it did matter," she said. "It mattered terribly." She wasn't even aware that she was saying what she had sworn never to say to Cabe. She looked at him. She saw a large man, his shoulders sagging, his gray head thrust toward her in a suppliant way. She saw the longing mouth, the cold brave eyes. She did not see the boy who had kissed her. She saw this man who was not that boy.

She was full of confusion, suddenly. Her hand went to

her glasses hanging around her neck. She picked them up and began to tap them nervously against her breast. "Well, dearest Cabe, that was a long time ago," she said then, drawing up a long practical sigh with which to stabilize herself, to bring them both back on course, "that was a long time ago," she repeated, cheerfully, almost maternally, as though childishness must be consoled. "And here we are, fifty, or no," she spread out her hands and counted with waggling fingers, "let's see, no, forty-six years later. That seems like such a long time. Here we are, and we're different, aren't we? We're not that boy and girl."

"I don't see that it matters now at all," he said. He still felt the bitter taste of humiliation, but he was refusing to feel debased. Proud, he was going on with it. There was everything to go on with. He had a sudden flash of memory: he was sitting in his living room with Celeste, the day of his recital, telling her that there had been an incident with his mother in which she had been despicable and Catsy courageous. He had never told Celeste the story of the step-ins of course and he never would. And now he understood that he hadn't needed to. Simply by knowing him, she had found him out. Striding out was the essence of her nature, and she could not have failed to realize that he was a man who always sat back. So there they were. Celeste knew him inside out. There was almost relief in realizing this. She knew him through and through, and yet they had gotten on with it nevertheless, and were still getting on with it. And after all, need he settle for sitting back? "I don't see that it matters now at all," he repeated.

"I guess that's what I mean." She drew another deliberate, loud sigh and leaned over and riffled through a pile of photographs as though it were a pack of cards. "I want to see that one of Turck again," she said in her loud strong way.

"Ah, here it is." She picked up the snapshot, looked at it a moment, turned it over and read on the back: *James John Turckman, US.S Army Hospital, 1938.* "Amazing how he looks like a young Cary Grant. I'll bet he was a good surgeon," she murmured. "And a good person to have as a surgeon." She looked again at the photograph, at the tall, dark-haired, rakish young man, the young eagle she had only known as the old eagle. "And a good person to have as a lover," she murmured. She looked up at Cabe and gave a little shrug, and smiled, self-consciously. "They *were* lovers, don't you think?"

"Oh, I think so. Yes. I'm quite certain." He was impatient with irrelevancies.

"How nice," Celeste murmured. She put the photograph down, on top of the pile—the young fierce-looking surgeon, in his operating room greens and skullcap, the ties dangling along his stern face. She looked up suddenly, candidly. "I had lovers," she said. "After Mort and I were divorced, I even had a black lover. For a year. He was a very nice man. But it wasn't like Tilly and Turck."

"You even had a black lover," Cabe repeated, calmly, unscandalized. "Why do you say it that way, Celeste? Like 'I had a blue Rolls-Royce?' Why do you say it that way?" he insisted.

"I *didn't*," she flared. "I *didn't* say it that way. Whatever do you mean by saying something so absolutely insulting to me?"

"I meant just what I said"—Cabe spoke imperturbably—"because I think *you* meant just what *you* said." He could stand off and be surprised at himself for his daring. Her remark had struck something deep and formerly unsummarized in him that knew all about her, it had illuminated the thing in her that plagued him. And though he wouldn't go so far as to say it to her, nevertheless he thought it tasteless and tragic that she had wanted to have an affair with a black man, not because of love, but as a kind of cause. He was achingly sorry for her. And more than that, he was shocked.

For a second, pure, reliable rage struggled in Celeste with another force, more powerful. Then quite quickly the force was winning and rage was losing, evaporating. Suddenly her mind was clear. She began to laugh. She sank back against the couch and laughed helplessly, shaking her head from side to side with her eyes wide and incredulous. She grew, in fact, rather hysterical. She laughed herself into weeping, dabbing at her eyes, shaking with gusts, shudders of laughter. But gradually she stopped. "Well," she said then, and blew her nose. She smiled, a smile at once apologetic, and relieved, and wonderfully candid. "I can see that it did sound that way," she said. "How really awful."

She was exhausted. Empty. They were both quiet. Beyond the windows, the evening sky was an intensity of vibrating peacock blue, bottomless. Cabe saw it. Received it. Felt splendor. And he felt splendor in this room, he felt a kind of pride in the inadequacies and the determination of the spirit.

There was a spread of silence as deep as the sky. And something was happening to these two, as they sat side by side on the floor, in this room grown almost dark. They had generated something newly alive between them. They had for the first time seen themselves, and each other, wholly and unshrinkingly. And it had settled them into a different kind of closeness. Celeste felt safe, content, even jubilant about this merging, this settling into together. What a powerful front it felt like, it was even a lark, to be so fortressed together against life. And Cabe was feeling failure as something that perhaps had to be cajoled, even tolerated, while power, like an older brother, was taking it in hand, instructing it, telling it that someday it must learn to go away, or if not, to lie low. He could settle back and be safe. Enormously unified, both of them were settling into a wonderful conjugal acceptance of their separate infirmities, and of the promise of enduring them and challenging them and facing together what they would bring about. Once, on the way to Tilly's the day Turck had died, they had felt a fusing which had made them, separately and together, enormous. That was what was here now. It was so immediate, so dominatingly alive, that nothing beyond this room seemed to exist at all.

Cabe reached over and took Celeste's hand in both of his. He had never done this before. It was such a momentous act, and yet he did it naturally, and without thought. Neither of them spoke. Celeste's heart seemed to be beating loudly in the back of her neck, in her cheeks. Silence quivered between them like sound. His hand touching her hand, this miracle of the touch of consenting flesh, sent a soft fire through both of them. As well as being wholly instinctual, this taking of her hand was ceremonial and confessional, the proper initial little step. But Cabe was unprepared for what touch would do. It filled him with a wild happiness so new that rules of conduct were immediately nonexistent. He put his mouth to the palm of her hand, and began to kiss it in a roaming, surprised, famished way.

She was amazed, she was in rapturous terror. She was resolved. Beneath her head, there was his gray head, its strange musty smell of warm scalp and hair. He was kissing her hand as though it were a mouth, wooing her hand as though it were she herself. She had a moment's impatience with what felt to her like indirect and unsure overtures, promising no more than this. Oh get on with it, everything in her cried. Her own feelings, at the moment, seemed to her so much more urgent than she felt his to be. In the midst of a tremulous excitement she was actually critical of him; she would have leapt in, he was creeping.

But then it came to her in a wave of compassionate impatience that perhaps she must be the one to leap in. She bent and put her lips on the wiry pungent hair, and felt the warmth of skull beneath it. She was light as air and all aflame. She began to feel a great simplified tenderness about Cabe. She put her hands on the sides of his head and pulled it up to lie against her breast, finding a serene dedication in herself to following this through to the end. At long last here it was, and she would see to it that this time it would become what it was meant to be.

His head was absolutely still against her breast, listening to the pounding of her heart. It was amazing and wonderful to him to feel Celeste's heart. It was something else, for a moment, besides desire that he was feeling. Veneration. Pity. He raised his head and looked at her for a long time. He saw a face which was purely open and concentrated, all the veils of flippancy and guardedness gone. He saw some fear, too, and a faint uncertainty, and a suffusing of desire that made her eyes dazed and enormous and dark. He felt the magnitude of his love for her now that she was letting herself be as she was. The fire in his blood was intensified and deepened and had a fuller purpose. Sensually and respectfully, he brought his mouth to hers, and slowly pressed it there, and left it there.

It was unbelievable to Celeste that that wonderful mouth could be so endlessly more wonderful than her fantasies about it, or even her memories of it. It was something else now, and not what it had been all those years ago. It was more than rivers of sweetness. It was not sweet. It was a sweeping fire. Every part of her opening body was swelling and bursting into a fiery blooming.

But it was even more than that. Cabe knew this too. He knew, they both knew, that what they were experiencing was the utmost kiss. They knew, in their own ways, that in it was all of their lives, a scalding joining of longing flesh at last, along with a time-deep consciousness of the aging, suffering minds and hearts that were bringing it about. Both body and spirit were fully in this aging man and woman's kiss. That was its perfection. And it was becoming totally consuming. There was nothing on earth but this devouringly consenting connection of their mouths. And then as though fearful of breaking this seal of completion, still with the hungry growing of their mouths together, they slumped to the floor.

Their bodies, then, began a loving that was at first fearful and slow. Not a youth but a proud private passive fastidious man of sixty-six, taught in his proper and passionless upbringing that what he was about to do was not done, Cabe for a moment was aghast with himself. And yet he was helplessly aroused, and solemn with love. His thrust, without the propulsion of seeds to strengthen it, was painfully unsure at first, discouragingly unpromising to them. To have waited all their lives for this—not for this together, but simply for fulfillment with someone both desired and loved—and then to have the loss of seminality as well as old fears flaw it was cruel.

Though no, not cruel, Celeste would not let it be cruel. She helped, with an instinctive, passionate determination. And with her abandoned, spirited ministrations, something in Cabe gave way, exploded with fascinated incredulity, with admiration, with relief. He was wanted. And so he was freed. He came into her in an unflawed whole revelation. Surprisingly painful to Celeste, after being so long unused, but only for a moment. Then there came a soaring, bursting, purifying singleness. For a second, everything that was wrong in their lives was transcended by this one thing of absoluteness, of cosmic rightness.

And with it came from Celeste a long-drawn-out shuddering faint bellow, unearthly.

The room was almost in darkness, though a pale light from the early evening radiance of a rising moon made everything in it visible. They lay side by side, as they once had, long ago. Underneath them and around them were the faces and words of the past. Their arms were flung out limp over the litter of old photographs, over bundles of age-speckled letters. And their faces were stern and peaceful as faces carved from stone.

Part Ten

THE only thing to do to pull herself together was to go outdoors. Indoors she couldn't put her mind to anything. Each room clamored with a confusion that came from her head being hard-packed with what she was trying not to acknowledge, and this made the known beauty and comfort of the rooms hostile and unfamiliar. There was nothing reliable in them; the living room, the kitchen, her cubicle, particularly her cubicle, froze her by their defection from familiarity.

But I am adept at pulling myself together, Lidi told herself jauntily. And with this fist of purposefulness, she punched herself into action, and went from the brooding inertness of her cubicle, with steps that felt solid to her, the only solid thing around here, to the hall closet for her coat. She would walk out to the mailbox, she told herself resolutely, just for a breath of air, just for a change, even though it was probably too early for the mail. But then again it might not be. You never knew. In any case, she would be outdoors.

But outdoors didn't help. There was no surcease, out here,

from that scene that had taken over her head utterly. It was worse, out here, because there were trees. And it was trees she was trying to get away from—tall dark trunks of trees, a lace of dark branches over the roof, two cars, dark, Cabe's house, dark—dark and still. And upstairs, the brazen shout of a lighted window.

No use trying to get away from that lighted window. Last night, driving along the dark road, past Cabe's house, coming home from the late movie, the jolt at seeing another car in his driveway, behind his jeep, the triumph that her suspicions about Cabe and Celeste were after all not groundless, Celeste's car, no mistaking it. Celeste's car in Cabe's driveway at eleven-thirty at night. All the windows of the downstairs, dark. And upstairs the window of Cabe's bedroom, a blazing square of light.

The afternoon had become overcast. There was no wind. There was no cloud to interrupt the soft, blanketing spread of gray sky. In the stillness that hung, that oppressed, there were only two sounds, the unceasing spring chorus of birds and the monstrous pounding of the sea. But the birds claimed everything—the high-up chuck and trumpet call of the red-wing, the honeyed incessant chipper of finches, the plaintive meu, meu of the mourning dove—they were the only vividness, the only thing that seemed to Lidi to be present in a flat gray-gauze motionlessness. She felt that everything about the day, and in herself, matched in color and mood the grayness of it, except for an ache underneath her heart, where disaffection for Celeste coiled alive and savage.

She walked with her stiff little groping steps, trying to deal with the lighted window. She did not deal with it in terms of imagining what had been going on in the bedroom behind it. Rather, she was attempting to handle a formless

292

but ravaging sense of displacement, a feeling that two people had agreed to become lovers only for the purpose of shutting this one person out in the cold. The connivance of two had blasted her out, sent her flying in pieces. It was as though they had disposed of her. As though Celeste had disposed of her. It was Celeste she blamed. She had never known precisely what it was she wanted from Cabe but now she saw that whatever it was, she would never have it.

Yet she was trying, trying very hard, to pull all the pieces of herself back together. There's too much focus on this, she scolded herself, and then she assured herself in a cool, flippant way that she was absolutely unconcerned, free now of whatever aberrance she had let herself in for, and free to get down to the good, the wonderful reality of being alive and well on a spring day at the age of seventy-two. Misery lay in her stomach, but she was pretending to an outer shell of unconcern, for herself and for Freddy, particularly for Freddy. "Well, that should settle any lingering doubts," she had said to him last night, when she could find her voice. "See what I mean about their flaunting it, leaving the bedroom light on like that?"

"More power to 'em," Freddy had said.

She trudged along the road, hard-packed now with the frost out of it, and the sand settled down to a seasonal firmness. A cardinal darted across the gray sky, lighted on the branch of a pine tree and began his long-drawn-out, sucking whistle. She tried to divert herself from her tumult by imagining that she was curious about the ornithological explanation of a cardinal's call. She tried to pretend to be someone carefree, outer-directed, perhaps a typical bird-watcher. She asked herself, almost believing in an interest, whether the crescendo of rapid chirps interspersing the long whistles was a come-hither call. A mating call. Of course, she said to herself with a pretense of dedicated ornithological inquiry, of course it's a mating call. Unmistakably.

She sickened away from the thought. And the cardinal's bold, compelling clamor mocked her, its taunt pursued her along the road—more power to 'em, more power to 'em.

Not a leaf moved, not a blade of grass. The sound of the sea, undeviated by any movement of air, was a heavy persistent roar, like high wind. The sea is here, the birds are here, spring is here, I will overcome this, Lidi said.

She came to the end of the driveway. She stopped. She looked to the left and then to the right, up and down the road. Then, hesitant, tense, because the unsteadiness of her walk and the anxiety of getting safely to and from that source of hope always made her incompetent, she crossed the road to the mailbox.

She had a moment of being aware of the air. It was mild. In it was the fresh fragrance of the green that was coming. And the tang of the sea. She longed to be rid of everything but this. She could feel the goodness of right-now, the solid realness of being here, in this moment, on this earth. She wanted to be only with this. She could be. For a second she was sure that there was, really, some way of being rid of everything but this, if she only kept trying.

But here was the mailbox, to be opened. It was here, inexorably, to be opened. Every day.

Inexorableness was the word for it, she thought, particularly today. And then there was an appearance densing in her stomach that was like a pushing cloud, a vaporlike queasiness forming and welling up throughout her, into her throat, into her head. Something had overtaken her. She was more amazed than worried at this strangeness, which was now twisting and rising up and sharpening from an amorphousness in her stomach to something in her forehead that was a shape. Suddenly the shape was that word, inexorable, and it was blending strangely into Cabe. Vaguely, persuasively, that word had to do with Cabe, as well as with the mailbox. That's what this still gray day was all about, she thought, it was all about the inexorableness of her dependence and her nonarrival, both of which would go on forever.

She felt impure, jarred. She stood there in her chunky padded brown coat, suspended, nothing under her, though her feet in shiny little brown boots stood on solid ground— the only pure thing here, she thought, knowing that this ground was something else, and that she was on it for something better than promises, knowing that the earth was real and that the mailbox was not. It had an awful, a sledgehammer shape, this weatherworn wooden post and on top of it a rusting metal box, with LUHIN painted across the side of it in flaking black letters.

In this honest moment, Lidi knew that honesty felt good. It felt as sound as the earth she was standing on. But then a great uneasiness overrode it, a bottomless uneasiness sweeping over her and weakening her, so that she had to put a hand on the mailbox for support. There would never, she told herself, be a letter of acceptance in this mailbox, there had never been the slightest chance of it. She would never have Cabe, there had never been the slightest chance of that, either. And yet, inexorably, she would continue to come out to the mailbox every day, hoping that there *would* be a letter of acceptance in it, and she would always look at Cabe and hope that there was the possibility of acceptance there, too.

She heard geese honking. She looked for them, and saw the line of them high and far off, like a ribbon of smoke floating and drifting in the sky over the sea. The line seemed to be heading somewhere and at the same time seemed insubstantially to be condensing and then expanding and then dissolving while remaining always in the same spot.

Suddenly that line of geese felt to her maddeningly, allegorically definitive. It felt like her own life, rising and sinking, rising and sinking, forever inconclusive, forever only the promise of what she could become. Cabe, Freddy, this mailbox, everything—only promises.

So, that was it. And she couldn't do a thing to change it. "Forever striving, forever nonarriving," she said aloud, feeling a grimness she would scoff at and disregard. Heavens, she liked that couplet! It perked her up. She could use it in a poem. Or use it just as it was. Just those two lines. Or maybe, "Forever Striving/ and Never Arriving" had a better sound.

Mechanically her mood was changing; warming to the reliability of being in the old grooves. And then, because she was here to do it, mechanically, she opened the mailbox.

It was empty.

She felt a bland relief. As she had anticipated, she was too early for the mail. But she could come back for it in an hour. It would surely be here in another hour! She shook her head, and sighed, half-humorously. "This is not my day," she said. And then, with mock despair, "No day is my day," she said.

She slammed the mailbox door shut with an emphasis that was meant to say, to hell with you and, to hell with me, but which represented, too, a certain angry vigorous determination. She felt easier now. She stepped out into the road, staggering a little because she was still weak, looking to the right and then to the left, and back again, quickly, with a snap of her head that made her dizzy. She began to cross the road with careful, planted steps, giddily. She heard a car coming and she broke into a panicky, stilted run, making soft sobbing sounds of effort and terror.

A matting of slippery dried brown pine needles lay in the sand of the driveway, blown there by winter winds and embedded there by winter snows. There it was, she had walked over it a hundred times this winter to and from the mailbox. But she was running now, heedless, panicked. The glass-smooth sole of one of her boots skidded on it. A convulsive sideways lurch. Her arms shot out to save herself. Impossibly, she lunged for the gatepost that was not close enough. She lost her balance and she fell.

Her head struck the sharp point of a small stone rising like a tiny volcano from the matted leaves at the driveway's edge.

Part Eleven

McCABE KINGSLEY, PIANO

Sunday, March 8, 1981

THREE INTERMEZZI, OP. 117   *Johannes Brahms*
(NO. 1 from a Scotch folk song "Sleep sweetly, my
baby so quiet, so pure.")

RHAPSODY, OP. 79, NO. 2

PAPILLONS, OP. 2   *Robert Schumann*

THREE ROMANCES, OP. 28

INTERVAL

CONCERTO (in the Italian style)   *Johann
Sebastian Bach*

   Allegro Animo
   Andante Molto Espressivo
   Presto Giojoso

IMPROMPTU, OP. 90   *Franz Schubert*
   In G Flat Minor, Andante Moso

The spring flowers are in honor of Lydia Pratt Luhin.

The roses have been given by Celeste Cunningham Hunter
in memory of Mrs. Agustus Bernhard and Dr. James John
Turckman.

The proceeds of this concert, for which McCabe Kingsley is very generously donating his performance, will go to the Seahaven Committee on Hunger. The committee wishes to express gratitude to the trustees of the Sydenham Congregational Church for permission to use it for this concert.

*T*HE concert is about to begin.

Every pew of the church is full. The Committee on Hunger has many well-wishers, and Cabe, around whom some mystique has grown, is a drawing card. The ladies in charge of tickets, fussing excitedly at the still wide-open church doors, are circumspectly jubilant.

Three o'clock. Outside the church, the day is soft, misty. The lowering sun is a pale diffuse radiance in a smoke of gray clouds, and its pallid light fills this lofty eighteenth-century room with its large-paned windows. Everything, inside and out, is softly gray, the sky, the dove-gray walls of this sedate and luminous and hushed interior. But three splashes of color flank the piano—a bowl of red roses at each corner of the dais, and in the center of it, an enormous arrangement of red tulips, yellow jonquils and blue iris.

There is a buzz of muted talk. And vibrations of expectancy. A smell of damp wool is present, and the faint pervasive fragrance of roses opening.

Celeste sat with Freddy at the back of the church. Because her emotions were heightened and because she was nervous for Cabe and knew she ought not to count on composure, she had chosen the least prominent spot she could find. And there she sat, surprised at herself, nettled, holding the program in a hand that shook. She wore a bulky white wool cape, and there were pearls in her ears for the occasion.

She raised her chin in the proud, smiling way she had and surveyed the audience, seeing the Durands, the Tates from the store, Evangeline Eliot, Marie who did Cabe's housework, the Lattimers, old Mrs. Kline, but . . . "Good heavens," she whispered suddenly, and bit her lip. She was realizing that for days she had not thought of the concert in connection with the hungry people it was being given for. It had only been Cabe she had thought about, and was thinking about now. She was appalled and amused. How much could she have cared about the hungry of this island if she could so completely forget that this concert was for the purpose of providing them with food? She was indeed appalled. But also she was perversely pleased. She thought very carefully for a minute and then she shrugged her white-draped shoulders and smiled.

A hush was settling over the audience now. Everyone had come. They were waiting. Celeste looked at her roses beside the piano, and saw how richly red they were against all the gray. She saw Turck's red roses pinned to Tilly's shoulder. She saw Tilly smiling.

And now abruptly the door beside the chancel opened and Cabe came out of it, looking unlike himself in a dark suit and a clean white shirt and a necktie. A polite flutter of clapping began as he walked in his plunging way to the dais, head pressed forward, eyes for nothing but the piano he was going toward. He reached it and turned there, stood still with one hand on it, his eyes roving composedly over the audience, coming to rest finally on Celeste. He bowed in that direction first, then he bowed once to the right and then slowly to the left, including everyone with perfect courtesy. He sat down. He put his hands flat on his knees, as though pulling his scattered exterior self together to go down into the center of himelf. After a moment he raised his hands, and shot them out from his sleeves, once, and then brought them down to the keyboard.

The serenity of Brahms stole into the church. It came to Celeste like a quiet surprise, buzzing blurred depths, a modified emotion, unsparkling in tenderness. Had Cabe known that the opening music of the concert should play into the mood of churchly quiet? To Celeste, this lullaby was absolute peace. She thought of the Virgin Mary and the Christ child, and felt grateful to Cabe for giving them all this pure little cosmic prelude to whatever was to come. And she saw with relief and pride that he was perfectly at ease. That's Cabe, she thought, admiring this elegance of composure and detachment. She hoped others were noticing the man as well as his music.

Her eyes swept over the audience. People listening. Their heads still. Pale sun came through the windows, but the deeper glow in this church was the tranquil amber flow of Brahms, spreading over these listening heads.

She glanced at Freddy. His eyes were closed and his mouth was slack, his face gaunt and sad. She thought of Lidi with a visceral pang, trying not to see the little body flung out limp and lifeless. And she made an effort to substitute for that grimness, the memory of Lidi laid out in her long red taffeta skirt, which Freddy had wanted her buried in because she had worn it on her last birthday, and because it was the color red, and it made a sound, he had said, and it felt alive to him. And he had ordered the lavish presentation of tulips and jonquils and iris for the platform "in memory of Lidi because she loved music, and because she'd been looking forward so much to Cabe's concert," he had told Celeste emotionally, and then had bent his head into his hands and started to cry with rough, shamed, helpless gasps.

Freddy liked this music. He looked at his program and read the poem about it again, nodding his head in agreement. A very tender piece, he thought, wanting to cry. He sat pressed against Celeste—there were ten people fitted tightly into the pew—glad in a numb way to feel a warm female body against his. He liked the feeling of the church. Not a religious man, nevertheless he was comforted by this place. And the presence of all the people around him, most of them his friends, comforted him. He felt wrapped in people, and succored by something anciently reparative. He was no longer in shock as he had been for almost all of the week. He had come out of shock and into a new place, which he was finding destitute of anything he could put a name to. It was as though he had lost the clothes he had worn for years, and was naked and cold. Yet he had waked up this morning knowing that he would make an effort to go to hear Cabe play.

He had dressed carefully, in a heather-mixture tweed jacket and gray flannel trousers, and had plastered down his wild white hair with a wet comb, feeling so strangely lost performing these habitual acts in an empty bedroom. And for whom? And for what reason? The house was empty. There was nothing to do. There was no one to be with, for better or for worse. And yet a greater ache was not for himself, but for Lidi, who had so outrageously, and in so picayune a way, been denied the remainder of her life. The only thing he could be even remotely grateful for was that she had been spared the rejection of her poem, which had come the day of her funeral, a grimly appropriate coincidence—the burial of Lidi, and the burial of her hopes—both on the same day. But even in the stupefaction of his grief, he had allowed himself, for a second, to feel that rejection of such an ambiguous little jingle had been justified.

The manner of her death he simply could not, would not, deal with. He thought it was an idiotic affront to the value of human life, a trifling little thing like a stone, on which her blood had been found. Such a trivial, inconsequential weapon of death, without dignity. Celeste had suggested that perhaps Lidi might not have thought of it that way, but might have thought instead that there was something poetic about having death caused by a little rock rising up out of the spring earth. And he had had to concede that she might have. Yet he couldn't really believe this. He felt her death to be brutal and small.

Celeste was putting her hand on his knee. He put his own hand on top of it, and found it cold and tensed, and so he took it up and folded both his hands over it, and held it.

Applause—a shocking sound after the quiet spaces of Brahms. There was a wait, now, before Cabe would begin the second Intermezzo. He sat in a tranced stillness, his hands on his knees, and then finally he brought them up and began again to play. Brahms was here again, dense, veiled, dulcet.

Cabe's hands . . . This was their separate existence, Celeste thought. They hurled a stone into the sea. They slid along the hollows and mounds of her body. They played this vast music. The same hands did all these things.

She pulled her cape close around her throat, for there was a draft here at the back of the church. Unable to let herself go completely in listening, she was remembering Cabe's hands. She was tensed with the effort not to think of his bare body as he sat up there playing from his spirit. She felt a great passionate knowledge of him and a possessiveness that no other woman in this audience could possibly feel, and she felt that she had an advantage over every one of them because she knew the entire man—his body and his spirit, because she could see his hands playing, and hear the music they were making, and remember the ways they had loved this body of hers sitting here so properly clothed but feeling undressed—feeling as lushly naked as a Lachaise sculpture.

I must listen, she thought. Brahms is not about physical passion, it is about spirit.

She turned to thinking about how brilliant the piano sounded in this high-ceilinged church. Next she drifted to thinking about the acoustics in her living room.

"What on earth are you doing, Cabe? What are you doing going back and forth like a caged lion? I'm fascinated."

"Soon I've got to move out of Aunt Tilly's house. She's left it to Albert who will sell it. So I'm trying to see if there'd be room for my piano in this living room, if you'd let me come live with you and be your love. This is hypothetical, of course."

The world had spun. Here it was. Then the spinning ceased, and she found, first, astonishment in her head, and then admiration. Cabe had spoken out. The fact that he had was suddenly of enormous importance. Cabe had spoken out. Could speak out. Hypothetically, of course. Yet she saw something emergent in him, tentatively new. Shiningly unsure, but at bottom, positive.

The spinning had begun again, the blotting out. Then again it subsided, leaving panic. She felt stormed, overrid-

*den. How did he dare so boldly to get to her like this? She
refused it, with terror, absolutely. I won't say yes. I won't
be forced. Never again, "Love Lies Dreaming." No. I won't
be forced . . .*

*"Dearest Cabe. Look. I cannot commit myself. I am ab-
solutely unable to commit myself. I can not."*

My heart is pounding at this concert, she thought. Now
suddenly there seemed to be too much here for her to surround, too much everywhere. But here was this music, which
seemed complacently and sagely to surround everything.
Stop thinking and listen to it, she urged herself.

So for a moment she listened. And she felt as though she
were in a deep golden ocean of peace, and that everything
was there.

"How would you feel about marriage, Celeste?"

*If only, forcefully he would say, "Marry me." Then it
would perhaps make all the difference. Why can't he do it?
Everything he says is a sort of question. Leap in, Cabe. I
need you to leap in.*

*"Marriage? Oh, dearest Cabe, not those meaningless words.
I don't see any point in marriage vows."*

*"Meaning you wouldn't want to use my name? This is
hypothetical of course, isn't it, Celeste?"*

*"Yes, it's hypothetical, Cabe. And no I wouldn't want to
use your name. Anyway, I think standing up in front of
people and saying words to each other is pointless and splurgy.
Show biz. And just think, Cabe, you'd be marrying beneath
you for a second time in your life. Heaven forbid."*

"I only think of you as beneath me in the one sense."

Here in this sacrosanct place among these deeply listening
people, beside a grieving Freddy and in the midst of Cabe's

playing, Celeste buried her face in the scarf of her cape and began to shake with an awful laughter. She couldn't stop. And the sobbing snorts were shockingly not muffled by the thick wool scarf. It was awful and she knew it and yet it was such fun. Oh, stop, stop! She made a superhuman effort and in a minute was able to control herself, and to sit up straight and then to tether herself to the music, though she shuddered a few more times with convulsions of soundless mirth.

Finally, because there is no room for laughter in the latitude and longitude of Brahms, and because one must go peacefully along with the scope of it in which there are no eruptions, finally she felt no more mirth.

"I keep thinking what it would be like to live with you day and night, Celeste, not just at night."

It had been possible to see, in the depth of Cabe's eyes, something stubborn, something he was adhering to, in spite of the question in his voice.

"Oh, dearest Cabe, dearest Cabe, I can not. I don't have enough in me. I'm not full enough." I'm full of sexual love, but nothing else. I want to feel something for you as powerful as the joining of our bodies. I want trumpets to blow all day, as well as all night. And I want to feel all the time what I felt when we sat on the floor in your living room going through Tilly's papers, and it was as if you and I were grown together, like Siamese twins, as though we were two people but one thing, and that we were absolutely huge. But it didn't stay. And I want to feel for you what I felt for Tilly when I rubbed her feet. And that didn't stay. And I want to feel what I felt for you when I touched your knee in the jeep, on the way to Tilly's the day Turck died. But that didn't stay either. And I want to want to share your life,

not hoard mine. I want to be directed by my heart, but I want to stay inviolate in the process. I want not to fill your need with my brand of compassion, because it's been the fakery of my life.

"I'm incomplete, Cabe."

"Funny. And I think the very same thing about myself. That you have this exceptional full wonderful thing I'll never possibly have."

"I wish I could have even a glimmer of what it is you mean. I just feel incomplete."

"I'd take what you have, my dear love. The truth is, it seems to me we wouldn't lose. We'd both gain. Simply by being together. Don't you think that perhaps together we could make things happen we couldn't make happen alone? I wonder if we couldn't have a nice old age, we two? Have you ever thought that marriage in one's sixties, or even seventies, or like Tilly and Turck in their eighties, could be a kind of ideal thing? The best time for loving? Most marriages lose their shine over a long period of time. Inevitably. But if you marry in your sixties, let's say, it's bound to be, perhaps providentially, a short thing, and perhaps always shiny. The honeymoon doesn't wear off, there's not enough time for it to, and anyway, you feel so deliriously lucky, to have love happen to you, sex and all, at last. And you've grown up, somewhat. You've grown up enough to deal with all of it, and you could feel, I could anyway, that you'd really hit the jackpot, after a lifetime of petty cash. It's astonishing to me, Celeste, that because of you I find myself these days awfully much in favor of old age. Its possibilities."

Old age. That's what this Brahms felt like, quiet and wise old age. It was beyond the fire of youth. It had reached the boundless land of tranquility. It wrapped her in golden fleece.

Perhaps trumpets weren't necessary? Was that what Cabe was telling her, through Brahms? That trumpets weren't necessary?

"I dread old age, Cabe. And yet I can see what you're saying."
"I don't dread it anymore. I did. I've stopped dreading it. Because as I see it, we both fortunately have those motors in ourselves that generate our going forward. That's all there is, really, as I see it. I suspect there's only one human attitude that's worth its salt."
"What's that?"
"Never take no for an answer."

This Brahms feels like the sea when it's quiet, deep and immense and peaceful.

She was shot through, suddenly, with the memory of Dearie.

Yesterday, lying in the dark, wide awake. Cabe beside her deeply asleep. And the growing compelling urge to get up and go out to the living room and clear out the chest of drawers, because those drawers must be emptied. For the reason that what was in them must go, to make room for whatever needed to be put there, sometime.

Quietly, not wanting to wake Cabe, she looked at the luminous dial of her watch on the night table. Six o'clock. She got up and went into the living room, closing the bedroom door softly. She turned on a lamp and went over to the chest and got down on her knees, pulling open the bottom drawer. Relics. A drawer that could easily be cleared. All her useless evening bags. And city gloves she never wore. And the box with Dearie in it.

She took out the box and pulled at the white satin ribbon that tied it. And then she lifted the lid. "Hello, Dearie."

"Hello, Celeste."

"Dearie." She lifted his paw and pumped it down dutifully, and had him say, "Humpf," but in a toneless way, no feeling. So she saw that they were entirely finished, he-she. An aging teddy bear in a box. An aging woman on her knees on a cold floor. Their game gone. The emptiness of its being gone was peaceful and absolute and as it should be for both of them. Dearie—why had she named this first and most precious of her stuffed animals that plain name—Dearie? Had her mother called her that? She had never until this moment wondered about it. Perhaps she had always known. Or her father? That felt right. Yes. It was her father who had called her Dearie.

She looked at the lumpy little bear, no fur left, only worn canvas stitched and darned—"operations" she had called her stitchings—and a few slits, "wounds", from which sawdust trickled. And the toppling neck. And shoe buttons for eyes now, his bright glass eyes long gone.

What was she to do with Dearie? It was time to empty this drawer, and to decide what to do with Dearie. She would not throw Dearie in the wastebasket. She would not discard Dearie. Nor would she ridiculously dig a hole in the earth and bury him there.

"As a bear's life goes, Dearie, you are now four hundred and twenty years old." There was only one thing to do with Dearie. She picked him up for one last hug. She kissed the stiff shabby little snout.

In the grayness of the sky, a strip of orange was expanding like something alive. She walked across the wet grass and then onto the dirt path that led to the dune, hugging the box inside her cape.

She came to the dark stones of the dune, and then to its brink. The sea washed there, hissing up the sand, sliding back. She took the lid off the box and scooped up a handful of stones and let them drop in a rattling blanket over Dearie. Then she closed the box and tied it tightly with the ribbon.

She slid with a lurch, but knowledgeably, down the short slope of stones to the sand, hugging the box against her breast. Strands of smoky clouds were softening the headlight of the rising sun. It would not be an orange ball, she saw, but simply a gold spread in the midst of grayness. She went straight down to the water's edge. A spent wave rushed up to where she was standing, scalloping almost to her feet then fizzing away, leaving the sand silver-wet.

Raising her arm high, she hurled the box. She heard the little thunp of Dearie's body and the clatter of the stones inside it as it went spinning out over the gray water. She heard the splashing thug as it hit, but turned away so that she would not see it vanish.

∽∾ II ∽∾

THE first concert of his life. It is utterly peculiar to be walking across a church floor to a piano, and to be turning to look out across hundreds of faces, all an anonymous blur except for Celeste in the back. Her white cape, white face, white hair make her easy to find in the audience, a brilliant little oasis of whiteness in a mass of variegated color and darkness. Before he turns to bow to the rest of the audience, he sees her childlike eagerness and nervousness, and senses how joined she and he are, whether she knows it or not. She has a wife's look of investment in how her man will perform and how he will be received. It increases his nervousness. He is imbued with the fact that this is the most important moment of his life. Finally, after forty years, a concert of his own. But he doesn't believe it or feel it. It is unreal. The experience of playing to so many people is totally unreal. He doesn't feel like himself, and there is no comparable experience with which to measure this one. He almost dislikes this strange disorientation. The windows through which he sees trees are not windows, and the trees are not trees. And he, standing here and bowing, is not Cabe Kingsley.

He sits down at the piano. Instantly he has forgotten the audience. Here is the piano, and here is himself and there, a small mass of whiteness in the back, is Celeste. He feels that this is enough, that it is all he wants or has ever wanted.

And so he begins to play. He has chosen Brahms because Brahms in its fuzzy authority tells him of arrival at a place of wisdom—no sharp joys there because emotion is muted by layers of experiential depth at the very bottom of which ultimate peace can be sensed.

This is what Brahms tells him, and so he has chosen to play him as an expression of the place he himself is arriving at, a realization of the boundlessness of aging. Brahms is his declaration to himself, and to Celeste, and to these people, most of whom are white-haired, that aging is arrival but that in it there is everywhere to go.

He has been so entirely in Brahms that when he stands up at the end of the Rhapsody, as applause bursts forth, he is amazed at where he is, and what is happening. Astonished, he thinks that applause is not what he wants, and never has been.

But in a minute the applause, which keeps on, is pleasant. Celeste is clapping extravagantly, her hands high up in front of her. People are putting their bodies and their lavish smiles into their vigorous clapping, which subsides all of a sudden, with one last clapper continuing then stopping in sudden self-consciousness.

Cabe sits down again, reinforced. He begins Schumann's "Papillons." The jubilant octaves leap up, steplike, joyously explosive. Cabe himself is joy, it is he mounting these steps. He has felt the audience now, through their response to him, and he has begun to feel that he is taking them up the steps with him. He and everyone here are joyously bounding up these steps. He senses the willingness of this collective soul to soar with him. That is what they want, why they came. It is what music is for—to reveal to oneself the feelings that are mostly hidden.

The Schumann has been a great heart-lifting lark for Cabe. When he finishes it, and before getting slowly up to bow, he sits in a glow of happiness, as the applause this time storms over him. He is in a trance of happiness. Yes, now the applause of people has gotten to him. It has told him what he knows himself—that the most fundamental law of his life has been the need to perfect within himself the art of his senses, and then to relate to others with it. To dignify, and yes, to glorify, through himself and to himself, and thus to others, the matter of the human soul. To define the untouched, the pure, in man, to make known the capacities hidden under ledgers. There has never been any doubt in Cabe that music glorifies, and that the innateness of man deserves glorification. Cabe has not been making himself, and Celeste, into something that they are not. And he is not taking this audience into make-believe places. He has only wanted to expose them to what is there.

The applause makes him believe that he has done this.

After the intermission he plays the Italian Concerto, which is a shade less jubilantly received, since for this audience Bach is harder to approach, it comes less easily, less familiarly to them in terms of known emotion. He has anticipated such a response, though he is disappointed not to have this, to him, most brilliantly beautiful music be less than enthusiastically and knowledgeably received. Never mind. He has played it to his satisfaction. He is glad the concert is almost over, because he is suddenly light-headed, disembodied.

And now the Schubert.

The putting of his fingers onto the keys with the first five notes, those beginning voices which stated surely, and implored, and venerated what they were stating, were the pulsating of Cabe's circulation in and with the vibrations of the hammers striking the strings. Buzzing like the strings of this piano were his nerves and arteries, oh, more than that, endlessly and profoundly more—his heart, his essence. So that he and the piano strings were the same thing, pulsating veins and pulsating strings identical, interchangeable, as though vibrating strings were in the arteries of his arms, in the blood pumped into and out of his heart, and the flow of his blood was in the vibrations of the strings.

He puts a finger on a key. And there is an immediate connection of resonant finger and resonant key. A unison. The man's life brings to life the instrument's life. But one thing emerges, not two. Not man and piano, but man, who can make this instrument duplicate himself—man communicating to woman that he knows his love for her and wants her to hear it, so that she will know it fully at last. He can feel the supplicating passion of the appeal of those first five notes as he puts his fingers to the keys and hears, and at the same time knows, that that is what is sounding.

He has chosen the Schubert because it is a declaration of what love feels like to him, more so than any music he knows. Indeed it is the only music he knows that so competently explains his sense of love. It has been his favorite piece of music ever since Mrs. Turnbull had given him a deeper recognition of it. "Play my Schubert," she would say, sitting monolithic in the beige brocade chair, after dinner, after Adelia had adroitly borne off the coffee cups on the monogrammed silver coffee tray. Mr. Turnbull would light his cigar. Catsy would suppress a yawn and fold her hands patiently. And he would play the Schubert for Mrs. Turnbull, while from underneath her closed eyelids two tears would appear, like tiny pearls, and make their way stealthily down her great cheeks.

Today he is playing the Schubert for Celeste. The whole concert has been largely for her, because *he* now is largely for her and so whatever comes out of him must reflect this. But the Schubert is exclusively for her.

As he plays those first five notes, he immediately knows that what he hears is equating what he feels. This has always been his goal, not to achieve greatness, not to captivate audiences, but simply to achieve a sound that duplicates the immensity of what he himself experiences in his living. He has a momentary surge of elation which won't develop into anything useful, and won't last. And yet existence is altered for him now, if only subtly. He will not tell himself that something unfound has been found, although fractionally it has been. For even though being now in possession of that fraction, he has no actual recognition of what it means, nor any sensation other than a momentary elation and relief, nor any feeling of conclusion. On the contrary, because there is everywhere to go he has no permanent sense of arrival. Ending something, he is only beginning something else.

Celeste sat with her white cape hugged around her neck, her lips parted pleasantly expectantly at the corners, no public expression on her ardent attentive exposed face; listening, waiting.

As the song stated, then mounted questioningly, she began to feel an actual softening in her diaphragm, as though muscles were relaxing, or as though a soft push of heat were expanding there. The music was in there. It was taking place in that part of her, like something growing. This was an experience of sensation undefined by words. Within the walls of her body there was perfect understanding of what the music, through Cabe, was saying. Questioning, answering, it informed her repeatedly of sorrow, and the climb to a transcendance of it. Over and over again, it told her about keeping on, about going up, then down, then up again, always higher each time. Her mind could not have said to her that she was listening to a song about growth through the pain of living. Nor could she possibly have said to herself that the music sang of an enlargement of being that was finally unalterable. However, she knew all this thoroughly as she listened. It was an experience of total absorption, through Cabe, of the celebration of archetypal pursuit and arrival.

The music came to her like a tender counseling. It came to her like Cabe's voice, his hands, his self. She had a complete sensory acceptance of it—Cabe's fingers touching the keys, Cabe's self speaking through his fingers, the sound vibrating across the church and touching her as though his hands were doing the touching. She was totally connected to Cabe by these bands of sound. She felt Cabe, all of him, reaching across this room and coming into her. And what she felt was his essence. Which trivialized his flaws absolutely. It seemed petty, ridiculous, to be attentive to flaws in the face of the sum of this man. Here was Cabe, all of him, and yes, the best of him. And the product of all this was the way he played, and the way he loved her.

A rage of feeling for Cabe for playing this shook her. A shuddering sound, part sob part gulp, rasped up through her belly into her throat. She bent her head into her hands and began to cry. She cried for sorrow, for Mort and herself, and for Cabe and Catsy, for the tragedy of waste and the nobility of trying not to have life be waste. It was sorrow her tears were for, for Freddy's kind body pressed against her like sun. For Lidi.

Now she was sobbing helplessly. It seemed that all the tears she had never shed for deep and personal sorrow were rising in her and pouring out. Her guts were being ripped out by the sobs. It was ugly. Wonderful.

Gradually the sobs quieted. Then stopped. She was purged, empty. Though perhaps not purged and empty except for this time. Defenselessly, she knew these tears could come again. The whole arrangement of her body felt different, as though now accommodating a river of tears which could at any moment pour forth. And she felt, soberly, that she had washed nonsense out of her body. She had a small relieved feeling of coming to an unclouded place. She felt small and lost there, queer. And yet this felt to her like the place she wished she could always be in. Every part of her body was strange with it and tiredly peaceful with it. Like the emptiness of having given birth.

An explosion of applause.

The audience rose with the sound of wind rushing, clapping emotionally, yelling "Bravo" and "encore, encore." Cabe stood by his piano, bowing, bowing, his eyes pale and burning with joy. Celeste sat up, confused, flat. Then tiredly she stood. Clapping was not in her. Freddy beside her blew his nose. "Nice tune," he said sternly.

Then Freddy saw that the flowers on the dias were quivering from the concussive din of applause, and for a second he pretended, more, he even let himself believe, that those trembling red tulips were Lidi. Reincarnated. And purified. Lidi reincarnated in purification. Exaltedly, he told himself that they were, in fact, Lidi as she had always wanted to be, and at last was. He saw all the years of her imperfections wiped out.

III

CELESTE and Cabe. Jouncing along in the jeep. The gray head, the white head. Spring is in the evening air. Grass turning green along the roadside is vivid in the diminished light.

"Cabe, I wouldn't dream of trying to put into words what your playing was like." She was hollow. She was someone else.

"I'm glad."

"Look how green the grass is getting," she said, "and how light it still is, at five-thirty."

"Yes," he said. "The days are getting longer."

She was drained. Almost cross. Sober with emptiness. "Your playing moved Freddy very much."

"I'm glad he came."

"We can be sorry for Freddy for a while, but we'll soon be glad for him. Freddy won't be single long."

"No. I'm certain of that."

"Cabe." She put a hand on his knee. It turned out that this was all she had to do in order to feel better. "Cabe, I want to tell you. I've cleaned out the bottom drawer of the living room chest for you." Her voice made light of this. She was not done yet with nonsense. But the innocence of her eyes disclaimed flippancy.

His body, and his face, seemed to lower. To settle. He took one hand from the wheel and put it on hers, and held it as he drove along.

"One mingy little bottom drawer. But I'll clean out the rest of it. I was thinking you could put your music in it."

He found his voice. "Yes, I could. I will." He had not let go of her hand. She gripped it so that he wouldn't.

They drove along, taking their wedding quietly.